Praise for Kristin von Kreisler and Her Novels

A HEALING JUSTICE

"Von Kreisler explores the deep and compassionate bond between humans and dogs. Like her previous novels, *A Healing Justice* will touch the hearts of readers."
—**Best Friends** magazine

"If you love animals the way I do, the way that officer Andrea Brady does, and the way that our author, Kristin von Kreisler, obviously does, you'll love *A Healing Justice*." —**Delilah**

"A perfect homage to people in law enforcement, exploring the split decisions that they must make. Another pet lovers' delight, along with an enticing developing romantic relationship." —**USAToday.com**

"In chronicling Andie's journey to recovery, this wonderful story powerfully renders the post-trauma road to healing while offering a touching and honest representation of the strength and loyalty of our amazing canine friends."
—**Modern Dog** magazine

"Be sure to set aside a quiet secluded time to read this book. You won't want to put it down and you will resent any interruption. *A Healing Justice* is a terrific novel and a great addition to Von Kreisler's canon."
—**Susan Wilson**, author of *One Good Dog* and *The Dog Who Saved Me*

"Kristin von Kreisler is spot-on delightful when she writes, with uncanny sensitivity, from the point of view of Justice, who is not 'just' a dog but a fully realized character. *A Healing Justice* demonstrates why dogs are, and always will be, man's (and woman's) best friend."
—**Amy Hill Hearth**, *New York Times* best-selling author

"Kristin von Kreisler writes masterfully about the connection between a police officer and her dog in this gripping story of heartbreak and redemption."
—**Helen Brown**, *New York Times* best-selling author
of *Cleo* and *Bono*

"When a book as wonderful as *A Healing Justice* brings tears to my eyes and warms my heart I know I have a 'keeper' in hand. *A Healing Justice* is that kind of book. I have no doubt that I will read this book again and again because I personally experienced how a dog's love and devotion can see you through the darkest days of your life."
—**Fern Michaels**, #1 *New York Times* best-selling author

EARNEST

"Dog lovers will adore this beleaguered Lab, who only wants to preside over a united household in his favorite 'library lion' pose." —*The Seattle Times*

"A sweet and appealing story of a pet's effort to bring his pack together again!" —**Heroes & Heartbreakers**

"Delightful . . . Von Kreisler's strength in her earlier works—penetrating character developments and tantalizing story lines—are prominent on this emotional, bumpy ride. She is an incredible storyteller." **—American Kennel Club**

"An insightful and uplifting story . . . a great read for those who know the power of pets." **—*Modern Dog* magazine**

"A highly readable story of what devotion and love really mean. Once again, von Kreisler, one of the best authors of animal-related fiction and nonfiction out there, brings readers a dog and a book they will cherish."
—*Best Friends* magazine

"The best part of von Kreisler's novel is Earnest . . . a sweet, lovable canine." **—RT Book Reviews**

"Earnest lives up to his name. He is a dog who earnestly desires only one thing, to keep his family intact. Kristin von Kreisler deftly spins a tale of human failings and canine devotion that will have the reader reaching for the tissues."
—Susan Wilson

"Kristin von Kreisler captures the emotional intelligence of Earnest, a dog who provides much needed guidance to a human couple spiraling into catastrophe. When Anna and Jeff both feel the depth of betrayal, only the steady loyalty and unwavering love of Earnest can save them."
—Jacqueline Sheehan, *New York Times* best-selling author of *The Center of the World*

"Be prepared to fall in love with Earnest, a yellow Labrador retriever adopted from a shelter who teaches his humans a thing or two about resilience, loyalty, and forgiveness. A truly charming story sure to please dog lovers everywhere."
—**Amy Hill Hearth**

"If you've ever wondered whether animals were smarter than humans, Kristin von Kreisler's *Earnest* is the book for you. This charming tale (pun intended!) leads us through the kind of conflict real families face and shows us, through the wisdom of a dog, what matters most in life."
—**Nancy Thayer**, *New York Times* best-selling author of *The Island House*

"Kristin von Kreisler's deep understanding of both people and dogs shines through in her compelling new novel, *Earnest*. Animal lovers will fall for the yellow Lab who saves his favorite humans from heartbreak."
—**Jeffrey Moussaieff Masson**, *New York Times* best-selling author of *Dogs Never Lie About Love*

AN UNEXPECTED GRACE

"A heartwarming and beautifully written tale about trust and compassion. Grace provides the story with a wonderful balance of humor as her heroine, Lila, poignantly brings the reader into her frame of mind. Dog lovers will be particularly enthralled with the novel."
—**RT Book Reviews,** 4 Stars

"With colorful metaphors, detailed descriptions, engaging scenarios, and a lively narrative, von Kreisler creates a landscape that's a natural metaphor for the humbling struggles between trust and torment. A soulful dog serves as a sobering inspiration and comfort pillow—and a poignant relief valve for the reader." —**Seattle Kennel Club**

"*An Unexpected Grace* is beautifully written. Kristin clearly knows dogs. The novel is filled with compassion. All pet lovers will relate to the story." —**Pet News & Views**

"Devoted dog parents will read *An Unexpected Grace* and relate to the deep bond and heartfelt connection that can develop between the human and canine species. Von Kreisler's passion for dogs is the underlying theme throughout the book and easily relatable by dog lovers wanting a happy ending."
—*Seattle P-I*

"A terrific, uplifting novel . . . Von Kreisler deftly shows how the love between a dog and a person can prove transformative." —*Modern Dog* **magazine**

"Kristin von Kreisler is an acute observer of dogs and a fine novelist. Her novel about the healing powers of dogs is enchanting. I was captivated from page one and I learned a great deal from this heartwarming, thrilling book."
—**Jeffrey Moussaieff Masson**

"Kristin von Kreisler weaves a modern tale that seems at first to be a relentless search to understand a workplace shooting. But wait; von Kreisler takes us deeper into the powerful connections between humans and animals who are wounded by the incomprehensible and bound together by love."
—**Jacqueline Sheehan**

Books by Kristin von Kreisler

A Reason
for Hope

KRISTIN VON KREISLER

KENSINGTON
PUBLISHING CORP.

www.kensingtonbooks.com

ISBN: 978-1-4967-3734-2 (ebook)
ISBN: 978-1-4967-3733-5

First Kensington Trade Paperback Printing: January 2022

10 9 8 7 6 5 4 3 2 1

Printed in the United States of America

For my dear nieces: Katherine von Kreisler, Paige Henry, Elizabeth von Kreisler, and Lonnie Matheron.

With much love.

Although the world is full of suffering, it's also full
of recovering.
—Helen Keller

Fall down seven times, stand up eight.
—Chinese proverb

PROLOGUE

2013

For a year, Will had imagined Hope lounging at his feet under his office desk between her appointments. And on weekends, in the field beside his house, he'd throw her a Frisbee, and, true to her Labrador retriever genes, she'd tear after it, her ears flapping, and drop it at his feet—*kerplunk*. The picture was perfect. A man and his dog. A beautiful bond. All good.

While Will had been imagining Hope, she'd been training to become a courthouse facility dog in the Prosecutor's Office of Nisqually County, across Puget Sound from Seattle. And Will had waited to become her handler. His colleagues would take her to comfort stressed-out people at trials, interviews, therapy sessions, and forensic exams, but he'd watch after her the rest of the time—twenty-four/seven, three hundred and sixty-five days a year. Who could ask for a better arrangement than caring for an impeccably trained dog who did important work? Will would have a friend at the same time that he supported a good cause.

But as he parked his Jeep, grabbed his ancient suitcase, and made his way along the stepping-stones toward the craftsman-farmhouse headquarters of Washington Facility Dogs, doubts hissed in his ear. *What have you done? You don't have time for a dog when your work saps nearly all your time and energy. It's not like you've got a wife at home to share the load.* Will wouldn't even own Hope. Until she retired, she'd legally belong here.

Applying to be her handler had been hard enough. He'd filled out forms that asked for everything but his mother's maiden name, and to judge if he'd be suitable, he'd weathered interviews by phone and in his home on San Julian Island. Sometimes he'd felt smashed between specimen slides and peered at through a microscope—and now for two weeks, the scrutiny would continue while he trained here. He'd have obedience sessions with Hope, daily lectures on dog psychology and care, and mandatory written exams. He'd have to learn commands he'd never heard of for dogs but that Hope already knew—such as "settle," "kiss," and "visit."

Gulp. Staring at the stepping-stone ahead of him, he hesitated.

But the Marine-sergeant discipline that had gotten Will through law school pushed aside the doubts, poked his chest, and barked at him, *You can't back out now, buddy. You're in it for the long haul. Full-time.* Truth be told, Will was stuck. He had to take on Hope, even knowing that maybe it was *not* all good.

No matter what, he reminded himself, he had good reason for Hope. As Harry Truman once said, "If you want a friend in Washington, get yourself a dog." Will could use a friend during the legal wrangling and uphill fights required for his work in the Domestic Violence and Sexual Abuse Unit. As a deputy prosecuting attorney, his specialty was incarcerating slimeballs.

When Will knocked on the door, he heard dog toenails click on hardwood, and they were moving closer. A woman shouted, "Coming!" just as the skittering toenails reached the other side of the door. A dog's excited pants and whimpers seemed to shout, *A visitor! A visitor! Hurrah!*

The dog's excitement was contagious. Will's heart sped up. A door lock turned. When a peppy thirty-something woman appeared, a streak of blond fur bounded onto the porch.

Hope was beautiful! Her fur was champagne blond, the color of moonlight—except for darker biscuit-beige from the top of her head down her back, and then again, like an afterthought, on the tip of her tail. She was sturdy, and a faint blush of pink appeared on her licorice-gumdrop nose. Under the gaze of her gentle brown eyes, Will's worry about the responsibility he was taking on evaporated like mist. Her velvety triangle ears flapped as her exuberant wiggles shouted, *Pet me!* Of course, Will obliged. The whole back half of Hope's body wagged when she wagged her tail.

"Hope!" Will sank to his knees to welcome her into his arms. Trained to cuddle, she melted against him and exuded the kind of soothing calm that could turn a snorting bull into a docile pug. Hope pressed her head against Will's chest, just as she would press her chin on the laps of victims in his office when they wrung their hands and tears streamed down their faces and she was told, "Snuggle." Her soulful eyes would say as clearly as anyone ever said anything, *Don't worry. I love you. I am here, and everything will be all right.*

Sometimes everything *did* turn out all right. Like now. With Hope. And that's what kept Will going.

CHAPTER 1

April 2014

"Here's your breakfast! Come and get it, sweet kitties!" Tessa called.

She didn't have to wait long. In the April sunshine dappling the forest floor, wary eyes peeked from behind trees and under bushes, and noses twitched at the delicious smells emanating from her wicker picnic basket. The feral cats now knew that they were about to dive into shredded sautéed chicken and chopped hardboiled eggs sprinkled over their favorite homemade kitty kibble. Their chorus of meows demanded, *Hurry! Feed us!*

Tessa quickly counted the cats, as she always did at feeding time. Six of her seven had shown up—Dickens, Alcott, Wharton, Melville, Fitzgerald, and Austen—but Bronte, a silvery, ladylike part-Siamese, was missing. A contemplative sort of cat, she enjoyed climbing madrone trees and gazing at the Olympic Mountains or meditating on the sun rising over firs. She had never strayed much till Tessa had recently trapped her and Dr. Vargas had spayed her. Now exceedingly mistrustful, Bronte began to wander.

Without breakfast, she'd be hungry. Tessa mentally begged

her, *Please, come home tonight for dinner. No one will hurt you. I promise.* Feral or not, the cats were her family—and a family among themselves. She often found them grooming one another, going off on expeditions together, and lying side-by-side in the sun.

She set her wicker basket on a cedar stump and pulled out a stack of aluminum pie tins. At each of her feeding stations, she exchanged a food-encrusted pan for a clean one, and she spooned out breakfast. Knowing the kitties would not come near if she stayed too close, she moved a respectful two car lengths away. In seconds, the cats dashed to the food, and the forest filled with smacking sounds.

"You be safe," Tessa told the cats as she did at every feeding time because they were vulnerable in a perilous world. Coyotes, eagles, dogs, moving vehicles, and cruel people could injure or kill them. They could eat a poisoned rat or sneak into a garage and lick antifreeze off the floor—and die. No wonder the cats were cautious. They had to be, to survive.

From a gallon milk jug, Tessa poured fresh water into the cats' community ceramic bowl, which was large enough for a goldfish school. "See you tonight," she called. Usually, she stayed to watch the kitties eat, but today she hurried across the field to her cottage to finish an important task. As she walked, she thought, *If only Bronte will be safe.*

At Tessa's cottage door, she paused, as she always did, to touch the tiny brass hand she'd bought at a garage sale and nailed to the wall. The hand was shaped like a policeman's, held out palm forward to say *Stop!* It was meant to keep evil from sneaking into the cottage or barging into Tessa's life. She liked to think that it would make intruders, thieves, or assaulters take their business elsewhere.

Inside, she passed her faithful Bentwood rocking chair, in which she read all winter by her wood-burning stove. She went straight to her desk, a thrift-store antique with an iron key for the side drawer's lock and legs that curved out like a slew-footed tiger's. As she booted up her computer, she smiled to herself. She pulled her chair up to her desk and settled her fingers on the keyboard.

Name: Teresa Jordan. *Call me Tessa.*

Where she lived: San Julian Island. *Population eight thousand, about fifty years behind the rest of the world, across Puget Sound from Seattle.*

Occupation: Librarian. *In my bookmobile, whom I named Howard, I travel to out-of-the-way communities all over Nisqually County.* And amateur literary psychologist. *I recommend books and poems to help my patrons with their problems.*

Hobbies: Tending feral kitties. *I know what people say about crazy cat ladies, but I am nothing if not honest about it.* Reading just about anything. Walking beaches. Baking pies. *Every Sunday I also bake bread and make soup with my garden's veggies.*

A phrase that described her physical appearance: *How am I supposed to judge that myself?* she wondered. *People tell me that I am pretty, and that my face lights up when I laugh.* Her dark hair had a touch of auburn in the sunshine, but it frizzed in the rain. And though she was average height and slim, she could lose an inch around her hips. But never mind about pluses and minuses. She typed, "reasonably attractive."

Her age: "Well, go ahead and admit it," she mumbled to herself. She answered, thirty-six—not that she was anywhere near over the hill. But her mother had started reminding her that she was running out of time to find a husband. What, ten years ago? Not exactly a confidence boost. When she broke up with her fiancé two years ago, she'd been more worried about her mother's reaction than her own sense of loss.

Tessa glanced around her cottage at the dried hydrangeas in her copper vase, the crowded bookshelves, and the knitted afghan draped over her sofa's arm. As cozy as she'd tried to

make her home, sometimes it felt lonely when she returned
from work and no one was around. When Tessa's father had
drowned in a sailing accident off the Maine coast just weeks
after she'd moved in here, she learned not just that life could
change in a flash, but also that a crisis was harder to face by
herself. Those lessons she was still trying to digest.

But, then, she reminded herself that she had her "people,"
as she called her patrons, as well as her friends, the best of
whom was Emma. Last week she'd urged Tessa to sign up
for Northwest Singles. "You can't sit home and wait for some
delicious man to come along and ring your doorbell. You've
got to gird your loins and put yourself out there." *Maybe so.*

Tessa would let fate decide how lonely she'd be. She
pressed "submit," and her profile flew through the ether to
NWSingles.com. To amuse herself, she scrolled through the
site's photos of men she might contact. One looked like a
hamster was among his forebears. Another had leprechaun
ears. Another had a bit of werewolf about him—his tensely
closed lips could have been hiding fangs.

Oh, my. What am I getting myself into?

In Tessa's one-room-plus-bath cottage, her "bedroom's"
desk and Murphy bed were along one wall, and her "living room's" wood-burning stove, sofa, and chairs were in a
corner opposite her "kitchen." She stored dishes behind glass
doors in a cabinet above the sink, and pots, pans, and cleaning
supplies behind a chintz curtain under it. Next to her stove, a
butcher-block table served for meals and a countertop.

With her NWSingles profile on its way to God knows
where (possibly a werewolf!), she would make her weekly
soup. She began chopping onions, and, as usual, her eyes
stung and tears slid down her cheeks. To avoid those tears,
she'd frozen the onion before slicing into it, turned its sliced
side down on the cutting board, worn goggles, even kept a

piece of bread in her mouth, as recommended in a cookbook. Nothing had worked.

Wiping her cheeks with the back of her hand, she put down her knife and crossed the room for a tissue. A ping sounded on her computer. Blinking against her watery eyes, she sat back down at her desk and found in her NWSingles message box an email from Nicholas Payne. *San Julian's Nicholas Payne?* In yards all over the island, campaign signs urged people to vote for him for City Council in a special election this summer. His message to Tessa: "Meet up for a glass of wine? Planet of the Grapes downtown tomorrow @ 4?"

Tessa expected a leprechaun or hamster, but Nick Payne? His bio said he was the forty-two-year-old Rainier College professor she'd read about in the *San Julian Review*, and he enjoyed sharing a good bottle of wine with friends. She studied his online picture: an honest face, a neck as sturdy as a marble column, intense gray eyes behind his horn-rimmed glasses. He was wearing a black turtleneck, and his dark, layered hair was mussed just enough to keep him from looking stiff.

Scarcely believing her beginner's luck, Tessa replied that she'd meet him tomorrow, and she gave him her cell number in case of a last-minute change of plans. "We'll probably recognize each other from our NWSingles photos, but just in case, I'll be wearing black jeans, a blue sweater, and a scarf with butterflies printed on it."

Two minutes later, another ping. "I'll be easy to recognize by the red carnation in my teeth. (A joke!)"

Tessa fired back, "LOL!"

CHAPTER 2

In Planet of the Grapes, 1950s stools that looked like chrome mushrooms were the only seating option, at wooden tables that had seen better days. "Question everything" had been chiseled into the table where Tessa waited by a window. Someone had stuck plastic flowers in a wine bottle for the centerpiece and nailed old out-of-state license plates to the wall behind her for art.

According to Nick Payne, who arrived ten minutes late with no carnation in his teeth, Planet of the Grapes' selection of wines was exceptional. At the bar, he ordered a premium 2006 merlot for himself and a special Italian zinfandel for Tessa and brought them to the table in mismatched glasses. "Your zin is going to explode a cherry fruitiness. It has a smoky finish, and its high acidity makes it taste bold," he said.

Tessa took a sip. No fruity explosion—in fact, no explosion at all, as far as she could tell—though if she let loose her power of suggestion, she might detect a tiny whisper of cherry. And as for a smoky finish? She wouldn't know one if she shook hands with it. But she simply nodded and smiled as she put down her glass. "It's great! Very bold!"

"I knew you'd like it." He glanced around the room as if looking for prospective voters. Then he fixed his eyes on Tessa.

He was even more attractive in person than in his photos on NWSingles.com and "Vote for Nick Payne" signs. He exuded confidence—even boldness, as evident as the high acidity was supposed to make Tessa's zinfandel. She thought he was the kind of man who took command, and that seemed good to Tessa because, though determined, she was gentle and quiet—and, as everybody knew, opposites attracted.

"Okay, let's play 'Get to Know You' for ten minutes so that part's out of the way," Nick said.

"Don't you always keep getting to know somebody? I mean, isn't it an endless process? Ten minutes isn't long enough."

"Tessa, you're splitting hairs." Nick's chuckle was as smooth as melted butter, and she liked that he had used her name. She also liked the lock of hair that fell onto his forehead when he leaned toward her as if he wanted to get closer, attentive to her every word.

"All right, then." Tessa smiled. "I'll ask you questions. Where are you from?"

"Chicago. I came out here when Rainier College offered me a great job," Nick said.

"Family in Chicago?"

"My mother."

"How'd you get to San Julian?"

"I was dating someone here."

"I saw online you're a professor. Do you like teaching?"

"Yeah. I do. I like sharing all I've learned and helping the kids." He chuckled again. "I say 'kids,' but a few are older than I am."

"People go to college now at all different ages," Tessa said.

"True," Nick said. "I like the older students best. They get my jokes."

"So why are you running for City Council?"

"To serve the community. That means more to me than anything. I've always felt I was put on earth to help people."

He cares about the world. Tessa pressed her heels against her chrome stool's base.

"Enough about me. My turn." Nick's gray eyes on her were mesmerizing. "Your questionnaire said you were a librarian. That can't be true."

"Why not?"

"You don't look like one. You don't have thin lips or a bun with chopsticks stuck through it."

"That's an old stereotype!"

"And your hair is pretty hanging down like that."

The compliment boosted Tessa's confidence. "I've been a librarian for ten years. I drive the county bookmobile. I'm surprised I've not seen you before." He was the kind of man she'd definitely remember.

"I get most of my books at the college or order them on Amazon."

"What do you like to read?"

"History. Politicians' bios. Novels."

"Favorite novelist?"

Nick looked like he was mentally sifting through a list of names. "Definitely Hemingway. I like his spare prose."

"Didn't you love *For Whom the Bell Tolls*?" Tessa asked.

"And *The Sun Also Rises*."

Nothing better than talking books, Tessa thought.

They talked books and politics while more than an hour slipped by. Nick licked his lips. "Hey, listen. Next Saturday my brother and his wife are coming over for a barbecue. You want to join us? I want you to meet them, and I have a great wine you should try."

When Tessa's face warmed, it wasn't from the zin. *Today isn't going to be a one-off. Another date so soon!* "I'd love it."

She thought, *Thank you, Northwest Singles, for a match beyond my wildest dreams.* She'd never have believed that the Internet would lead her to Nick Payne.

CHAPTER 3

It was the gorgeous kind of April day that Will had waited for all winter. The sky was as clear a blue as was allowed on the earth, his apple and plum trees were blooming their heads off, and the birds were belting out songs they'd repressed for dreary months. The air smelled of spring, everything fresh and green, including the knee-high grass that Will was mowing in the three-acre field next to his rickety Victorian farmhouse.

Last year, he'd bought his nearly new drivable mower for fifty-five dollars at San Julian's Rotary Auction, to which island citizens donated unwanted items. Somebody must have died or downsized from house to condo to have given away such a steal. It had already saved Will scores of sweaty hours.

Hope rode behind him on the covered grass-collection trailer, which she loved even more than picking blackberries with her teeth and licking peanut butter off a spoon. As Will turned the mower for another pass across the field, she gazed into the distance as if she were surveying her kingdom, the mower her gilded coach, and Will her minion in black livery and polished boots.

Will slowly worked his way over to the deer fence he'd

put up to corral Hope, and he checked his watch. *Damn.* He had to get the grass cut before summer came and dried it out—one match, and his neighborhood could go up in a blaze—but he had no time to finish today. Because of his job, there was never enough time for all he had to do, including repairs on his house before it gave up and fell in around him. He could count on one hand the weeks in the last year when he'd worked only forty hours.

This very afternoon, piled on his kitchen table, were tasks he had to finish before jury selection in the morning. He'd be up till after midnight, combing one last time through the jury list, snooping on the social media of prospective members, pre-ranking them. Tomorrow he'd brace himself for what some said to weasel out of serving: "Based on my religion, I believe that only God can judge someone." "I don't believe in the criminal justice system." "If that man is here in this courtroom, he must have done something." No excuse was too lame. Will had heard them all.

"Ready to call it a day, Hope?" he shouted back to her over the mower's roar. If she could speak, her answer would have been an emphatic "No!" Instead, she relied on body language to convey her opinion, which she gave with her tragic look—her posture drooped, her forehead rumpled, her moist eyes averted as if she could not bear to look directly at someone who could be so cruel. Had he no understanding of a dog's need of sunshine?

Will wasn't ready to leave the field, either. He could have used an afternoon off. Nevertheless, duty-bound, he headed back to the barn.

When he turned off the ignition, Hope, who forgave anyone anything, leapt to the concrete floor and began to patrol for interesting objects to sniff. Will pushed his sunglasses to the top of his head and picked up his plastic water bottle. As he climbed off the mower's seat, he heard scratching sounds in the loft, where he stored his college trunk and old kitchen chairs that should go to this summer's Rotary Auction.

He stopped, craned his ears, listened. More scratching. Hope looked up at the loft, then back at him as if she, too, believed something was amiss. Her worried eyes unambiguously declared, *A vagrant in our midst!*

"Please, don't let it be a rat," Will muttered. It was the last thing he needed. He didn't have time to deal with it.

CHAPTER 4

"Welcome," Nick said as he helped Tessa remove her corduroy coat. In the manner of a gentleman, he worked it onto a wooden hanger and left it in his entry closet. "Any trouble finding my house?"

"Your directions were perfect," Tessa said. *Kind of like you are, if you want to know the truth.*

All week, she'd eagerly anticipated seeing Nick again. This evening, he was dressed in dark slacks and a pale blue shirt that complimented his gray eyes and draped over his chest like silk. It was as elegant as you'd ever find at a barbecue, and she felt a little frumpy in her denim leggings and long-sleeved striped T-shirt.

She handed him a cherry pie in her wicker basket. "I made our dessert."

His smile revealed even, white teeth. "This is a definite step up. All you were going to get from me was some rocky road ice cream."

"Cherry pie à la mode would be good."

"We'll see what we want later," he said. "For now I've got some sorry news."

"Oh, no." But then Tessa thought the news couldn't be too sorry. Maybe the power was out, and he had an electric stove, and all they'd have to eat was barbecue and cherry pie and rocky road.

"My brother cancelled on us. A tenant started a fire in his rental house in Ellensburg. He and his wife had to race over there to meet with the insurance people."

"That's a shame," Tessa said. "I was looking forward to meeting them."

"And they, you," Nick said, as if he'd told them all about her. "They'll be back next week. We can always get together with them later."

A hint about a future!

"Hey, you up for a tour?" Nick asked. "I've put a lot of sweat equity into this house." When he took Tessa's hand, a tingle traveled to her elbow. He led her into his living room, which was bigger than her entire cottage.

It was masculine and as elegant as his shirt—hardwood floors, neutral colors, a leather sofa facing two matching leather chairs in front of a granite fireplace—all tasteful, subdued. In his study was more leather furniture and floor-to-ceiling shelves crammed with books that Tessa itched to peruse. But Nick hurried her off to his sleek, modern kitchen, all black granite and stainless steel. He pulled a fire-engine red towel off the rack and joked, "My one bow to flamboyance."

"Your house belongs in *Nisqually Life*," she said, because the magazine featured the lifestyles of influential people. "It looks like you had a decorator."

"I consulted a friend sometimes."

Nick took her hand again and led her through a sliding glass door onto a deck. His garden was immaculate—emerald green grass and beds of sword ferns in front of carefully pruned rock rose bushes. Someone had pulled every weed that had dared show its face.

"Here. Sit." He gestured to a chaise lounge with a black

canvas pillow, where Tessa could extend her legs and lean back, relaxed. "I've got it all warmed up for you." He pointed to flames hissing from a gas stainless steel heater nearby. "How about some wine?"

"What kind did you choose for me this time?"

"Wait and see."

While Tessa waited, she studied the exterior of Nick's house. It had two stories, and she noted that he must be playing the gentleman, not taking her upstairs—a sign of his respect for women. The exterior color was a soft, dove-breast gray. *Was the friend he'd consulted a former girlfriend?*

"Here you go." Nick handed her red wine in a large glass, the kind that made her want to plink her finger on the crystal and listen to the ring. "It's Petite Sirah. It's got blackberry and sugarplum notes—and plenty of antioxidants. They're a good excuse to drink all you want."

Nick pulled up a deck chair close to Tessa and rested his tasseled loafer on the chaise lounge's wooden edge. He was drinking the same Petite Sirah that she was, he told her—a new kind he just found through his wine-tasting club. "To your health," he said, and they raised their glasses in a toast.

Tessa took a sip. She couldn't detect blackberry, and she didn't know what a sugarplum tasted like, so the Petite Sirah's notes whizzed by her. But it felt good to be here with Nick.

"Your garden is lovely. I don't see how you ever get yourself to leave here," Tessa said.

"I hike a lot. Yesterday after my classes, I walked a beach along the Hood Canal. Did you know the floating bridge there is the third longest in the world?"

"I'll remember that. People ask me questions about that kind of thing all the time," Tessa said. "Do you know what language is spoken in New Guinea?"

"Can't say I do," Nick said.

"There are supposedly eight hundred and thirty-two of them. It's the most linguistically diverse place on earth. The most widely spoken is Tok Pisin. I looked that up yesterday when someone wanted to know."

"You'd think your patrons could Google it themselves."

"Not everybody has a computer, at least not in the rural communities where I go."

"I'll mention that at the women's club where I'll be speaking next week. They're raising money for iPads for disadvantaged kids. I don't see why they couldn't help some of your patrons, too."

So thoughtful! "That would be fantastic."

"We'll see what I can swing. There are lots of good projects going on around here," Nick said. "I'm starting an afterschool program for kids of single mothers. They need a lot of help."

As Tessa and Nick discussed his program, they kept sipping. When Tessa finished her wine, he left to get another glass for both of them. She wished he would offer her some nuts or crackers, but she didn't know him well enough to brazenly request food. She wondered when he would serve dinner. There were no hot coals in the grill on his deck and no smells of something cooking in the kitchen.

"Here, pretty lady." Nick handed her another glass.

He called me pretty! "I usually stop at two."

"Remember the antioxidants. They protect you from free radicals. You don't want cancer." Another of Nick's heartwarming smiles.

When Tessa got halfway through her second glass and Nick was telling her about a fundraiser that a friend was having for his campaign, she began to feel mentally fuzzy. She noted that Nick was watching her. It wasn't like her to get drunk on a glass and a half of wine, but then, she'd had nothing to eat since lunch.

"What book's on your bedside table these days?" he asked. His voice sounded like it was coming from underwater.

"I'm re-reading *The Catcher in the Rye*." Tessa heard herself slur the middle of the word, so it sounded like *catch her*. She leaned her head back on the chaise lounge's pillow and closed her eyes.

CHAPTER 5

At dinnertime on a Saturday night, the Chat 'n' Chew smelled of hamburgers. If Hope had come along with Will, her nose would have quivered at the prospect of lunging at the meat, but he'd left her at home. On the way to his Jeep, he'd made the mistake of turning back and seeing her bereft face, framed by his back door's windowpane. She was a champion of heartstring pulling. Will had almost wished he'd not agreed to meet his sister, Maria, and her husband, Alex, tonight.

His parents used to claim the Chat 'n' Chew had not changed since the sixties, kind of like San Julian. Walking in here was like entering a time warp. There were tables covered with plaid oilcloths, flowers in candle-dripped Chianti bottles, and posters of Chairman Mao and Che Guevara.

Will saw Maria waving to get his attention. In the crowd, her bright pink sweater was like an exclamation point. All his life, friends had told him that he and Maria looked alike, but that was mostly because they both had ruddy skin and cerulean blue eyes—and when they wore cerulean blue, they could practically hypnotize people. But Will was a strapping and sometimes disheveled six-feet-two to Maria's delicate and always impeccable five-feet-one. His hair was chestnut brown, and hers ranged from black to platinum, depending on her mood.

Will pulled out a chair across from her and Alex. "I'm not late, am I?" Usually, he was the one waiting for them.

"You're right on time. We ordered you a beer." Maria slid a mug toward him, past salt-and-pepper shakers that had seen a few too many greasy hands.

"Thanks. Very thoughtful of you." Will took a slug. "Where are the boys?"

"We dropped them off at a birthday party," Alex said.

"They're doing okay?" Will asked.

"Great," Alex said. "They're at a fun age. Not old enough yet to cause much trouble."

The boys were six and eight, cute kids with freckles and rust-colored hair—definitely from Alex, who was fair and Nordic and looked like he'd descended from Eric the Red. Without the boys, tonight would be quieter than usual, not necessarily good. Maria would have more opportunity to fuss over Will, nose into his business, and shower him with un-solicited advice, as she'd been doing with abandon since their mother died last year.

"What are you going to order? We're having the calorie splurge," Maria said.

Will knew she was talking chiliburgers. He didn't have to open his menu because it hadn't changed since he and Maria were kids. "Same old for me," he said. Maria would know that meant a cheeseburger with fries.

Will waved over the waitress in a peach-colored uni-form and ruffled white apron. She took a pencil from behind her ear and wrote their orders on a pad. As she collected the plastic-covered menus, Will took another gulp of beer. "So how's business, Alex?"

"Too busy. I've got three landscapes to put in next week and not enough crew."

"It's his hardest time of year. His clients run him ragged," Maria said.

Alex did look a little green around the gills. Will told him, "It's tough. I don't know how you do it."

"I don't know how *you* stand up in court. I couldn't handle that kind of pressure." Alex shooed a fly off the oilcloth. "Who are you going after now?"

"A DV jerk. It's his third arrest for beating up his wife."

Maria shuddered, narrowed her eyes. "I hope you get him."

"I intend to."

"How do you deal with tragedies like that day after day?" Alex asked.

"I think about putting the perverts behind bars. It's rewarding."

"You work too hard," Maria said, steady eyes on him.

Oh, man. The food hasn't even gotten here yet, and here comes the campaign, there's-more-to-your-life-than-your-job. "I love you, Maria, but I've heard that from you before." *About a thousand times.*

"Well, you should hear it again. I don't want you to keel over dead from a heart attack before you're forty-five. I need a brother, and my boys need an uncle."

"Don't worry about me. I don't smoke, and I don't drink much. Hope makes sure I exercise."

"Yeah, but you're always thinking about work. It matters more to you than anything."

"That's not true," Will said, though maybe it was. Sometimes, anyway. Trish, his ex-girlfriend, had accused him of the same thing.

Last February, she'd called his office around eight one night. "I need you to come over and help me with my application." From the get-go, her demanding, whiny voice had bothered him.

Will had forgotten about the application. "When's it due?"

"I told you *yesterday*," she said. Will could imagine her put-upon expression, her imperious head toss. "It's due the day after tomorrow."

"You've got plenty of time. I'll look at it tomorrow after work."

"That's too late. I can't get it done," Trish said.

"You'll have the whole night." Given the last-minute complications Will faced in court, a whole night was a luxury.

"Some of the questions require long answers, like why I want to teach. You can lay out an argument better than I can."

"Maybe you shouldn't argue. Maybe they want a statement from the gut."

"I need help with that, too."

Will exhaled an exasperated breath. Trish had a good HR job. Workwise, she'd been around the block. There was no reason she couldn't fill out the application on her own. "Look, I'm really busy. I'll call you after a while."

A few minutes later, she called back. And half an hour after that. And again in another half hour. "It's clear your work matters more to you than *I* do," she said.

As Will paused to shift from his witness questions to her sulk, it occurred to him that he didn't feel like pacifying her. He'd done enough of it, and, furthermore, she was correct: He *did* care more about his work than her. He liked her, but he'd known for a while that she was never going to be the one. Will was looking for a woman with a kind and loving heart; if Trish's heart were a piece of paper, it would have something hard and scratchy written on it, like *thistle*.

Though Will was careful to break up with her on friendly

terms, that night was the beginning of the inevitable end. The curtain came down on a relationship that had never been right—and if a relationship wasn't right, forget it. He had no regrets. Rather than try to force something that was never going to work, he preferred to be alone.

CHAPTER 6

Tessa's eyes fluttered open. She felt as if someone had poured sand into her limbs and weighed them down so she could hardly move. Her head seemed filled with used and dirty paper towels.

She stared at an unfamiliar bedside lamp—a brass candlestick base with a black linen shade—and she couldn't figure out where it had come from. Or where she was. Sunlight was streaming through a window that was not positioned right for her own bed. Whose bed *was* it? How did she get here? The room had a cloying, unfamiliar smell of forced flowers in a hothouse.

With a start, Tessa realized that she was naked. From the sag across the mattress, she also realized that she was not alone in this bed. She marshaled her strength and rolled over. Nick opened an eye and grinned at her.

"Good morning, sunshine." His voice was husky. Stubble covered his cheeks. "How you doing?"

"I'm not sure," Tessa managed.

"You were fine last night. I can tell you that. You enjoyed it as much as I did."

Tessa tried to unscramble her thoughts, but still, she didn't understand. By "it," he must mean sex, but she couldn't recall it. How could she *not* remember something like that?

Deep inside, something as primal as earth urged her, *Get out of here.* Her survival instinct propelled her to sit up and swing her legs over the side of Nick's bed.

Her body ached all over, and she was sore between her legs. Feeling Nick's eyes on her naked skin, she grabbed her clothes off the carpet, hobbled into the bathroom, and locked the door. Her icy hands made it difficult to step into her leggings, and she fumbled with her bra's hooks. She shrugged into her T-shirt and slipped into her flats. For an instant, she wasn't sure where she'd left her purse, but then she remembered setting it on a table by Nick's entry closet, where he'd hung her coat. If her basket wasn't still on his kitchen counter, she'd go home without it.

"Leaving so soon?" Nick flashed Tessa a crooked smile. He looked rumpled—on a better morning, she might have thought sexy. She'd have pictured him in an ad for Jockey briefs.

"I have to go," she said.

"It's been great." Nick made no move to get out of bed and walk her to the door.

Outside, Tessa squinted at the sunlight, which was too cheerful, a personal affront. She walked, unsteady, to her yellow Volkswagen Beetle. After three tries, she fit her key into the door's lock. Perhaps she should calm herself before driving away, but she was desperate to leave.

As she started down the street, she glanced back at Nick's house. Through his bedroom window, she saw him in gray sweatpants, stripping his bed. Why the rush?

Did he strip me?

He must have because Tessa couldn't remember taking off her clothes. She couldn't remember anything, and that brought a chill to her bones.

CHAPTER 7

The sunny Sunday afternoon beckoned to Will, *Come outside and enjoy the spring!* Not an option. Yesterday he'd finished mowing the second half of his field, and Maria and Alex had kept him at the Chat 'n' Chew later than he'd wanted. Today he had to pay the piper and tackle his trial's closing argument. As he shuffled through a stack of notes, something thumped his knee. It was an urgent and familiar thump undoubtedly meant as a clearing-of-throat *ahem*, delivered by Hope's paw. The thump shouted as intently as the sunshine, *You can't work all afternoon! I am desperate! It's way past time for my walk!*

Hope had been hinting for one since Will had gotten up and stepped into his jeans. Being a highly intelligent dog, she recognized that they were not the usual slacks he wore to work on weekdays. When he neglected to put on a coat and tie, Hope was certain that instead of going to work, today she could be a normal dog. She pranced around the house with her yellow duck, her favorite toy.

In the last months, bit by bit, Hope had massacred her duck so that most of its stuffing was gone. The duck looked like roadkill, squashed flat by a panzer fleet. Will had brought home a new duck replacement, but Hope had eyed it with suspicion and spurned it. Ignored, it now lived at the bottom of her wicker toy basket.

After another thump to his knee, Will reached under the table and stroked Hope's velvety ears. He told her, "Later. Be patient."

Hope responded with a barely audible whimper, but it was clearly backed by her strongly held opinions. She could bring people to their knees with her convincing oratory, and today's tiny whimper let Will know that she wanted to go for a walk *now*. It reminded him that he *had* agreed with Washington Facility Dogs to walk her twice a day, and so far, he'd only let her out for her morning patrol of the field. She had been a good and earnest dog, and she had not bothered him for hours. Her self-restraint deserved his consideration.

Though Will could concentrate at his desk for hours without a break, Hope, like Maria, had her own ideas about his work habits, and she clearly believed that they should allow for extra-long walks on beautiful afternoons. Knowing defeat when he saw it, Will closed his file and resolved to finish up tonight, though he'd hoped to get to bed early. He pushed back from the table. Hope sprang to her paws and danced around his legs.

As Will started for the back door, his eyes went to a photo on the wall. His mother and Maria were beaming on each side of him in his cap and gown on his law school graduation day. Sadly, his businessman father, who'd never gone to college, had died five years before the photo, and he'd never know that Will had made something of himself. But his mother, whose life had revolved around her children, had kept reminding him, "Dad would be so proud of you." Though his father was gone, earning that pride was still important to Will.

Maria said Will was too focused on his work, but he believed that he'd been put on earth for it. His job was more than a job. It gave his life purpose and provided him with the personal crusade of making sure bad guys got what they deserved. If he didn't give so much of himself to his work, how else could he win the good fight? Prosecuting without passion got nowhere.

Even so, he knew there was more to life, and he was as aware as Maria was of what he was missing. He took Hope's leash off a hook by the door, the signal that, indeed, they were about to have a walk. Hope panted with excitement but sat quietly, as she'd been trained, when Will attached the leash to her collar. "Come on, girl!"

Squeak. Whine. A shuffle of eager, frolicking paws as he opened the door. Without question, along with becoming a lawyer, taking on Hope was the best thing Will had ever done.

"Does Waterfront Park sound good to you?" he asked.

As she bounded down the steps toward the gate, her paws answered, *YES!*

CHAPTER 8

Again, Tessa opened her eyes, but this time she knew in an instant that she was in her own bed. The blooming rhododendron's branches were brushing against her cottage window, and the familiar scent of her fabric softener lingered in her sheets. Like the Princess and the Pea, she would recognize her mattress's special softness anywhere. A framed silhouette said to be of Jane Austen, for whom one of her cats was named, was propped up on her desk next to the bed.

Once Tessa's whereabouts had registered, Nick Payne crashed into her thoughts, an uninvited guest. She could not escape her mental picture of him this morning, tangled in his sheets, his hair sticking out in tufts, his glasses on the night table. He was surely right that they'd had sex—she wouldn't be clammy and sore if they hadn't. But had she wanted it? How could that be? It was not like her to end up sleeping with a man she barely knew.

Feeling dirty and disoriented, Tessa checked her watch— four o'clock! She'd slept all afternoon. Gingerly, she climbed out of bed. On her way to the bathroom, she saw that in this morning's haste, she'd put on her long-sleeved striped T-shirt inside out. When she pulled it over her head and dropped it into her wicker laundry hamper, she noticed five fingerprint bruises on each upper arm. Nick must have gripped her and held on.

Something was wrong. No, more than wrong. Something was disturbing, unnerving. From the bathroom mirror, glazed eyes stared back at Tessa. It seemed as though inside her, nobody was home. Except for forehead creases, her face seemed as blank as the expanse of time that her mind could not recall.

Out loud, Tessa asked her image, "Did Nick drug you? Is that what's happened?"

The image replied, "That's ridiculous! He couldn't have. An upstanding man like him wouldn't drug anyone."

That conviction echoed through Tessa's mind as she showered for nearly thirty minutes. Soap and pure, clean water had never felt so good.

Outside, Tessa fed her cats plain store-bought kibble with a little canned Salmon Treat for their dinner. Just as this morning, she had no strength for a homemade meal for them. Bronte was back, thank goodness. Now Dickens, a sumptuous tiger-striped male, was missing. Though neutered, each spring he wandered off to go a-Maying—and in unfamiliar territory, he could get hurt. Bad things could come to cats just like they came to everybody else. Something more for Tessa to worry about.

"You be safe," she mumbled to her other cats.

Having no interest in dinner for herself, Tessa went back to her cottage and burrowed under her covers again—until the phone rang. Jangled, she bolted up in bed, then hesitated. What if Nick was calling? What would she say? With trepidation, she looked at the caller ID. Emma. Tessa picked up the receiver.

"Hey, Tess! I just got back from camping. You've been on my mind all day. How'd it go?" Emma sounded breathless, excited. Surely she expected no less than a joyful report of last night.

"I don't know what to tell you," Tessa said.

"What do you mean?"

"I got home this morning. I think something happened."

"Something bad?" The excitement drained from Emma's voice.

"I'm not sure. We were drinking wine, and this morning I woke up in his bed. In between, I don't know what went on."

Tessa heard Emma's sharp intake of breath. "You don't know *anything?*"

"I can't remember," Tessa said.

"That's not right."

"Tell me about it." The misery felt suddenly heavy.

"You must have made love."

Love didn't seem like the correct word. "My body hurts, and my arms are bruised, but this morning he told me I liked it, whatever 'it' was supposed to mean."

"That's not for *him* to judge, the arrogant—" Emma cut the thought, as if she'd been putting jigsaw pieces together and the image that suddenly emerged alarmed her. "You know what, Tess? I'll bet anything that horrible man drugged you. He raped you."

The ugly word made Tessa shiver. "I can't believe he'd do that. He seemed so honorable."

"Yeah, right. 'Honorable' men can do awful things as well as anybody," Emma said. "That creep took advantage."

"It doesn't fit who he is."

"Who you *think* he is," Emma corrected.

"He could get plenty of women into his bed without drugging them. I might have been a candidate myself once I got to know him better."

"Sex is all he was after. He didn't waste time getting to know you."

Tessa's mind flashed on his ten minutes of questions for getting acquainted. Perhaps Emma was right.

"Nick Payne is even worse than my boss. Lots of people think that man's a saint, but he's a lech. He keeps giving me his head-to-toe once-over, like he's devouring me. I feel like telling his wife," Emma said.

"At least he hasn't attacked you." *Did Nick attack* me?

"Yes, but he always says I look hot. He acts like it's a compliment, but it's a sneaky show of power. It turns me into his sex object." Emma paused. "Listen, Tess, I may have to put up with harassment, but you can't let Nick Payne get away with rape."

"I'm still not sure that's what it was."

"I am. And you need to report it. I'm coming over and taking you to the police."

"No! I don't want to do that," Tessa shot back. "Maybe he didn't do what you said. Maybe I agreed to go to bed with him."

"You couldn't have agreed if you were drugged."

"I don't know for sure if I *was* drugged," Tessa protested. "I can't accuse Nick and cause an uproar if I'm wrong. Nobody would believe me, anyway. Everybody admires him." If the phone had been a living thing, Tessa's grip might have squeezed the breath out of it. "Nick's wine could have fogged my memory. When the effect wears off, I'll figure out what happened."

"You're in denial, Tess."

"Maybe." *Am I?*

"If you change your mind, I can take the three o'clock ferry home tomorrow and get you to the police by four."

It was all too much. Tessa couldn't handle any of it. After she hung up the phone, she rooted under her covers and closed her eyes to block out the world.

CHAPTER 9

Tessa is walking along a wood-chip path in San Julian's Grand Forest. Fir trees are all around her. Ferns. As she breathes the cool, fresh air, she thinks that she is lucky to be alive in this beautiful place. But then, out of the corner of her eye, she sees something move just off the trail, and she whirls around—sometimes black bears swam to the island.

A man in gray sweats is watching her. Tessa can't make out his face, but she thinks he's wearing glasses. Without speaking, he starts toward her. A bead of sweat creeps down her spine, and she knows with certainty that he means harm—and he is evil. She runs, and he runs after her. His hands reach for her hair to drag her to the ground.

She screams. No sound comes out. She yells so hard her throat burns, but the only sound she hears is the man's ragged breath. Tessa is alone. No one knows she is in danger. No one can help her.

Tessa's shouts jolted her awake. She sat up, looked around in the dark. She realized that she was in her bed, panting and wet from sweat. Shivers of fight or flight were working their way from her chest down her limbs. Fear, smelling acrid and sour, seeped from her skin's pores.

Did Nick assault me? Is that what my subconscious wants me to see? Or was Nick right, and I enjoyed the sex—and the wine has erased my memory? How would Tessa ever know? One thing she *did* know: If everything was fine, the nightmare would be fading from her mind now instead of growing more insistent.

Tessa lay back down and bunched her blanket in her fists. Minutes passed as she tried to slow her pants to easy breaths. She closed her eyes and pictured herself lying on a sandy beach, the sun warming her skin, ocean waves lapping her toes. That had always been her way to calm herself, but tonight, peace eluded her. She thought of getting up for a glass of water, but she was too frightened to walk across the room.

Suddenly, as a meteor streaks through a black sky, a snatch of memory burst into her mind: Nick had thrown her onto his bed. He'd shown no gentleness—she could have been a log he tossed onto a fire. She remembered the solid weight of his body crushing her. Then nothing. Her memory screen went dark. That was all her mind was willing to give her.

Tessa lay there, holding onto those brief seconds, scared she might lose them again. She searched her mind for what they meant. They didn't confirm a sexual assault, but they showed that Nick had cared nothing for her. There had been no warmth or tenderness. He *could* have drugged her.

Maybe Emma had been right. Maybe Tessa should go to the police, though the prospect filled her with dread. She'd be embarrassed to show up and try to explain what had happened when it was so personal and she knew so little.

What should I do?

Indecision gnawed on her. But as she looked out her window at clouds blowing across the moon, she told herself that she needed to tell the police. She needed to be strong.

She'd call Emma in the morning.

CHAPTER 10

When Will woke in the dark, Hope was snoring beside him. As far as he could tell, there was no reason for his sleep to be disrupted—unless the tentacles of his current DV case had wrapped themselves around his brain. He checked his clock; the glowing 2:15 a.m. told him that he'd slept for only an hour. *Hello, insomnia, my sometimes friend. Here we are again.*

All of Will's cases involved others' pain and suffering—physical, emotional, maybe even spiritual if he dug down to the victim's soul. Across his desk passed a constant misery parade, and some cases were worse than others for the victim—*and* for him. He wasn't too proud to admit to himself that the misery sometimes shoved past his defenses, bored into him, and hung on, weighing him down and waking him in the night, like now. If he were a robot, his job might be easy. But he wasn't a robot, and some cases got to him.

Will wasn't sure why the current one had done so, unless it was because of the visceral disgust he'd felt for the bully when he'd swaggered into the interview room. It wasn't just the injury he'd inflicted on his wife on the three occasions when he'd been arrested—though recently knocking out four of her teeth, breaking her jaw, and smacking her across the kitchen with the back of his hand was reprehensible.

What also galled Will was the psycho's attitude. He'd acted like domestic violence was a God-given right, and he was entitled to keep "the wife" in line. "You're making too big a deal," he'd told Will. Never mind the two young children locked outside, watching through the kitchen windows and wailing because they couldn't help their mother. Never mind his carousing at the Tipsy Cow, drinking himself into a rage, and then assaulting her as if the violence were a nightcap.

Now Will had to get him. If he could.

On the wall across from his bed, he studied shadows made by moonlight filtered through his plum tree. They could have been a Rorschach test. A beheaded rabbit. A one-winged moth. An eviscerated buffalo's chest. As Will saw it, all pain and destruction. And projection of his concern for the woman he'd been trying to help.

Blinking in the dark, he reminded himself that he couldn't let the case get to him, no matter how much he detested the perp or how sorry he felt for the wife. Internal disturbance was not allowed on his job; if he let himself feel too much, he'd do no one any good. He had to stifle his emotions and stay detached. He had to keep his eyes on the prize of sending the lowlife to prison.

If Will was going to do that, he needed to get some rest. He rolled over on his side, put his arm across Hope's haunch, and began to count her breaths, like aural sheep. She shuffled her paws—perhaps she was dreaming of chasing a rabbit like the beheaded one on the wall. Or of running across the softball field of the Sons of Pitches, the team he played on all summer. One, two, three . . . He breathed in sync with her.

Washington Facility Dogs had trained Hope not to get on furniture unless invited, and Will was not supposed to allow her on his bed. But after she'd lived with him for a couple of months, she apparently decided that his bed suited her better than her own round one, which looked like a giant green pea after a face-off with a steamroller. At first, Hope was furtive about her decision; she snuck onto Will's bed and curled up next to him after he'd fallen asleep. But slowly, more blatantly, she took to jumping up beside him as soon as he turned off the light. Now before he even got to his bed, she sprawled across it as if she owned it; sometimes she stretched out her legs in front of her so her body formed a champagne-blond *C* and crowded him to the edge.

Tonight, she rested her cheek on his pillow, so close that he felt her moist breath on his neck. Will didn't mind. He liked her company. She made it easier for him to be alone.

CHAPTER 11

"Hi!" A woman's hand—nails short and square, no polish—came toward Tessa for a shake. "Sandy Johnson. I'm a detective in the Nisqually County Prosecutor's Office." Her hand radiated warmth.

She was short and stocky, and she had a chain tattooed around her neck. Her silver hair, cut in a punk style—Marine Corps length on the sides and cascading over one eye—also made her look tough. But her exposed eye, highlighted with violet shadow, looked sympathetic, as if in a long career she'd heard every story there was to tell, nothing was beyond her understanding, and she wanted to help.

"Tessa Jordan." In a police station for the first time in her life, Tessa could barely whisper her name.

"This is Hope." Sandy's pats on Hope's side sounded like she was thumping a watermelon. "I'm one of her handlers. Do you like dogs?"

"Yes."

"She's a sweetheart. Would you like to sit with her?"

"Sure."

Sandy gestured toward the Naugahyde sofa, where Tessa had been waiting since a barrel-chested policeman had asked if she'd rather talk with a woman than him. Her knees wobbly, she sank back into the seat, which felt as stiff as she did. Hope jumped up beside her. When Sandy said "snuggle," Hope rested her chin on Tessa's lap and glanced up at her so the whites below her pupils looked like crescent moons lying on their backs. According to an old wives' tale, moons like that announced good weather—an irony, since Tessa was in an emotional storm.

Hope seemed to pick up the storm, and her snuggle spoke whole paragraphs of compassion. *I know you're scared, but I am here. Don't worry. I care with all my heart.*

Tessa stroked Hope's triangle ears. "Has Hope been trained to love people, or does she naturally do it?"

"She's been trained, but I think she's truly kind. Her heart is as big as Texas." When Hope gazed up at Tessa again, Sandy added, "I think you've made a friend."

Tessa felt slightly better, though after Saturday night, "better" was a relative term. The interview room, which wasn't much bigger than a walk-in closet, felt like it was closing in on her. She wished as much now as when she'd arrived that she could run outside and disappear, yet something internal urged her on. She'd come this far to make a report, and she was determined to see it through.

"The officer who called me said you might have been sexually assaulted," Sandy said.

"I don't know what I'm doing here. I'm not sure if I was assaulted or not."

"A lot of women come in thinking that. Assailants can have a way of blurring the edges of truth." Sandy sat in a swivel conference chair across from Tessa so their knees almost touched. She pulled a spiral notebook out of her backpack. "You want to talk about it?"

Definitely not. "I guess."

"Do you mind if I record our conversation? It would help."

Oh, no. Please, don't. "Okay." Like an ostrich sticking her head in sand, Tessa closed her eyes and hid behind her lids. It was all too much, being here, and so embarrassing, even frightening. She didn't feel prepared.

Sandy pressed a button, and the recorder started rolling. "Whenever you're ready, Tessa. Take a deep breath. I'd like to know what happened."

Tessa's deep breath barely got as far as her trachea. There was no turning back. She opened her eyes. "Okay, I met him on NorthwestSingles.com," she began. Sandy scribbled notes but kept her violet-shaded eye fixed on Tessa while she poured out her story, as short and incomplete as it was. "You can see I don't remember anything except being thrown onto his bed. The rest is a blank." She pushed up a sleeve of her T-shirt and showed Sandy some of her bruises. "I guess these are his calling cards."

Sandy leaned forward and examined Tessa's arm. "They look painful. I'm so sorry," she said. "So tell me . . . Let's go back. You haven't mentioned his name."

"Nick Payne."

"Oh." The one syllable revealed that Sandy knew exactly who Nick Payne was.

"I still can't believe a man like him would assault anybody," Tessa said.

"From what you've told me, it sounds like he could have," Sandy said. "Where exactly did this happen?"

"At his house. On Bent Route Road. I don't remember the number."

"I can look it up," Sandy said. "What did the outside look like?"

"A two-story craftsman. Gray."

"What about the inside?"

"Tasteful. Lots of books. Leather sofas and chairs. A modern kitchen. There was a rubber plant in his living room, and over the fireplace was a print—part of the Sistine Chapel ceiling, you know, God's index finger reaching to give Adam life. I've seen the image dozens of times." Tessa re-crossed her legs. "Why do you need to know all this?"

"If it's a crime scene, your description can establish you were there and convince a judge to give me a search warrant. I'll need it to gather evidence."

Tessa stared at the station's wall of concrete blocks as "crime scene," "search warrant," and "evidence" rattled through her mind. There was no escaping that this interview was serious.

"You said Nick Payne gave you a glass of wine. Did you drink more than that?" Sandy asked.

"He refilled my glass once. I got about halfway through it."

"How much do you normally drink?"

"Maybe two glasses."

"What's your typical reaction to them?"

"I don't get drunk. My head doesn't spin or anything. I just feel relaxed."

"So how does that compare to how you felt when you finished half the second glass on Saturday?"

"My brain got fuzzy. Nick's voice sounded weird. My body went kind of limp, like I was losing control of my arms and legs. You know what I mean?"

"I've heard people describe that many times," Sandy said.

"I knew something was wrong, but I didn't have the strength to do anything about it. That's when I must have passed out," Tessa said. "Do you think he could have drugged me?"

"It sounds possible." Sandy flipped to a blank notebook page. "Do you remember consenting to sex with him? Anything you could have said to make him think you agreed to it?"

"I don't remember saying anything. Mentally, I wasn't even there." When tears Tessa had been holding back slid down her cheeks, Sandy handed her a box of tissues. She pulled one out and mopped her face.

"I know this is hard, but you're doing great," Sandy said as Hope, an expert reader of tears, pressed the side of her head against Tessa's waist. "I have more questions. Are you okay with that? We can take a break if you want."

"No, it's okay." *I want this over with. I want to go home.* Holding onto Hope, Tessa blew her nose.

"I have to ask, have you ever had voluntary sex before Nick Payne?"

"I'm thirty-six."

"I take that as a yes?"

"I lived with a boyfriend for four years. We were engaged, but it didn't work out."

"Okay," Sandy said. "Does your body feel different now from how it felt after voluntary sex?"

"Night and day different. When I woke up yesterday, it hurt to walk to Nick's bathroom. It still hurts."

"So penetration occurred?"

"I wasn't conscious at the time, but . . . um . . . penetration must have occurred."

Tessa squeezed her tissue into a ball and dug her fingernails into it.

"I don't mean to stress you, Tessa. Would a glass of water help?"

Tessa shook her head. "Do you think Nick raped me?" She could say that word a thousand times, but it would still sound awful.

"He sure could have. I know it's hard for that to sink in," Sandy said. "It's more of a shock if you were unconscious when it happened. It's hard to imagine being sexually assaulted when you weren't really 'there.'"

Tessa nodded, took another tissue, and swiped at more tears.

"Have you changed the clothes you wore?" Sandy asked.

"I couldn't stand to keep them on."

"Where are they?"

"In my dirty clothes hamper."

"Underwear too?"

"Yes."

"What about taking a shower or bath? Have you done that?"

"I took a long shower yesterday afternoon. Was that bad?"

"Nothing's bad here, Tessa. Nobody's judging you. You might have destroyed evidence, but I'm not the person to figure that out."

"Who does?"

"Mary O'Malley. We call her a SANE. It's the acronym for sexual assault nurse examiner," Sandy said. "Would you be willing for her to take a look at you?"

Tessa shrank back. She'd intended only to report what Nick had done, not to be physically invaded again.

"Let me tell you why I think it would be a good idea. Do you mind?" Sandy asked.

Tessa shook her head, an anemic *no*.

"What you've told me points to sexual assault, but the nurse needs to confirm it. You could be a walking crime scene. Your body might have valuable evidence that she needs to preserve and analyze," Sandy said.

"But I'm not sure I want to go ahead with this. All I wanted was to let someone know what could have happened. You know, document it, get it on the record," Tessa said. "I didn't mean to make a big deal. And I don't think anybody would believe me if I accused Nick of assault."

"I believe you." Sandy closed her notebook and returned it to her backpack. She fixed her exposed eye intently on Tessa again. "The thing is, if you're not certain what Nick did to you, an exam might answer that. And you can't predict how you're going to feel about this in the future. If you don't have the exam, we won't have evidence, and if we don't have that, we won't be able to help you. You'll have closed the door on legal options."

Tessa's gaze went to flecks in the floor's linoleum, which looked like dirty snow.

"I don't want to pressure you, Tessa. It's your decision." Sandy's eye slanted down at the outside edge with what looked like genuine concern. "But you might help us catch a predator. If the evidence points to Nick Payne, we can arrest him. Evidence is what gets offenders off the street."

"I don't know what to do," Tessa said. "When I came here, legal options weren't on my mind. I had no intention of going after Nick like he's a criminal."

"Somebody would be with you every step of the way . . . The exam is just another step, but it's necessary if you want justice."

Justice. The word felt hard and heavy, like a rock thrown into a pond—and the ripples would go on forever. Still, Tessa finally said, "Okay."

CHAPTER 12

The day felt like it would never end. That afternoon, Will had wound up the DV trial and gone back to an avalanche of work in his office—returning phone calls, answering emails, catching up on all he'd let go of last week. Everybody had wanted a bite of his time, including the Rotary Club president, who'd asked if he could bring Hope to star at a luncheon next month. Along with his legal work, Will kept community relations going with her, and that meant rides in parades, attendance at fundraisers, and portraits of her for charities' calendars.

Looking forward to a good night's sleep, Will turned into his driveway and drove through the field to his house. Hope and Sandy were waiting for him in her black Chevy Lumina sedan, which was unmarked so she could snoop without being noticed. It was time for what they called the "Hope Transfer."

As Sandy got out of the car and opened the door for Hope, Will's motion-detector light illuminated the parking area and path to his front porch. He left his Jeep in the barn and walked toward them. Hope's droop told him that she was as tired as he was. Her spine sagged slightly, her face looked weary, and she barely swished her tail to greet him. Stressful visits emotionally saturated her. She was petted out.

"Hard day?" Will asked.

"Long one," Sandy said.

Ditto. "Need to come in and talk about it?"

"Just for a minute. I've still got lots to do tonight." Sandy followed Will into the house. "Hope was hungry, so I fed her."

"Thanks." When Will took off her vest and officially relieved her of her duty, she shook her body as she did after a bath—perhaps she was shaking off the day's emotions. Once free, she usually hunted for her yellow duck and paraded it around, but tonight she headed upstairs, a signal she needed time alone. Will would find her conked out on his bed, belting out snores.

"So what's going on?" he asked.

"We need a warrant. Probable sexual assault. I just dropped off the vic for the forensic exam. Tessa Jordan. She drives the county bookmobile. You know her?"

"Can't say I do," Will said. "What happened?"

"She met the perp online. On Saturday night, she went to his house. She doesn't remember anything after a glass and a half of wine. Woke up in his bed yesterday morning."

"You believe her?"

"Totally. She seems like a good person. My gut says she wouldn't lie."

"Why'd she wait so long to report the assault?"

"Because she wasn't sure if she was assaulted, but I expect the nurse will verify it."

Will felt a slight stirring of his blood, the awakening of interest that accompanied the possibility of a new case. He welcomed any chance to take another pervert to court. "I'll meet you first thing in the morning. We can do the affidavit," he said.

"We need to get a move on. Seven okay?"

Will could get maybe six hours' sleep. *Goodbye downtime.* "I'll be there."

"I'm on my way to the vic's house for the clothes she wore. I'll bring them to Mary O'Malley."

"You've got a long night ahead of you."

"I'm used to it." Sandy pulled her Chevy's keys from her coat pocket. "Um, Will . . ."

"Yep?"

"The perp is Nick Payne."

Will's blood stirred faster. "Wow. Turn over a rock, and you never know what you'll find."

"Endless surprises in this business."

High-profile case. Got to do it by the book. Lots of eyes on us. If the case ever got to court. So few did.

CHAPTER 13

Tall, erect, and perfectly groomed, Mary O'Malley might have served in the military. Her nurse's shoes dazzled white, and her starched lab coat crinkled when she moved. In a corner of her exam room, which could pass any muster, Tessa fidgeted in a straight-backed chair while Mary typed on a laptop at a faux wood desk.

She asked Tessa to sign consent forms for an exam and for photos.

"Why photos?"

"They'll help if your assailant is brought to trial," Mary said.

"Assailant" sounded threatening and clinical. "Can't we just call him Nick?" Tessa asked, signing the forms without reading them.

"Whatever makes you comfortable."

With uncommon efficiency, Mary's questions came in a downpour. Some were similar to Sandy's, but others were aimed specifically toward the physical exam. In the last five days, had Tessa had sex with anyone other than Nick? Had she taken any drugs? Did she know if Nick had used a condom?

Mary took Tessa's medical and sexual history and listened intently as she told her story yet another time. When Tessa finished and stared, lost, at her loafers' stitching, Mary said, "You've suffered through a horrible experience. You're very brave to come here. Many sexual assaults never get reported."

Mary was understanding, but not sentimental. Tessa could see her, unflinching at wounds, in a field hospital. "Tonight I want to examine you and make sure you're physically all right. And I need to collect evidence. That sound okay to you?" she asked.

Tessa wasn't sure if any of it sounded okay, but she agreed. She presented her arm for a blood sample and provided urine in a cup. Mary took scrapings from under her fingernails. She told Tessa that her shower may have removed all of Nick's DNA, but she would still hunt for it because it would positively link them together.

Then Mary asked Tessa to remove her clothing and put on a hospital gown, which was folded on a padded table, covered with paper, across the room. When Mary left Tessa alone, she did as directed. Feeling exposed and vulnerable, she sat on the edge of the table and, shivering, dangled her bare feet over the side.

She waited. From the hospital's hall came snatches of conversation, rubber soles' squeaks on linoleum, and the clatter of passing equipment and carts. They let Tessa know that people were around, yet she felt achingly alone. She wrapped her arms around herself partly for emotional comfort and partly against the cold.

When Mary knocked and came into the room again, she must have seen the tension in Tessa's face. "Would you like some water?"

"No thanks."

"You must tell me if there's anything I can do to make this easier for you."

Erase the last two days from my life. Make all this go away. Take me home.

"I'm going to start by checking for signs of bruising or injury. Can you help me by pulling up your gown?"

As Tessa raised it and exposed her naked chest and belly, she said, "As far as I know, all the bruises are on my arms."

Mary found them and took photographs. When Tessa shivered again, Mary asked, "Are you cold?"

"Yes."

"I'll turn up the heat."

Indeed, Mary did. She returned to the table, fluffed up Tessa's pillow, and said, "I'd like for you to lie back." Tessa's mind flashed on her one small scrap of memory, when Nick threw her on her back. The image made her stomach lurch, but she did as she was told.

"You doing okay?" Mary asked.

"I guess." A lie.

"I know this is hard," Mary said as she covered Tessa with a sheet and pulled a steel tray on casters to the table. A white cloth hid whatever was on top. "As we're going along, at each step I'll tell you what I'm going to do, and you can always decline the procedure or ask to take a break. It'll be your call. You're in control. Nobody will be upset by anything you decide, all right?"

"Okay," Tessa said, grasping at straws of strength inside her. Even more than while she'd waited for Sandy, Tessa wanted to leave, but again her determination kept her there.

From then on, the exam passed like a bad dream, between each step of which Mary changed her latex gloves. Looking for evidence of Nick, she combed Tessa's pubic hair. She swabbed and poked Tessa's private parts, and she took internal images with a cringe-inducing colposcope's small TV camera, attached to an adjustable, beige metal arm.

"It's almost over," Mary said as Tessa glued her gaze to a poster of a snowy mountain taped to the ceiling. Mary removed her last pair of gloves with a snap of rubber and tossed them into a steel can. She pushed the colposcope aside.

"You're badly bruised and swollen, Tessa. Nick was way too rough. He injured you."

As Mary helped her sit, Tessa asked, "So it was rape?"

"It looks that way. If your lab results show a date-rape drug, we can corroborate that you couldn't consent to sex."

Tessa had come here partly to put the question of rape to rest, but actually hearing Mary's answer shocked her again. Her denial could no longer cushion the facts. She now believed that while she'd been unconscious, Nick had preyed on her in the worst possible way. She blinked a few times, but her eyes were dry. A numbness settled over her.

"Why did he do it?" she asked.

"Everybody wonders that," Mary said. "I'm no psychologist, but I've come to believe sexual assaults are usually about power."

"Why power over an unconscious woman? There could be no pleasure in that. It doesn't make sense."

"Yes, it does. If you were drugged, he'd have complete control over you. You couldn't defend yourself. That could have been what he was after. Power and control."

Tessa recoiled. "It's so sick."

"It is," Mary said. "He could be a power-assertive type of assailant. They may come across as confident, but they often feel inadequate with women, and they can be angry at them, too. Men like that assault women to validate their masculinity."

"I can't see how any man can be that way."

"I know. It's hard to understand." The kindness in Mary's expression helped Tessa, but not enough. Her gaze went to the floor.

"We need to talk about counseling and prophylaxis. Would you rather do that while you're dressed?" Mary asked.

CHAPTER 14

After two a.m., Tessa staggered out of the exam room and found Emma in a metal folding chair, her head bowed as if she'd nodded off. Usually, she exuded a spunky, can-do attitude—put her in a power suit, and watch out!—but at this early morning hour, messy tendrils hung over her cheeks and her normally sharp, bright eyes were red and dull. She had let Sandy into Tessa's house to get her clothes, then come here to wait.

In the jeans and sweater Tessa had worn all day—and would never wear again—she dragged herself to her friend and hugged her. "Thanks for being you, Em."

"I'm glad to help. Come on. Let's get out of here."

That was a rhapsody to Tessa's demoralized ears. As she and Emma made their way to Emma's Volvo across the street, they said little to each other. What was there to say after all Tessa had endured? Words couldn't help. Nothing could.

At the late hour, few cars were on the street. Emma pulled out of her parking spot as Tessa watched the Volvo's wipers go after drizzle splattered on the windshield. She clutched Mary's list of recommended counselors and the information for a sexual assault survivors' group, but Tessa had no intention of contacting anyone. Nor had she agreed to being assigned an advocate to help her while the investigation continued. She would manage whatever came on her own.

Emma turned onto Cedar Street toward Tessa's cottage. No lights were on in the houses they passed, and that made the night gloomier. "You okay, Tess?"

"People have been asking me that since you brought me to the police station. I don't think I'm ever going to be okay again."

"I was so worried about you. I'm sure it was tough."

Tessa closed her cardigan more tightly across her chest. "The nurse agreed with you. Nick *must have* raped me. He hurt me, too." Speaking it out loud wore down some of the shock and made the assault more real.

Emma's narrowed eyes glared at the road ahead. "I hope Nick Payne rots in hell."

"I hope so, too," Tessa said. "Everybody tried to help tonight, but I still feel humiliated and ashamed."

"Why ashamed? *You* didn't do anything to be ashamed of."

"I keep thinking it's somehow my fault."

"Are you *crazy*?" Emma almost ran a stop sign. She slammed on her brakes, even though no cars were around. "It could never be your fault."

"What if I gave Nick the wrong idea? Or I led him on without intending to? Maybe I shouldn't have accepted the second glass of wine."

"That's ridiculous. You can stop beating yourself up right now."

Emma's windshield wipers' squawks did not drown out Tessa's sigh. Emma could argue all she wanted, but Tessa knew better.

"Maybe thinking you're to blame keeps you from having to admit how unfair life can be," Emma insisted. "There's savagery out there. Bad things happen to good people all the time."

"But why Nick? He's attractive and smart. He doesn't need to assault women. I can't imagine why anybody would do that."

"Because *you* don't have it in you to hurt anyone."

"All the same, I don't get it."

Emma turned into Tessa's driveway and drove toward her cottage, which was located behind her landlady's house. The headlights illuminated her front yard. Nailed to a wooden stake was a campaign sign. It looked like a toadstool that had sprouted in the grass, and the words were dripping poison: *Vote for Nick Payne! A voice for our future! He's visionary! Smart! Principled!*

"Principled?" Tessa spat.

"Don't look!" Emma reached over to shield her from the sight. "Your landlady must have put that up this afternoon. What timing."

"I feel sick."

As soon as Emma left, Tessa hurried to the edge of the woods behind her cottage to feed her cats. They were all that could have kept her from crawling into bed. Usually at this time of night, they'd be curled up together, asleep in straw nests inside the A-frame shelters she provided. They'd be safe from coyotes and owls.

But tonight's supper was the cats' first meal she'd ever missed, and they'd probably given up on her and gone prowling for food just when roaming was most perilous. "I have your dinner, sweet kitties," she called. *Please, be here.*

In her flashlight beam, Dickens sauntered out of the forest—he was back from his sojourn, thank goodness. Alcott and Austen, Tessa's calico sisters, emerged from their shelter, arched their backs, and yawned. Fitzgerald, the friendliest, who looked like a miniature palomino pony, approached but not close enough for her to pet. The other cats were gone, including Bronte, whom Tessa hoped was safely up a tree again, waiting for a sunrise to meditate on.

"Sorry your dinner is so late. I thought I'd get home sooner," she said. "I'd much rather have been here with you." *The understatement of all time.*

She set down clean pie tins, poured in kibble, and spooned canned Tuna Delight on top. It felt good to be doing something normal, though "normal" seemed like a faraway land she'd never visit again.

"I missed you," she said. "Where are Bronte, Wharton, and Melville?"

With loud smacks of Tuna Delight, the kitties ignored her question and pointed out in no uncertain terms, *We were famished. We thought you'd abandoned us. It was terrible!*

"I'm sorry," Tessa said again. Tonight she was sorry about her whole life.

While the cats gobbled down their dinners, she emptied and refilled their water bowl. She told them, "You be safe."

As she started back to her cottage, however, she reminded herself that the cats were never safe. The males swaggered around as if duking it out with challengers was easy, and the females streaked away from danger on winged paws. But the cats had neither security nor a guaranteed defense. Every minute of the day, they felt threatened. They went through life afraid.

It would now be the same for Tessa. Nick Payne had crushed her sense of safety. And he'd sliced through her life's timeline; from now on, she would think of everything that happened as before or after the assault. In one night, he'd become the central fact of her life.

At her cottage door, Tessa did not pat the brass palm before going inside as she used to do. It had failed to ward off evil, and she couldn't trust it anymore. She locked the door behind her and leaned her desk chair under the doorknob so no one could push his way in and attack her. She checked every window to make sure it was locked.

She removed her clothes and wadded them into a plastic bag to toss into the garbage can tomorrow. She showered, and in her nightgown, she huddled in bed. Now that she was finally alone and quiet, her mind went into masochistic overdrive, and she began to imagine every horrible thing Nick might have done to her in her missing hours.

The mental pictures became so graphic that she got up and poured herself a glass of water to escape. But when she returned to bed, the images shoved their way into her mind again. She felt as if her life had shattered into pieces, and she might never put them back together.

Desolate, she stared at the blackness out her window until the sunrise pinked the sky—and Tessa finally fell asleep.

CHAPTER 15

William took a swig of coffee and worked his tie into a Windsor knot. He should buy a few new ties—Maria would insist that this one was too wide—but what the hell? It wasn't *that* wide, and he was a man. According to an unwritten law, men hated shopping. Getting to the grocery store was the most Will could ask of himself.

He set his unwashed cup into the farm sink with the skillet that had just fried his eggs—he wasn't wild about washing dishes. He put on his sports coat, opened the back door, and called Hope, who was roving the freshly mowed field and sniffing for rabbits and mice. She raised her head and looked at him. Her eyes clearly asked, *Me? Surely not. You must be calling some other dog.*

Hope knew from Will's clothes that a workday lay ahead, and she was too responsible to rebel. But she did express her opposition to his call by taking her sweet time to meander toward him, extending her morning patrol as long as she could. The instant Will snapped on her blue vest, however, her demeanor changed. No longer a pet, she shifted to a working dog.

In her vest with its Washington Assistance Dogs logo on the back, Hope seemed to know that she had an important job to do. She stood up straighter, and a serious expression overtook the carefree Labrador smile that had been on her face in the field. Now she responded to Will's commands in the flap of a hummingbird's wing. She put others' needs and wishes before her own.

Will said, "Let's go." With impeccable obedience, she trotted along beside him to the barn.

He opened the front passenger door of his Jeep Cherokee, which was elderly because his salary had paid off his student loans and was now covering his mortgage.

Just as Hope was about to scramble into her seat, a rat scurried across a windowsill and climbed up to the loft.

Hope knew as well as Will did that a rat had invaded the barn. As she pawed the floor, her whimpers pointed out, *Look! An interloper! Let me at him!*

Will held her collar. "We'll add rat detector to your resumé, Hope. Good job." He patted the front seat. "Jump on."

As she leapt into the car, he knew he'd have to plug up holes in the barn walls and replace missing windowpanes. Soon. Before the rat became a permanent squatter and invited his friends to join him in setting up an outpost. Maybe he would leave on his own, but Will doubted he'd have that kind of luck. He worried that the rat would move on to colonize his house.

When Will was a child, his parents had waged war on rats who'd gnawed their way through their home's wood siding and into the attic. They tunneled through the insulation. They wore down their incisors by chomping on cardboard boxes and plastic bins—but then, rats' teeth always grew back so they could continue the mayhem. Worse, the rats shredded family papers, photographs, and scrapbooks.

Will's mother had wept at the damage, and he had felt powerless to help. He'd never forget the turmoil. It left him with a lifelong rat revulsion, and now he'd have to fight back.

Will climbed into the driver's seat and gripped the steering wheel as if he wished it were his marauding rat's neck. He backed out of the barn and hurried down his drive. Soon, Sandy would be arriving in his office.

When Will was so busy, he had no time for a rat. But when was he not busy? Actually, when was he also not dealing with rats? He'd be dealing with Nick Payne, a rat, this very day. Will had to catch rodent rats in his barn and human rats on his job.

CHAPTER 16

After resting for a day, Tessa was determined to go back to work. She needed a return to routine and a distraction from brooding. She wanted to get back on her horse after being thrown to the ground. Though still feeling like she'd been whacked with a two-by-four, she gathered her grit, boarded Howard, and set off for the town of Bucksport, thirty miles from San Julian's library.

If Howard were an animal, he'd be a friendly rhino, whose personal infinitive would be "to galumph." Slightly smaller than a school bus, he commanded respect when he lumbered down a highway, sporting his sign on which was printed in bold green block letters: LIBRARY ON THE GO— DRIVEN TO READ. When Howard passed by, his friends gave him a thumbs-up.

Most people had never heard of Bucksport. Its two boasts were a lavender farm and a Bucksport High School graduate who'd become a Nisqually County deputy sheriff. Tessa passed the town's general store and only gas station, and she parked in her usual spot beside the post office, which was a small, unremarkable metal building, rusty at the seams. It looked like a large storage unit.

Tessa unlocked Howard's door so her people could climb

the three steps to her ever-changing book selection in shelves on each side of his green-carpeted aisle. Overhead was a sunroof, and at the back was her desk with a bust of Shakespeare and a pot of blooming hyacinths, anchored to the wood with museum putty. Next to her desk, a pile of pillows welcomed patrons of all ages to sprawl. And in the corner above the pillows was a bulletin board on which Tessa posted a weekly quote about reading, such as, "We lose—and find—ourselves in books" and "A reader lives a thousand lives before he dies." This week's quote was "A chapter a day will lighten your way." But now, Tessa doubted if that were always true. If she did nothing today but read, she'd still feel weighed down.

Usually, she started each day by thinking of a wish for one of her people who might be coming in. *Let Mrs. Jasper find peace with her hooligan son.* Or *help Billy Westerfield get the job he wants at Mr. Satterwhite's sawmill.* Today, however, Tessa needed the intention for herself. As she booted up her laptop, she thought, *Please, let me get through this day without falling apart.*

To her people, she would be the same Tessa as the last time they'd come here. She would still wear round red-framed reading glasses, have freckles on her arms, and weigh one hundred twenty-one pounds. But today's Tessa was different in ways her people might not note. Nick Payne had dampened her smile and robbed the pink from her cheeks. He'd stamped into her heart such adjectives as *used* and *dirty*—words that had stuck to her like burrs to her sweater when she searched the woods for a missing cat.

As Tessa was sorting through a stack of requested books, Lowell Settle, a six-foot-four paramedic, came into Howard, who shook under Lowell's size-thirteen feet. His head almost brushed the skylight as he made his way toward Tessa's desk, holding Alice, his Chihuahua, in one hand and a plastic bag of snow peas in the other. He held them out to her. "For you. From my garden."

Before Nick Payne, Tessa would have been delighted to see Lowell and Alice and to receive this gift, but she took the bag and drew back, anxious that she was alone with a man. She asked herself, *Could Lowell attack me? Is he the type to assault a woman?* But what was the type? If she'd been so mistaken about Nick, she could never trust her judgment of a man again. Her confidence in her good sense was gone.

"Thank you, Lowell," Tessa said as starch seemed to stiffen her words—and her bearing. She did not reach out to pet Alice in his arms as she usually did. "Tonight I'll stir-fry these with tofu."

"Tofu! I hate tofu." Lowell looked like he'd found half a worm in an apple he'd just bitten into. "Tofu is slimy. It doesn't have any taste."

"You can perk up the taste with soy sauce. I've brought a tofu cookbook today, if you want to take a look."

"Sorry. Not my thing. I like my snow peas straight." When Lowell picked out the latest *National Geographic* and settled onto a pillow with Alice, Tessa wished her desk were on Howard's opposite end. She was aware of every flip of Lowell's page, his every cough and breath. *Was* he the type?

All day she fought the same unease when she was alone with a male patron. She realized that her measure of a man was now going to be how trustworthy she could rank him— and today, given her newly jaded view, each man had scored in the minus range. In Howard, where she used to feel happiest and most secure, Tessa was afraid of who might come in.

At five o'clock, as she was packing up to drive back to San Julian, Sandy Johnson called her. "Just wanted to let you know that we've questioned Nick Payne."

"What did he say? Did he admit what he did?"

"He gave us the usual he-said-she-said. He acknowledged that you had sex, but he claims you consented to it."

Though Tessa should have expected him to lie like that, she reeled back. "I was unconscious! I couldn't consent to anything!"

"I believe you, Tessa. I've told you that. But we have to prove it," Sandy said. "I searched Nick's house and collected possible evidence."

"Will *it* prove anything?"

"We don't know yet. It has to be tested," Sandy said. "We had to release Nick while we continue the investigation. For now, we don't have enough to charge him."

Tessa leaned against her desk to steady herself. "Do you think you'll have enough to charge him *ever*?"

"We'll see. We've got to get your blood and urine test results. There's a lot to analyze yet."

"How long will it take?"

"Hard to say. Some results might be back in another day or two. Others can take longer," Sandy said. "We're on the case. Don't worry."

But when Tessa dropped her cell phone into her purse and made her way to Howard's front, she *was* worried. Nick Payne was out there, aware now that she'd accused him of rape, and he'd be furious. He was a constant threat, and she had no say in the investigation that could get him locked up. He could end up never charged with anything, and she'd have to keep going somehow.

For now, all Tessa could do was hang on tenterhooks and wait.

CHAPTER 17

Looking weary after comforting a child through a deposition, Hope wriggled under Will's office desk. Her blue denim bed waited for her under the windows across the room, but she must have wanted to hide close to him. So as not to hurt her accidentally, he took off his shoes. When she rested her chin on his socked foot, her breath warmed his toes.

Will was about to pick up his phone and return a call when Sandy walked in. "Got a minute?" she asked.

Usually, when people came into the office, Hope threw herself on her back at their feet, a blatant request for a belly rub. But today she stayed under the desk and irrefutably announced, *I've given all I've got. I need to be alone.*

Sandy eased into the captain's chair across from Will's desk and fixed her exposed eye on him. Today it was shadowed with silver that matched her hair and hoop earrings.

"What's up?" Will asked.

"Three of us went to Nick Payne's house. He wasn't exactly pleased to see us."

"No surprise there," Will said.

"They escorted him to the station while I searched his house and took photos. The interior and exterior match up with Tessa's description, so we can assume she was definitely there."

"What else?"

"We won't know what drug Nick might have given Tessa till we get the lab results. But, sad to say, I found no drugs in his house except Claritin and Advil in his medicine cabinet."

"He's too smart to keep date rape drugs around."

"Yeah. At least where we could find them." Sandy brushed dust off a knee of her gray slacks. "I went through his kitchen trash, garbage can, and recycle bin and found only one lousy wine bottle. We'll see if it has any drug residue. Same for the dirty wine glasses I took from his dishwasher. They might have Tessa's DNA and fingerprints."

"Any other physical evidence she was there?"

"The lab is looking for traces of her in the muck I got from Nick's washing machine and bathroom traps. I also brought in his sheets, but they looked pretty fresh. Your tech guy has Nick's computer and cell phone."

Will absently picked up his pen and pressed its point against his desk's blotter. "Have you had time to interview neighbors?"

"Not yet," Sandy said. "But I talked with Nick's brother, who was supposed to be at dinner with him and Tessa that night. He lives in California, and he hasn't spoken to Nick in nine years."

"So Nick lied to lure Tessa to his house."

"Looks that way," Sandy said. "I also sat in on the last hour of the officer's interview with him."

"What did you think?"

"He's guilty as sin. Arrogant. Self-important. He laughed when we told him Tessa's charge. You can see he'd be good at dishing out humiliation," Sandy said. "If you ask me, he's a sociopath. Scratch his charming exterior, and you'll find grandiosity out the wazoo. He thinks he's too smart for humble folks like us to catch him."

Will shook his head. "We see enough of that kind."

"Yeah. He admits Tessa was at his house and they drank wine and had sex. But he claims she wanted it, and she wanted it rough."

"Oh, right." Will tossed the pen back onto his desk. "If I had a nickel for every time I've heard that, I'd pay off my mortgage."

"Me, too."

"The drug test is going to be our only way to prove she couldn't consent," Will said.

"Stay tuned. I'll let you know when I hear anything." Sandy stood to leave. "I've gotta say, it hurt to see that jerk walk out of the station a free man. I hope we get enough to nail him."

"Keep on it. You never know where these cases might lead."

As Sandy walked out to the hall, Will thought that unfortunately, most cases never led anywhere, and it wasn't from lack of trying. The number of convictions was dismal because the vics couldn't identify the perps, or investigators couldn't scrape up enough evidence to prove guilt. Or—and this reason rankled Will personally—supposedly, three out of four vics never reported the assault in the first place because they feared retaliation, or they believed the police would be indifferent toward them, or they felt the rape wasn't important enough to report. Then the perps got off free.

Will leaned back in his swivel chair and clasped his hands behind his head. Along Hope's spine, he ran the socked foot that her chin wasn't resting on. Her presence radiated peace, and she wasn't even in her professional comforter mode. Whenever he thought of victims not reporting assaults, Will needed all the calm she could give him.

On the Sunday after his first final exams in law school,

he'd come home exhausted. His mother, Stephanie, a stout second-generation Italian with a heart like Hope's, sat him down at the kitchen table and said, "We need to talk about Maria."

The previous weekend, a popular high school senior football player had asked Maria to a party at a friend's house, and she, a gangly, introverted sophomore, had whooped with joy. She spent all afternoon styling her hair, putting on makeup, and picking out the perfect jeans, boots, and sweater. "When she took off her glasses, she looked smashing. Honest to God. Our little Maria," Stephanie said.

"After that buildup, don't tell me he broke the date," Will said.

"Worse than that."

Across the table, Will leaned toward his mother, worry carved between his brows. "How do you mean 'worse'?"

"At the party, he slipped her a drug. My doctor said it could have been a few Valium. We don't know. That boy took her upstairs in that house and raped her, and she was too spaced out to fight him off or run away."

Will's exhale echoed around the kitchen. "You're *sure*?"

"You should have seen her when she came home. He whisker-burned her face so bad it bled. Her boots were gone. If you'd seen her, you'd have had a fit."

Will was having a fit now. He wanted to pummel the thug to a bloody mass. He wanted to send the police to lock him up. "Why didn't you call me?"

"You were studying. I didn't want to bother you. If your father had been alive, he'd have agreed. All he wanted in the world was for you to get through school."

"I could have helped."

"I don't think so." From her apron pocket, Stephanie took a handkerchief that Will would bet had been getting lots of use. She wiped her eyes.

"You called the police, didn't you?" Will asked, as if any rational person would have.

"Maria wouldn't let me! She claimed the boy would be thrown off the football team—and the state playoffs are next week. If the school missed out on a championship, she'd be bullied and shunned," Stephanie said. "Maria was afraid. She didn't have the will to stand up for herself. She's still sad about Dad's death."

"Jesus."

Stephanie reached across the table and patted his arm. "I know you're distressed."

"Damn right. You bet I am," Will fumed. "You're talking about last weekend, right?"

"Yes."

"It's not too late to go to the cops. They need to know about that pervert. You can't let him get away with what he did."

Stephanie ran her thumbnail over a cross-stitched heart in the tablecloth. "Maria won't do anything, Will. You know how stubborn she is. I've begged and pleaded, but she won't listen. I don't think we should pressure her anymore. What's done is done."

Will talked with Maria anyway, but his arguing and pressing might have more easily worn down concrete. Without her cooperation, legally going after the damned football player was useless. Stephanie had been right—what was done was done, and Will could do nothing about it. His anger and powerlessness burned his insides.

When Hope stirred against his ankles, she let him know she'd picked up the agitation that coursed through him every time he recalled that incident. Nearly twenty years later, he was still angry about it. And guilty. After his father's death, Will had felt responsible for Maria, yet he'd not been able to protect or get justice for her.

But the nightmare had given Will a front-row seat on assault victims' trauma. While still in law school, he decided to make a personal crusade of going after perps like that teenage scumbag. If Will didn't get him, he'd get others who terrorized women. He'd do whatever it took.

CHAPTER 18

On Tessa's second day back to work, she drove Howard to Downhill, Washington, which was located on flat terrain, miles from any hill it could be down from. Like all her stops, Downhill was an out-of-the-way small town that ambitious residents had long ago fled. It was two miles after the turn-off to Point No Point along the coast—and unless you were driving a bookmobile, there was no point visiting Downhill, either.

Tessa parked and unlocked Howard's entrance. Just as she went back to her desk to set up shop, her phone rang, loud and insistent. She rifled through her tote back, but piled on top were books, papers, scarves, cans of cat food, a hairbrush, a cosmetics case, and an umbrella. By the time she dug out the phone, she expected the caller to have hung up. "Hello?"

"Thanks for causing me so much trouble." The voice had the quality of sleet-dusted granite. The voice also sounded menacing; the speaker might have been suppressing rage.

"N–N–Nick?"

"I want to tell you something."

Tessa didn't want to hear what it was, but she was too jangled to hang up. Adrenaline shot through her. Her mind raced. *I forgot I gave him my number . . . It would take nothing for him to find out where I live . . . He could call the library and ask where I am today . . . He could show up here . . . and I'm alone . . . and . . .*

Like a rabbit in the shadow of a hawk, Tessa froze.

"Just so you know, on Saturday night I took photos of you. Naked. In my bed. 'Compromising' doesn't begin to describe the positions I put you in. They're the dirty pictures that teenagers and old men love." Nick's chuckle sounded sadistic.

Sinking into her desk chair, Tessa felt like she'd been slugged in the stomach.

"I'm warning you—I can post the photos on the Internet and send them to your boss. I'll be glad to make sure everyone knows the prim librarian is a whore. That sound good to you?"

"But—"

"If you don't go to the police and admit you've lied, I'll ruin you. I'll make your life as miserable as you're trying to make mine. It's your choice. Do you understand?"

Tessa opened her mouth to answer, but nothing came out.

"I take your silence as a yes."

Click.

Tessa's heart pounded like it intended to break out of her chest and run down the street.

This can't be.

Yes, it can. Nick could ruin me. Besides being afraid of his photos, she was more afraid than ever of him. She was trapped. There was no way out. Dread pushed aside her horror at the pictures and engulfed her. With trembling fingers, she dropped the phone into her tote and buried her face in her hands.

Tessa, who'd never bitten her nails, was tearing at the one on her left thumb when old Mr. Wheeler, one of her favorites, clumped up Howard's steps and came toward her in his signature jeans, red suspenders, and white long underwear, which he was still wearing in May. This morning, he'd been burning trash again; he reeked of smoke, and it had darkened his white hair.

After Nick's call, Tessa's heart had finally stopped pounding, but she still felt quivery inside. She tried to gather her wits enough to do her job. "Hello, Mr. Wheeler," she managed.

"Are you all right?" He peered down at her. "You look like your last patron was a ghost."

"I'm fine." *Liar, liar, pants on fire.* It was impossible for Tessa to force a smile. "What can I do for you today?"

"You've got to help me."

Mr. Wheeler, I've got to help myself. "What do you need?"

"I can't take it anymore!" he said. "The TV news! It's all about volcanoes, hurricanes, floods, fires, earthquakes, atom bombs, murderers, hackers." Mr. Wheeler's list made him breathless. His eyes darted around Howard as if he were searching for danger. "It's getting to be doomsday on this planet. You know what I mean? Military buildups. Nuclear buttons. Never-ending conflict and threats."

I'm all too familiar with threats. "Lots of people have been telling me they've stopped watching the news because it's too agitating. A fast from it might help you."

"The news is reality! I have to be informed about what might be coming at me. I need to be ready."

"Sometimes things happen that you can't be ready for." *Such as rape.*

"Maybe, but I have to do my best." With a boisterous honk, Mr. Wheeler blew his nose into a red bandana. "Do you have any information about emergency preparedness?"

"If you'll wait a few minutes, I can print up some from the Internet," Tessa offered, knowing he didn't have a computer.

Mr. Wheeler watched over her shoulder while she opened her laptop and Googled "emergency preparedness, Nisqually

County, Washington." He was so close that she could smell the smoke on his clothes. Still, he was one of the few men she trusted. Though excitable, he was a muffin. He adored his cat, Millie, and he'd show photos of his grandchildren to anyone who wasn't blind.

Tessa clicked on the Nisqually County Department of Emergency Management and printed its Disaster Preparedness Handbook. It offered tips on surviving natural catastrophes, from mudslides to tsunamis, and terrorist attacks with bombs, radioactive materials, and chemical and biological agents. The handbook listed what items to put into an emergency kit and what plans to make for shutting off gas and staying in contact with family.

"You'll need food and water for three days." Tessa took the handbook from her printer, stapled the pages together, and gave them to Mr. Wheeler. "I hope this makes you feel safer. I guess forewarned is forearmed."

"Thanks," Mr. Wheeler said.

Tessa got up from her desk, pulled *Taming Anxiety* off one of her shelves, and gave it to him. "Sometimes it's hard not to be frightened, but maybe this book could make your life easier." Her voice was quivering again. Though she often suggested books to help her people, not even this one could help *her*. "Physician, heal thyself" seemed out of her reach, like the gold ring on someone else's merry-go-round.

What have I done to deserve this disaster? Am I being punished for something? Tessa asked herself as she checked out *Taming Anxiety* for Mr. Wheeler and watched him walk down Howard's aisle to the door. When he was gone, she sat at her desk, still frozen in dread. But slowly, it melted, and anger that had been lying dormant inside her burned through.

How dare *he?* Wasn't it enough that he'd assaulted her? Did he also intend to taunt her for the rest of her life? She would not let that happen.

I want that evil man locked up forever. I want him never to see the light of day again. Sandy had urged Tessa to have the forensic exam because she might want justice someday, but she wanted it *now*. She'd earned it. She deserved it. If she had any say in the matter, Nick Payne was going to prison for years and years and years.

Tessa fished her phone out of her purse again. When Sandy answered, Tessa blurted out between clenched teeth, "Something awful just happened."

CHAPTER 19

As Will stuffed papers into his canvas messenger bag, which had carried home his work the last twelve years, Hope panted happily by his office door. She could read the signal as clearly as an Apache understood an all-is-well column of smoke halfway up a distant hill. Messenger-bag packing meant that Hope could soon go home and be freed from her vest.

She'd prance around her field, then take her yellow duck on a tour of the house. Far more important, she, a world-class glutton, would have dinner! Hope would dive into her food and gobble it down. In a quest for every kibble crumb, she would lick the glaze of her ceramic bowl till it shone.

At Will's office door, she smiled her retriever smile and ratcheted up her tail wags from swishes to circles, like a pro-peller, reserved for moments of greatest excitement—such as at Starbucks, where Hope got a Puppuccino, a shot-sized cup of whipped cream that she polished off in two slurps.

But then Sandy bustled into the office and dashed Hope's dream of food. Groaning the groan of a starving dog, she did not ask Sandy for a belly rub, but instead threw herself down on the carpet, her face turned to the wall. She unmistakably declared, *I am famished. I may not last another fifteen minutes. You are heartless not to take me home and feed me* now!

Sandy pulled up the captain's chair to Will's desk. "I've got some new lab results." As she sat, her punk cascade of hair swung to the side long enough for a rare glimpse of both her eyes, which were walnut brown. Today she'd shadowed them with beige, like her khaki shirt.

Will leaned back in his black leather swivel chair and crossed his ankles on his desktop, making visible the Labrador retrievers on his socks. "Go on."

"The DNA from Nick's saliva matches the DNA in the semen collected from Tessa's underwear and in a hair found in her combings. Tessa's own hairs were in his washing machine's catcher drain."

"So all that supports what we already knew from both of them—Tessa was at Nick's house, and they had sex."

"Yeah." Sandy looked tired. Under her lone exposed eye was a dark semicircle, and her hair, which wasn't sticking out quite right, didn't look as counter-revolutionary as it usually did.

"What about the drug?" Will asked.

"No traces of anything in the empty wine bottle from his garbage can or the used wine glasses from his dishwasher."

"I guess that would have made life too easy for us."

"You want me to give you the really bad news?" Sandy asked.

Snowball's chance in hell of a case without some. "May as well."

"There was no drug of any kind in Tessa."

"Damn." Will wedged his thumbnail between his two front teeth while he let that test result sink in. Hope stirred in her spot by the door.

"Nick must have given Tessa something that was out of her system by the time she got to the hospital," Sandy said. "Could have been a roofie or GHB. Maybe Ambien. Who knows?"

"No drug, no proof she couldn't consent." For a sexual

assault, a lack of consent was the most essential—and often the most confoundingly tricky—thing to prove. It provided Will with no end of frustration. "Looks like this case is going nowhere."

"It's a bitch that some drugs don't stay in the body longer," Sandy said. "I still believe Tessa. All of it."

Without ever having met her, Will pretty much believed her, too. Though false accusations happened, ninety-two to ninety-seven percent of the time, women brave enough to report a sexual assault were said to be telling the truth. "What about the photos of Tessa you mentioned last night? Any found on Nick's computer or cell?"

"Not yet. I'll let you know."

In the front passenger seat, Hope peered out the windshield and kept tabs on the world. Besides looking for landmarks, she relied on her internal global positioning system that let her know where they were going—and whether Will would be taking her straight home for dinner or cruelly forcing her to wait somewhere again. They passed Waterfront Park, where she could sniff captivating messages left by other dogs and hunt for delicious bits of food that had fallen from picnic tables. Will drove by the Barkery, a doggy bakery that sold Woof Supremes and Beef Ecstasies, but, sadly, he didn't stop there.

He did not make the turns that would take them home, either, and, with disappointment, Hope's expression became downcast. He drove half a mile down Rainier Avenue, and just as he clicked on his turn signal for DIY Hardware's parking lot, Hope perked up. They were about to visit Mr. Allen, the kind man who always welcomed her with a treat! It would tide her over till supper! She thumped her tail on the Jeep's seat, then padded beside Will into the store.

Mr. Allen, whose straining belt suggested he liked treats

himself, leaned over his checkout counter and handed Hope a large Milk-Bone, which she accepted with an eager, though gentle chomp, careful not to bite his hand, as she'd been trained. While she crunched the biscuit to rubble, Will and Mr. Allen discussed the weather warming up and the recent run on charcoal grills. Will's father had owned the store before his death; Will always felt at home here.

"You'd think animals would want to be outside in the spring, but a damned rat has moved into my barn," Will said. "Yesterday I found his droppings all over my workbench."

"Rats are most active in the fall, but they can cause trouble any time of year," Mr. Allen said.

"I hoped he'd leave on his own," Will said. "Any advice?"

"Quickest and easiest solution, put out poison. I've got pellets that'll do the trick." Mr. Allen pointed to the other side of the store. "Baits and traps on aisle three."

He didn't have to tell Will. For years, he'd worked here on Saturdays with his dad, and since buying the store, Mr. Allen had left it mostly as it was.

Though reluctant to leave her human Milk-Bone dispenser, Hope walked across DIY Hardware with Will. He picked up a Rat-B-Gone bait station, into which he could load Mr. Allen's pellets, but Will worried that Hope might eat them, and he didn't want a slow death even for a rat. He also examined and rejected a snap trap, which would be quicker, and a glue trap that was supposed to terrify a rat into a fatal heart attack. Will was no sentimental softy, but he was not big on animal abuse. Ideally, what he wanted was to send "his" rat miles away so he'd never come back, like the Brits used to send convicts to Australia.

Will finally found the solution: a have-a-heart trap, which was a small cage with a door on one end and a steel plate on the other. He could set the trap and place some cheese on the trap's plate, and the instant the rat stepped on it, the door would slam closed. On his way to work, Will could drop off the incarcerated rat in the woods. Voila! Problem solved.

As soon as Will turned into his driveway, Hope, barely able to contain her excitement, began marching her front paws in place on the passenger seat. They shouted her joy at her forthcoming supper and urged, *Get me to my kibble and chunky chicken! Now!*

Buoyed with hope for catching the rat, Will turned into his barn and helped her out of his Jeep. "When have I ever neglected to feed you, Hope? Dinner coming up."

Chapter 20

The caller ID said Margaret Jordan. Tessa stared at her mother's name and gathered courage for a step into the unknown. She never knew what to expect. Sometimes Margaret could be loving; at other times, she unleashed her resentment, which was always crouched just below her surface. She'd never forgiven Tessa for leaving Maine, much less for living on the other side of the United States. And Margaret's rancor had sharpened after her husband's death when Tessa, her only child, had not moved back home.

Margaret had quietly sulked, and she found ways to shoot passive-aggressive arrows at Tessa. They were oblique, but they hurt. If her annoyance reared its head today, only a week and a half after Nick's assault, Tessa was too emotionally raw to dodge it. She wanted to get this conversation over with so she could finish browning hamburger for her kitties' breakfast and leave for work.

Tessa picked up the phone. "Hi, Mother." She forced herself to sound cheerful.

"It's still cold here," Margaret grumbled. "Summer is never going to come."

"Oh, it always does. Wait a few weeks. You'll see."

"Hummph. I've been sitting here missing your father."

It was a bad day to dredge up that sadness. "I miss him, too."

"The wind has been whipping his memorial tree. It's too young to survive that kind of attack."

"They told us at the nursery that Honeycrisp apples would grow fine where you live."

The instant "you" came out of Tessa's mouth, she pictured her mother arching her signature judgmental eyebrow. "You" emphasized the divide between her and Margaret—Margaret was living in Maine, and Tessa wasn't.

Tessa rearranged the sizzling hamburger for even browning in the pan. "What have you been up to?"

"Same old same old. I made macaroni and cheese for the Knights of Columbus dinner at church. Everybody liked the comfort food."

"I'll bet they did."

"Have you baked the bread I sent you the recipe for last week?" Margaret asked.

"I haven't had time."

"Why are you always so busy? You're not taking care of a family."

In other words, you poor wretch, you have failed to have *a family.* The hamburger splattered grease on Tessa's hand. "Have you been playing much bridge, Mother?"

"Every other week. Same as always. Yesterday the ladies asked if you were dating anybody."

If Tessa could have relied on her mother's support, she'd have answered that her last date had been a disaster and she wasn't sure if she'd ever go out with a man again. She'd have told her that all she'd been thinking about was RAPE, all capital neon letters, and it might take her a lifetime to process what had happened. As for healing, many lifetimes might not be enough.

But Margaret would use that information to argue why Tessa should come home. Margaret would claim that Maine was safer than Washington, and some of the nice boys Tessa had known in high school were still single.

"Tessa, is anything wrong?"

"No." She tossed chopped kale into the hamburger to wilt.

"You seem a little odd today."

"I'm hurrying to go to work, and I've got a lot on my mind."

"Like what?" *Press, press.*

"Like turning in my budget for the next six months."

"That shouldn't be a big deal. You've been doing it for years."

"I've got a lot of book requests to fill. They take time."

Tessa could hear the disbelief in Margaret's exhale from three thousand, one hundred, forty-five miles away—the distance between San Julian and Portland, Maine. Margaret was too perceptive not to notice that Tessa had lied. She probably knew something was wrong. When Tessa hung up, her tense shoulders, which in the last few minutes had risen almost to her earlobes, lowered two inches.

If only my father were alive, Tessa thought as she turned off the stove's burner. When she'd told him about her San Julian job, he'd hugged her and said, "I'll miss you, but it's time for you to spread your wings. Get out there and make yourself a beautiful life."

He'd have been enraged to learn what Nick had done. But after his fury had passed, he'd have helped her find her way again. "Everything'll be all right," he'd have said, as he had all her life.

But Margaret? No way could Tessa be honest with her. Tessa never crossed her, and she always tried to be kind to her, because that's what her father would have wanted. Still, it was hard.

Even harder was waiting for Sandy's investigation to end so Nick Payne would get what he had coming to him.

CHAPTER 21

In the staff lounge of the County Prosecutor's Office, Will and twenty of his colleagues were gathered for Hope's third birthday. Wearing a royal blue wizard hat, she propped up her torso with her front legs and sat on a gold-and-white-striped pillow provided by Sandy, who'd organized the party. She'd also invited Hope's friend Ranger, a black Lab from the County Prosecutor's Family Support Division. Today, Ranger worked the room looking for handouts, while Hope's human friends stopped to offer congratulations, which she graciously accepted like a pope did kisses on his ring.

Behind Hope on a Formica table was a pile of birthday gifts from her handlers: a red Frisbee from Sandy, who'd taken her to comfort a DV victim in an interview that morning. A box of gourmet cheese-and-bacon dog biscuits from Valentina Herrera, the sexual assault advocate, who shepherded victims through the legal process. And a squeaky carrot from Louann Evans, a psychologist, who led assault survivors' groups. Will had given Hope a stuffed snake that she could drag around when her yellow duck needed some peace.

Next to the human cake—devil's food with HAPPY BIRTHDAY, HOPE and a trail of pawprints in the chocolate frosting—Sandy clinked a spoon against a bottle of sparkling apple juice to get her colleagues' attention. When the buzz of conversation stopped, she said, "It's time for Hope's doggy cake. We have one for Ranger, too."

Sandy set loaves of browned hamburger, iced with mashed potatoes, in front of Hope and Ranger, and the staff started singing "Happy Birthday." The dogs attacked their food with lusty chomps and nosed their plates across the floor as they seemed to compete over who could finish first. Soon after the singing stopped, the cakes were gone, and both dogs were looking at Sandy with soulful eyes that begged, *Can we have more?*

Valentina cut and served the human cake and licked icing off her fingers. Sandy brought a plate, fork, and napkin to Will, who was leaning against the staff's refrigerator, his arms crossed over his chest.

"Thanks." He shoveled a large bite of cake into his mouth. "This is delicious."

"The Sweet Time Bakery never fails," Sandy said.

"I'm going back for another piece."

"I don't know how you stay so slim."

Will shrugged and shoveled in another bite.

"I hate to mix business and pleasure, but I didn't have time to stop by your office earlier," Sandy said.

"What business?"

"I finally heard from our tech guy. He found porn on Nick Payne's computer."

"To be expected." Will wiped the napkin across his lips.

"Tessa's phone records show that someone called her the same day and time she claims Nick made his photo threat, but the tech guy found no record of that call on his landline or cell."

"He must have used a burner phone for that," Will said.

"Yeah. Covered his tracks."

"Any compromising pictures?"

"Zip. Nothing on his electronics," Sandy said. "When I went back and searched his house for a SIM card or flash drive, I couldn't find a thing. Looks like Nick was bluffing. It's good news for Tessa."

"Yep. But a dead end for the investigation." The photos had been a last chance to go after Nick. "Looks like he's slipped through the system. We can't get him."

"Breaks my heart for Tessa," Sandy said.

It bothered Will, too. In his years as a prosecutor, he'd lost count of the women brave enough to report an assault and start the forensics process, only to be let down like Tessa was going to be. That the women had no recourse weighed heavily on him. But then, the law was the law, and he wasn't God. He couldn't manufacture evidence they didn't have.

"I wish the assaults with drugs were easier to prove," Will said. "Don't leave Tessa hanging. You need to let her know we don't have enough of a case to file charges."

"Will do."

Insistent squeaks of a rubber carrot interrupted Will and Sandy's conversation. Will reached down and petted Hope, who'd been circling around the room's forest of legs. She helped him weather demoralizing moments like this, but she couldn't cancel all the disappointment. So many damned setbacks on his job. In times of failure, it was easy to lose sight of the successes.

As Will pulled into his barn after work, he told Hope, "You're going to have a birthday bonanza. We've got a Sons of Pitches game tonight." She'd see more friends and retrieve out-of-bounds balls, to say nothing of receiving cheese bits and happy-birthday pets.

Her "cake" had been her dinner, but Will would have to get some peanuts for his own. He had ten minutes to change into his green-and-white uniform and head back out to the softball field, so he climbed out of his Jeep and opened the passenger door for Hope to leap to the concrete floor. When he unfastened her vest, she bucked and danced, rejoicing in her freedom. He glanced at his workbench. *Damn!*

The rat had designated it as his personal toilet, as evidenced by ever more droppings around the have-a-heart trap. Worse, the cube of cheddar that Will had set on the steel plate had disappeared. The rat had speared the cheese with his teeth and whisked it away. He'd escaped!

The empty trap seemed to mock Will: *This ain't working, Buddy. You're going to have to try harder.* One touch of the rat's paw could have closed the door and imprisoned him. But Will's rat was apparently the Houdini of rats.

Will set his jaw in grim determination. "I'll get him sometime," he told Hope as they hurried toward the house. If cheese wouldn't reel in the rat, Will would try peanut butter that would require being licked in place and couldn't be stolen away. It was Will vs. the rat. *By God, I'm going to win. Just you wait.*

CHAPTER 22

Tessa backed Howard out of his parking place in front of Fall City's general store, which sold groceries and animal feed and housed a small branch of the U.S. Postal Service behind a special counter. As the small town's hub, the store also attracted patrons to the bookmobile, and many of them had filed through today. Tessa's stomach growled because she'd been too busy for lunch. Eager for dinner and rest, she would try to ignore the Damocles sword of Nick's photos, which still hung over her and unnerved her.

As she shifted gears to pull out onto Fall City's unpaved main street, a black Chevy stopped in front of her and blocked her way—and startled her. The people here were never so rude.

Sandy got out of her car, her silver-skull earrings dangling against her neck. She slammed her door and motioned for Tessa to let her into Howard.

Since "The Night," as Tessa had come to think of the worst one in her life, more than three long weeks had crawled by. With ever-growing impatience, she'd been waiting for the investigation to wind down and for Nick finally to be arrested and put away.

Tessa turned off Howard's motor, got up, and opened his

door. "Hello," she said, backing into his belly to give Sandy room to board.

Sandy climbed his steps and emerged on his green aisle. "You were probably leaving for home. I'll only keep you a minute. It took longer to get to Fall City than I thought."

"It's definitely out of the way," Tessa said. "Do you have any news?"

"Yes, I'm afraid so."

"Afraid so" latched onto Tessa's brain and bored in like a tick. "Are you going to tell me that Nick has posted the photos online?"

"No, and nobody can find them anywhere. We feel sure he was bluffing."

"But that's great!" Tessa's heart, which had beaten its way to her throat, retreated to its rightful place inside her chest. "Why did you say you were afraid you had news?"

"I wish I didn't have to tell you." Sandy's gaze lowered for a moment before she fixed her eye on Tessa again. With rare formality, she said what she must have learned to say at times like this: "The prosecutor has determined that he can't move forward with your case at this time."

"How can that be?" Tessa held on to Howard's magazine rack. "It's not right that nobody believes me!"

"I've told you I believe you. He does, too. That's not the issue."

"What is it, then?"

"He doesn't have enough evidence to press charges. Whatever drug Nick gave you had gotten out of your system by the time you went to the hospital, so the prosecutor has no way to prove you couldn't consent to sex. He wouldn't have a leg to stand on in court."

"Surely a *jury* would understand."

"Maybe they would in their hearts. But to prove sexual assault, the prosecutor needs more. Otherwise, Nick's defense attorney would tear him to pieces," Sandy said. "The prosecutor regrets this—"

"He's a *jerk*!" Tessa interrupted. "He's hanging me out to dry! I can't believe no one will help me."

"The prosecutor would like to, Tessa. He's not cold-hearted. He understands what you've been through. I promise. He'd love to see Nick go to prison."

"I don't believe that. And now Nick's free forever!"

"He is for now. Something could change."

Tessa didn't believe that, either. She bit her lip to keep from shouting more. What would be the point of arguing with Sandy? The prosecutor couldn't care less about Tessa. It wouldn't matter to him that his decision not to go after Nick traumatized her again. *Why did I ever go to the police?*

Scowling, she muttered, "Nobody seems to get that I need for Nick to be punished before I can recover."

"I get it. Of course, you feel that way. Every woman in your situation does," Sandy said. "Have you contacted Louann Evans, our psychologist? She's helped a lot of women through their pain."

Nobody could help. And now Tessa was abandoned, humiliated, furious. She felt the annihilation of hope. She felt alone. Her pursuit of justice had ended in nothing.

After Sandy left, Tessa returned to the driver's seat. She closed her eyes and rested her forehead on the steering wheel. Sometime later, she didn't know how long, she raised her head and looked at the fir trees across the road. Early evening fog had turned their promising green to a dingy gray. The sun had fallen out of sight behind the trees and brought on a chill.

When Tessa returned to her cottage, she was unable to muster energy to whip up a fresh dinner for her kitties. She walked over to the woods and spooned into their pie tins the leftover Mackerel Medley she'd made the day before with mackerel, brown rice, steamed broccoli, and sunflower oil. As she stepped back, pandemonium broke loose. Because the cats' dinner was later than usual, they dove into their meal as if it would be their last.

Though Tessa had been feeding them for years, they always seemed to remember hunger from lean times. It was as if the suffering had been indelibly stamped onto their brains, and the cats would never trust that their needs would be met or their lives would turn out right. On the drive home, Tessa had arrived at similar conclusions. She'd permanently removed her rose-colored glasses and been forced to admit that fairness was a mirage. She'd tossed her optimistic nature out Howard's window. From now on, she'd be as mistrustful as her cats.

CHAPTER 23

In Mel's Market, Tessa pushed a shopping cart down the pet-supplies aisle. Only a need for cat food could have gotten her to leave her house on this Sunday night. Sandy's Friday visit had sent Tessa into a tailspin. On Saturday morning, she'd gotten up to feed her cats and gone back to bed. Even now, her eyes were still swollen, her face puffy from crying. She hadn't washed it or brushed her hair in forty-eight hours, and she wore the same yoga pants and crumpled sweatshirt she'd had on all that time. But her kitties still expected—and needed—to eat.

As usual on a Sunday night, the market was crowded with professionals, storing up food for the week when they'd commute by ferry to work. Their hands gripping lists, they pushed their carts down the aisles with the resolve of kamikaze pilots. Tessa sidestepped to stay out of the way.

She stopped in front of the cat food, and into her cart she tossed three cans each of Salmon Sensation, Chicken Delight, Tasty Turkey, Beef Grill in Gravy, and Fussy Eaters' Feast. She picked up a small bag of Kitty Kibble, whose ingredients made her shudder when compared to what went into her homemade kind. Mission accomplished, Tessa headed for the checkout line but then remembered she needed lettuce. Better to get it now and save herself a trip here tomorrow after work.

Dodging shoppers, Tessa turned a sharp left to the fruit and vegetable department and found the romaine piled into a pyramid, the fresh leaves facing out. She grabbed a romaine head. Who cared if the leaves drooped? A quick soak in her salad spinner would perk them up.

As she set it with the cat food cans, she glanced across the pyramid toward the cantaloupes, which were a little on the green side this early in the season. Looking over them, in jeans and a blue fleece jacket, was Nick Payne. He had the same imposing posture and clean-cut good looks. As usual, self-assurance seemed to drip off him.

Tessa skipped five breaths. As she stared at him, her stomach listed. She watched him examine one cantaloupe, then another, pawing them as he might have Tessa's breasts. Perhaps he sensed that someone was watching him because he looked up. His eyes met Tessa's. He blinked like he may have met her during his campaign, and then he squinted, as if trying to remember who she was.

How could that be? He ruined my life and doesn't even recognize me? To defend herself from his squint of unrecognition, she turned away. Had she been braver, she might have stomped over and punched him, but just as when she'd woken in his bed, all she could think of was getting out of there.

Tessa abandoned her shopping cart by the lettuce and hurried through the crowd to the exit. Outside, she ran to her yellow Beetle, and trembling, she locked the door behind her. As she gulped for breath, her heart thumped all over her chest.

She was as traumatized as she'd been after "The Night." As vulnerable. As tangled in a snarl of emotions. Fear, resentment, fury, shame, despair. In nearly a month, nothing had changed.

★   ★   ★

Half an hour later, Emma arrived at Tessa's cottage. "I'm glad you called me," she said as she unloaded cans of cat food onto the butcher-block table. "I looked all over the produce department but couldn't find your cart. I hope the cat food flavors I picked out are okay."

"They'll be fine. Thank you, Em." Tessa watched from her rocking chair, too emotionally scrambled to get up and put them away. "Was Nick still there?"

"Not that I could find, but I only know what he looks like from his campaign posters. I see his face in your landlady's yard every time I come over here."

"I keep thinking about stealing that abominable sign."

"I could do it if you want." Emma hung her lime-green shopping bag on Tessa's front doorknob, ready to take with her when she left. "Tess, I hate to say this, but you look awful."

"Who wouldn't after being told Nick would get off free— and then running into him? It doesn't get worse than that."

"I'm worried about you."

"So am I," Tessa admitted. "Nick is out there without a care to his name. And I'm here in chronic distress. I don't see how I can keep living on this island. I'll run into him all the time." Tessa circled her fingertips on her right temple to stop the throbbing.

"It's easy to understand." Emma sat on the edge of Tessa's sofa and set her elbows on her thighs. "I really believe you'll be okay, but it's going to take time. It'll get better."

"Never," Tessa said.

Later, when she walked Emma to the door, the porch light glinted off the brass palm, which had failed to ward off evil. She scorned it for falling down on its job. She felt like knocking it off its nail, sending it flying to the porch floor, and grinding it with her heel into the wood. Any target for her anger. But the brass wouldn't even get a scratch.

At least I can get rid of it, she thought as she got ready for bed. In her nightgown and slippers, she went back to the porch and yanked the palm off the wall. By moonlight, she walked to the woods behind her cottage and flung the palm into a blackberry thicket. She'd never have to set eyes on that useless brass again.

In bed that night, Tessa tossed and thrashed. Repeatedly, she turned her pillow over, only to have her feverish cheek heat the new side. Each time she looked at her clock, only a few minutes had passed. At two in the morning, she got up and warmed milk, but her usual ticket to the Land of Nod didn't help.

Finally, as a hint of gold began to lighten the sky, Tessa had an anxious dream, most of which she didn't remember. But one piece of it woke her with a start: Nick Payne's photo was lodged under the skin on the back of her left hand. When she clawed and scratched to get it out, his face looked up at her, mocking and gloating that he'd gotten away with raping her, and—*too bad, honey*—she was going to have to knuckle down and accept it.

In an agitated sweat, Tessa turned on her light and inspected her hand to make sure that Nick was not really there. He wasn't—not literally. But when she pondered what her subconscious might be telling her, she could not dispute the stark possibility that Nick had gotten under her *psychological* skin. He'd taken up residence in her head, pushed everything else out of the way, and settled down as if he intended to live there forever. Power-hungry sadist that he was, he would enjoy inflicting torment.

Nick's presence was destroying her. As Tessa lay there until the sun slowly rose, light also dawned on her, and she came to a conclusion: If she intended to live on the earth for what was left of her natural life, she had to evict Nick from her mind. It was bad enough what he'd done; she couldn't let him also drive her crazy. She couldn't go on as she was.

Tessa got up, and in her bare feet, padded to the desk, rummaged through the top drawer, and took out a plastic bag of business cards that people had handed her for years. She flipped through the cards to the ones that Mary O'Malley had given her, and she found Louann Evans, the assault survivors' group psychologist. Louann Evans was Tessa's last hope.

CHAPTER 24

Two weeks later, Tessa raked the courage out of herself to open the door of the meeting room, which in itself invited her to be upbeat. Potted begonias bloomed on the windowsills, and strings of multicolored paper butterflies hung from the ceiling and urged goodwill. Inspirational posters reminded her: "Sometimes you win. Sometimes you learn." "Believe in yourself!" "The future is female."

The cheer was out of sync with Tessa's mood. The last to arrive, she walked into the room dragging a ball and chain of wariness behind her. She felt awkward and out of place, a giraffe unsure how to sip from a cup at a ladies' tea. She would guess that all four women at the round table in the center of the room felt the same way she did.

Certainly, they were all vulnerable because at this table there would be nowhere to hide. As Tessa pulled up a chair to join them, she thought that they also represented variations on a theme of sexual assault; it was their common denominator, along with loss—of trust, hope, security, self-worth, and confidence that life could be good. Loss showed on the women's creased brows and downturned mouths. Tessa understood immediately that she was among her own kind.

"Welcome!" Louann Evans's smile added to the room's

warmth, and it rose another degree when Hope wriggled out from under the table to greet Tessa. Hope's tail swished like an ebullient windshield wiper; her triangle ears flapped with joy. Delighted to see her again, Tessa sat down at the table and hugged her. "You remember me," she murmured.

"I bring Hope here on Monday nights because she always knows when someone's troubled and she comes over to help. You'll see," Louann said.

Aware of the other women's eyes on her, Tessa nodded hello to the two women she'd be sitting between and noted their name tags: Carmen, whose dark eyes seemed like they'd known grief, and Gail, who was fair and blond and wore a small gold cross around her neck.

Louann slid a box of chocolate-chip cookies into the center of the table. "Have some sugar therapy. Pass them around. You have to finish them before you leave. If I take them home, there won't be a crumb left by midnight."

Around the table, a few lips turned up into semi-smiles. "I think we can force ourselves to help you out," Carmen said.

"Not me. I've gained eleven pounds since it happened." Across the table, Samantha, who was knitting a hat, didn't have to explain the antecedent of *it*.

"Well, then, the rest of you do your best to finish these. My waistline will thank you." Louann patted her belly, which, along with her wide hips and large breasts, gave her the appearance of a Paleolithic fertility goddess. In Birkenstocks and a loose denim smock, she looked like she'd been put on earth to nurture.

"Tonight I'd like for us to start with each of you telling us one important thing about yourself. We'd like to get to know you, but if you want to pass, that's okay," Louann said. "Anybody want to be first?"

Silence. Downcast eyes. Hope watched from under the windows on her orange corduroy pillow.

"It can be just one sentence. No threat." Looking peaceful, Louann waited. So did Hope.

"I'll start. My parents brought me to the U.S. from Mexico when I was a baby. I've gone back there to see my family twice." Carmen glanced at Louann. "Is that enough?"

"Sure," Louann said. "Welcome, Carmen. Anybody else?"

"I'm a vet tech, and my face is sunburned because I went hiking last weekend. People call me Sam. Ignore the Samantha on my name tag."

"Okay, Sam," Louann said.

"I teach sixth grade at St. Ignatius School. I love my kids," Gail said.

Not quite at ease, Tessa quickly mentioned that she loved the patrons of her county bookmobile. A fact like that was safe to reveal.

Then LaKeisha, who had light brown dreadlocks and coffee-and-cream skin, took a bite of a cookie and explained that she worked at a printing company to support her little brother, Jason. "My father ran off when Jason was born, and my mother is living in Michigan with her sick sister. So I'm in charge."

"Good for you for measuring up," Louann said, and everybody nodded agreement. "So now we know one thing about each other, and see, it wasn't hard to share." Hope must have agreed because she stayed in her library lion position, front legs straight out in front of her, and kept a careful eye on the group.

"What about you?" Sam asked Louann.

"Well, you know I love cookies. And I have a daughter and two young grandchildren. I've been leading survivors' groups for the last five years." She took a small dog biscuit out of her purse, got up, and handed it to Hope. "We've got to make her feel welcome, too." Hope responded with a grateful crunch. Everybody smiled.

"I expect it was hard for all of you to show up tonight," Louann said, returning to the table.

If you only knew. Tessa eyed the string of carefree paper butterflies, the opposite of her.

"Difficult circumstances have brought you here. You and I know they're not easy to discuss, but I hope you'll help each other by sharing your stories. Leave advice and 'shoulds' at the door—we get enough of them out in the world—but feel free to tell us about your feelings and insights," Louann said. "This is a place for honesty. We want to hear about what's helped you or held you back while you've been recovering from trauma."

"What if I'm not recovering? I'm as unnerved now as when it happened," LaKeisha said.

No truer words, Tessa thought.

Louann asked, "You want to talk about that, LaKeisha?"

She closed her eyes for a second, like she was deciding how open to be. "Okay, one afternoon after work, my boss cornered me in the stockroom and groped my breasts. I told him to stop, and he got mad. If I'd yelled, nobody was around to hear. I don't have to tell you what happened after that."

"I'm so sorry," Gail told her.

"I'm scared he'll rape me again, but I have to act like everything's cool so he won't fire me. Which would be almost as bad as what he already did because Jason and I would starve to death by the time I found another job without a reference."

"What would you say is your strongest feeling right now, LaKeisha?" Louann asked.

"Fear. I'm afraid to go to work. Every time I have to walk into the stockroom, it takes ten years off my life. My boss has my address—he could show up at my apartment."

"You should never be alone with him." Gail clapped her hand over her mouth. "I'm sorry. I said 'should.'"

When Louann chuckled, her breasts jiggled. "That's not a capital offense, Gail. Could you rephrase what you said? Use your own experience?"

"Ummm . . ." Gail absently fingered her gold cross. "I went to an evening meeting. A man I thought was a friend offered to walk me to my car. It was parked a few blocks away by a deserted warehouse, so I was glad for his company—till he pushed me into the backseat and put his hand over my mouth." Grimacing, she skipped over the rest. "I haven't filed charges—long story—and because of my work, I still have to see him sometimes, but I'm careful *never* to be anywhere near him alone."

"So having somebody around is a good way to protect yourself. LaKeisha, maybe you could get a co-worker to go to the stockroom with you." Louann broke down and took a cookie. "Has anything worked for the rest of you?"

"My ex-boyfriend let himself into my apartment with the key I stupidly forgot to get back from him. I was sleeping, and he woke me up and raped me." Sam's sunburned cheeks darkened to an angry red. "I stayed with my best friend till my landlord changed the locks and put in a deadbolt, and I posted my ex's photo in the elevator. I asked neighbors to call the police if they see him."

"Has he come back?" Tessa was still afraid that Nick might show up at her cottage.

"So far, he's stayed away, but I'm expecting him," Sam said. "At least he can't get in now."

"What about a protection order? Would it help?" Gail asked.

"I got one, but it's just a piece of paper. It doesn't make me feel any safer," Sam said.

"I'll bet my karate class at the Y would," Carmen said. "The jerk of the world ran up behind me when I was jogging one morning—and he dragged me behind a hedge. If I'd known how to defend myself, I'd have kicked his cojones. Any man dares come at me like that again, and he'll be sorry."

"Karate wouldn't have helped me." Tessa had intended only to observe tonight, but now she felt compelled to add her story. "A man I met online at Northwest Singles invited me to his house and drugged my wine and knocked me out. I couldn't run or fight him off. I had no way to protect myself."

"That's the pits," Sam said. "The coward."

"You can say that again." Tessa reached into the box for her second comforting cookie.

"I wish I'd been unconscious. I mean, it would have been like I wasn't there," Gail said.

"Except it's beyond disturbing not to know what happened. I've imagined all the dirty, awful things he could have done. Sometimes it feels like my body is a stranger to me, and it will never be fully mine again," Tessa said.

All around the table, heads nodded with understanding.

"So I see fear and anger in our group," Louann said. "I'm wondering what other feelings you have. You're all carrying a heavy emotional load."

"I feel isolated because now I'm different from everybody," Sam said. "I can't talk about what happened. No one understands how bad it was."

"I've found that, too," Carmen said. Nods all around.

"I feel like everything's my fault. If I hadn't gone into the stockroom when my boss was there, I'd be fine today," LaKeisha said.

"You didn't know he'd assault you." Sam's knitting needles clicked.

"I should have known," LaKeisha said. "He stares at women's breasts and tells stupid dirty jokes. Now I see all kinds of signs I should have noticed."

"Remember, no *shoulds*," Louann said gently with a tilt of her head.

"You can't blame yourself for not reading your boss's mind." Tessa realized that the same applied to her with Nick. She couldn't have known what he was going to do. Beating herself up didn't help anything, just like she could see that it wasn't helping LaKeisha.

"I *do* blame myself," LaKeisha said. "I feel used. Like some filthy dress nobody wants to buy at Goodwill."

"It's not right to judge yourself by what your boss did to you," Sam said.

"It sounds like you feel guilty and ashamed, LaKeisha. That's a common reaction," Louann said.

"Her boss is the one who should feel ashamed, not her," Gail said.

"Amen," Carmen said.

"Am I right that all of you have blamed yourselves for what happened?" When Louann looked around the table, everybody nodded yes.

Realizing that they all shared those feelings—and they weren't justified or deserved—Tessa felt like hugging Louann. Tessa felt her whole body relax. She wasn't alone.

"What about hate? It must be a common reaction, too," Carmen said. "I wish I could cut off my attacker's penis, like Lorena Bobbitt did."

Sam gasped. "Who was *she*?"

"A woman in Virginia. Some of you may not be old enough to remember her," Carmen said. "One night she came home wiped out from work, and her macho husband John wouldn't take her 'no' for sex, and he raped her. After he fell asleep, she did it!"

Tessa smiled. Last year, she'd looked up the Bobbitts for a patron. "The story gets better."

"Yeah, it does. Lorena drove off with his penis and threw it in a field!" Glee shone in Carmen's eyes. "Later, she felt guilty and called nine-one-one. Way after midnight, a policeman found it, and doctors reattached it. The surgery took nine hours."

"Did he go to prison for rape?" LaKeisha asked.

"Sadly, he got off," Carmen said. "But so did Lorena. It came out that he'd bullied and abused her for years, and she finally snapped. She claimed temporary insanity."

"Thank God she wasn't found guilty," LaKeisha said. "I wouldn't have called nine-one-one. I'd love to see my boss go through the rest of his life minus his prick."

As chortling traveled around the circle, Carmen said, "At least one sicko in the world got what he deserved."

"Here's the best thing," Tessa said. "To raise money for his medical bills, John Bobbitt started a band called The Severed Parts. He named his penis Stumpy!"

The chortles mushroomed to cackles. Tessa shook with mirth. Imagining Nick with a Stumpy of his own was delicious, though she wouldn't admit that to anybody but the women in this room.

Hearing laughter, Hope rose from her pillow and looked around as if to check whether anybody needed her, but tonight, at least for now, nobody seemed to need anything. Since the meeting had validated Tessa's fear and anger, she felt freer than she had since Nick had slashed and burned his way into her life. And she felt lighter. Her heavy heart seemed to have lost a few ounces.

As she drove home, she clicked on the radio, and the oldies station greeted her. She turned it up full blast and sang along with Queen—"We Are the Champions."

Yes, we are.

CHAPTER 25

The day after the survivors' meeting, Tessa was still buoyed as she drove down her driveway after work. For the first time in six weeks, she had gotten through the day without an onslaught of despair. It was something, and she welcomed any progress she could get.

When she approached Nick Payne's campaign poster, which neither she nor Emma had gotten around to yanking out of her landlady's lawn, Tessa averted her gaze as usual. She would not subject herself again to the poster's lies, and she would not allow Nick to ruin her first decent mood in six weeks.

But as she rounded her driveway's bend, her determination faltered. A San Julian police SUV came into view in all its crisp, no-nonsense black and white. She'd thought her case was closed. Had Nick tried to break into her cottage? Had her landlady called the police? Just when Tessa's life was looking brighter, stress returned with a vengeance.

An officer climbed out of the SUV, came toward Tessa, and left a German shepherd standing in the backseat kennel area. The dog peered at her as if he were sizing her up for possible criminal acts. His eyes warned, *If you're on the lam, you're doomed.*

The officer's bulletproof vest made her look barrel-chested.

Her red ponytail, threaded above her baseball cap's adjustment strap, bobbed as she walked. "Tessa Jordan?"

"Yes." Tessa gathered up her books and thermos and climbed out of her Beetle. From a madrone tree next to her driveway, a flock of crows cawed. To scold? To warn?

"I'm Chelsea Bishop. San Julian P.D. You got a minute?"

Anxiety blossomed inside Tessa. "Anything wrong?"

"Yes, unfortunately."

I can't take more bad news.

"Your cats. You feed them in the woods back there?" Officer Bishop pointed behind the cottage.

My cats? "I feed them there, but I'm not hoarding them or anything. I take good care of them. They have shelters. There's no cruelty going on."

"I'm not concerned about cruelty, Tessa, but your neighbors are complaining. They say the cats hang out in their yards and yowl at night. They attack birds at their bird feeders and scratch around in their flowerbeds. Last week, one of the cats attacked a woman's tabby. People are scared they have diseases."

"They don't! They're healthy!" They'd be in perfect health if they'd let her catch them and take them to the vet for inoculation updates.

"Your neighbors say the cats are pests," Officer Bishop said. "We've gotten several calls at the station, and so has Animal Control."

A dark cloud passed over Tessa's face. Couldn't the world just leave her alone? For once? "The cats are my family. I love them."

"I don't doubt that for a minute. I love my dog the same way." Officer Bishop's gaze seemed to soften with concern. "The problem is regulations. Cats need to be licensed. Strays are considered a nuisance. We're supposed to seize and impound them."

"You can't do that! My cats aren't strays," Tessa nearly shouted. "They're mine. I watch after them."

"Can you move them somewhere? Find them homes?"

"They're feral. Nobody but me would want them."

"That's a problem." Officer Bishop rested her hands akimbo on her utility belt, from which hung a scary-looking holster and gun. "It's Tuesday, and I'm supposed to give you till Saturday. If you haven't found another home for the cats by then, Animal Control will have no choice but to take them to the pound."

Tessa's heart slid to her toes. Her thermos's metal edge jabbed into her arm. "That's a death sentence. Feral cats never get adopted. If they end up in a shelter, they're always put down."

"We wouldn't want to do that, but we may have no choice," Officer Bishop said. "I understand this is awful news for you. Tell me, is there anything I can do to help?"

"I don't know. I have to think." Tessa rubbed her forehead as if she were trying to dig solutions from her brain.

Losing her cats would be bad enough, but if they were put down? The very thought caused her physical pain, which settled in her chest like pneumonia. For the first time since moving here eight years ago, she hated her neighbors, Judases who cheerfully waved to her, then stabbed her in the back. How could they be so mean to needy, innocent cats?

Officer Bishop handed her card to Tessa. "I'll contact you in a few days and see how things are going. Call me if I can help."

Tessa mumbled to herself, apropos of nothing, "The kitties are terrified of traps." Thanks to her neighbors, she was trapped, too.

CHAPTER 26

In the June sun through Howard's skylights, dust motes floated through the air. For most of the morning, Tessa had been helping her people, but now, alone at her desk, she had time to stare at the motes and worry about her cats. All she could think was: *What am I going to do?*

For breakfast, she'd fed her cats their favorite scrambled eggs, garnished with bits of a salmon steak thawed in the microwave. After the cats had finished eating and grooming themselves with fastidious licks and swipes of paws, she sprinkled catnip around the bushes for them to roll in for dessert. She told the cats about Chelsea Bishop and promised to fight till her last drop of strength to save them from Animal Control.

But now that the fight was about to start, anxiety sprang up again. How could she convince someone to adopt *seven* feral cats? And if Tessa failed, as unspeakably sad as that would be, how could she live with the cruel injustice of her kitties' deaths? The questions bombarded her.

If she dwelled on them, however, they would immobilize her. She herded them to the darkest corner of her brain and locked the gate. She may have lost the fight against Nick

Payne, but as she'd promised her cats, she would work to her last breath to save them. Today she would ask everyone she could think of to help, beginning with all Nisqually County vets listed online.

Tessa dialed San Julian's generous Dr. Vargas, who had spayed and neutered her cats at a discount. She knew his receptionist well.

"Heather!" As Tessa aimed for a confident tone, she mentally begged the universe for kindness. "I've got a horrible problem. I'm wondering if you can help."

"Is one of your babies sick?"

"Worse. My neighbors are complaining about them. I have to move them by Saturday, or Animal Control will come and get them."

Heather gasped. "That's terrible."

"Would you see if any of your clients or their friends could take them? Or even just one? I have seven who need homes."

"Oh, dear. I must have lost count." Heather was a quintessential crazy lady. She'd crowded so many cat photos on her desk that there was hardly room for a computer. "You know how people are about ferals," she said. "Even the most dedicated cat lovers don't want them. They think enough domestic cats need help in the world without worrying about wild ones."

"Will you at least ask around?"

"Yes. I promise. But I'm pretty sure what everybody's excuses will be," Heather said. "Just last week a woman came in here and claimed feral cats were tough enough to survive on their own. That's what a lot of people think."

"They're wrong. Feral cats are nearly always desperate."

"You're preaching to the choir," Heather said. "Are you going to make some fliers?"

"Later today."

"Bring me a few. I'll put one in our waiting room. Tomorrow I can leave a couple in the ferry terminal on my way
to Seattle."

A ray of hope. Tessa clung to it as she worked her way
down the online list of veterinary clinics. In every spare minute all afternoon, she also posted on the San Julian citizens'
Facebook page and contacted by phone and email the local
cat rescue and adoptions groups, such as the Nine Lives Soci-
ety, the Nisqually Cat Coalition, and Alley Cats and Friends.
Their responses, though predictable, crushed her.

"All our foster homes are full up with springtime kittens."

"Nobody here would be willing to take on a colony."

"You'll have to put the cats down. The likelihood of
someone adopting a feral for a pet is zero."

Like water dripping on a rock, the negativity carved a
canyon of dejection into Tessa's spirit. At the end of the day,
she called Emma, who railed at the callousness of county rules
and regulations, but she couldn't help because of a no-pets
clause in her rental agreement.

Unwilling to accept defeat, till late in the night Tessa
worked at her computer on a flier for her kitties.

Below CATS NEED YOUR HELP in red block letters, Tessa
printed a picture of Fitzgerald, who was part Siamese and her
colony's friendliest, most photogenic member. His buck fangs
were endearing, and the depth of soul in his blue eyes could
bring cold-hearted brutes to their knees. She wanted his sweet
face to draw in people for a closer look so they would read
about her cats' plight and melt with sympathy. On fringe cut
into the flier's lower inches, she supplied her phone number.
All anybody had to do was tear off one and call her.

On Thursday morning, Tessa told her patrons that she
was looking for homes for her cats, but no one volunteered
theirs. To cast a wider net, on cat-rescue websites throughout

Washington, she posted photos and begged pet fosterers for a stay of execution. After lunch, she took off from work and set out with sixty-five copies of her flier.

For hours, Tessa searched every San Julian road from north to south for posting spots, though she avoided Nick's neighborhood. The stack of fliers on her Beetle's passenger seat grew steadily thinner as she attached them with pushpins to telephone poles and tree trunks. She taped fliers onto stop signs' poles at intersections where potential cat adopters might pause in cars or on foot. She left fliers at the Aquatic Center, the Island Winery, the Elks' Clubhouse, the Grange, and in every church vestibule she found unlocked.

Downtown along Rainier Avenue, San Julian's main street, she pinned her cry for help to bulletin boards and taped it to the inside of businesses' windows, facing out. Now Fitzgerald could lure pedestrians who passed Say Cheese, Loose Ends Hair Styles, the Improv Comedy Club, and the Reel Good Movie Theater. By eight o'clock, her pin-pushing thumb ached, and her stomach growled for dinner, but she kept working her way down Rainier toward Planet of the Grapes, where she'd first met Nick.

For six weeks, she'd avoided coming near it because she could run into him as easily there as at Mel's Market. But tonight she would not cave to that fear. No, sir. As she got closer and her stomach's knot tightened, she jutted out her chin and reminded herself that she had to do everything she could think of to save her cats, or she'd be forever sorry. She forced herself to cross the street.

She pulled open Planet of the Grapes' heavy speakeasy door. A lingering smell of aftershave told her that a man had just walked through. *Nick?* She searched the dimly lit room for him. *So far, so good.*

In the center of each table, candles flickered "romance" and made her wince. Customers in animated conversations leaned toward each other as she and Nick had done. She checked each face, then looked a second time to convince herself that Nick was not there. She was safe! All clear.

She showed the bald cashier a flier and asked if she could post it.

He gave Fitzgerald a contemptuous glance. "Don't much like cats. Who in their right mind would want a whole damn pride of them?"

I would, you twit, Tessa thought but didn't say. In order not to rile someone she was asking for a favor, she politely answered, "I guess people have different tastes."

"Whatever." He shrugged. "Put it on the left sidelight." He aimed his index finger toward the speakeasy door.

Tessa taped the flier next to announcements for the Rotary Auction and the Daylily Club's annual sale. Now Fitzgerald would greet every customer and steal his way into their hearts. She begged, *Work your magic, sweet boy,* and went back to the street.

Tessa gulped in cool air. Proud for facing down her apprehension, she started toward her Beetle. She passed an elderly woman walking her sheltie and a jogger lost in thought. In front of the Sweet Time Bakery, a teenager with a pierced tongue sang "Amazing Grace" and plunked awkward chords on his guitar.

Tessa buttoned up her cardigan. Going into Planet of the Grapes had taken courage she had not known she had. But it was there. Though Louann would correct her for saying "should," she told herself she *should* remember that, in spite of everything, she was brave.

That evening, Officer Bishop, looking end-of-shift frazzled, knocked on Tessa's door. "Just checking in. Any takers?"

Tessa shook her head. "I need more time."

"I wish I could give you years, Tessa, but I have to follow protocol."

"Protocol" sounded cold and official. There was no humanity in it. It was a word that a robot might use.

Officer Bishop held up crossed fingers. "Maybe something will turn up. Good luck."

Tessa thanked her, closed the door, and dropped wearily into her Bentwood rocker. *Two days to go.*

CHAPTER 27

On Friday, Tessa took off work and called local cat-rescue and adoption groups again. She wanted them to know that the deadline was approaching, and her cats still needed homes. The luck that Officer Bishop had crossed her fingers for might be kaput; Tessa got only a few *sorrys* and *wish-we-could-helps*.

She drove around the island and walked downtown to see if her fliers were still posted, and found every one exactly where she'd left it. Out of sixty-five fliers, only one person had cared enough about the cats to tear off her phone number. So far, that person had not followed up.

As evening closed in, so did Tessa's realization that within twenty-four hours, her kitties would likely be chased down and shot, gassed, or injected with a lethal drug. Each possibility was unthinkable—an outrage—and urging herself to believe in miracles or eleventh hours didn't help. What hurt most was that she could think of nothing more to do to save her cats. Her well of ideas was dry. All that was left for her to do was make the most of the short time she had left with them. If tonight's supper would be their last, she would make them a feast of their favorite foods, like a death-row inmate's last meal.

She mashed canned sardines into oatmeal and patted the

mixture into Fishy Loaves. She combined raw ground beef with pureed broccoli and added hot water for Steak Tartare Stew. She grated zucchini and tossed it with alfalfa sprouts and canned-tuna oil for Kitty Salad, which she garnished with minced catnip from the potted plants on her front porch. For a new and yet unnamed treat, she scrambled eggs and added chicken pieces.

Tessa piled the feast onto a tray and carried it across the field behind her house. She could not cry. She did not want the cats to see her tears and sense that anything was wrong. She would not allow her grief to ruin their last night together.

When she got to their feeding stations, she set down her smorgasbord in clean pie tins and backed away. Delicious food was her last way to show her love. "Here, kitties!"

Their bodies quivering with anticipation, all seven tore out from under bushes. Alcott and Austen, the calico sisters, led the way.

Fitzgerald and the sensitive Bronte dove into the Kitty Salad. Wharton, the colony glutton, raised her mouth toward the sky and swallowed bites of Fishy Loaf as a seal would gulp down herring. Melville, a pugnacious cat with sawtooth-edged ears, stepped into the Steak Tartare Stew and scooped up bites with eager teeth. A chorus of the cats' smacks drifted through the air.

Tessa watched, pleased but sad. She tried to stop from thinking that this meal was probably her kitties' last, but her mind latched onto that terrible truth and refused to let go—until her cell's ring cut through her gloom and startled her. Maybe the caller was the person who'd torn her number off the flier. Or Alley Cats and Friends, or Dr. Vargas. Tessa scarcely dared hope.

"Hello?"

"Tess, any news?"

For the first time in their long friendship, Tessa was sorry to hear Emma's voice. "No news, and I can't think of anything else to do."

"You put up all your fliers?"

"Everywhere I could find."

"Outside the post office?"

"Yes."

"What about City Hall?"

"Did that," Tessa said with a little impatience. Emma was trying to help, but Tessa *had* gone everywhere.

"Did you go to the bulletin board behind Mel's Market?"

Tessa straightened up. "I forgot about that."

"Get your body over there, girl. The market's open till ten. Lots of people could still pass by there tonight."

Tessa hurried back to her house to print another flier.

CHAPTER 28

After working late, Will stopped at DIY Hardware. Last weekend, he'd glazed three barn windowpanes and filled in half a dozen wall cracks. Now he bought a second have-a-heart trap to set in the loft, and he'd leave the first on the workbench. Two traps doubled his chance of capturing the rat and his friends, who had grown into a mob, as evidenced by their droppings. The little thugs had also begun gnawing on his windowsill.

After DIY Hardware, Will drove to Mel's Market to get kibble for Hope and a strawberry-rhubarb pie for himself. Finding no empty places in the parking lot, he pulled into a spot on the street behind the store. He patted Hope. "Wait here. I'll just be a minute."

As usual, Hope's mournful eyes let him know that she did *not* like being abandoned. Furthermore, she suffered chronic FOMO, a fear of missing out. She was sure that Will was embarking on an exciting adventure, and where would *she* be? In his Jeep, locked up, deserted and alone, that's where.

"I'll get you some people crackers," Will said as he climbed out of the driver's seat.

Her dejected eyes informed him, *Your middle name is "Meanie."*

As Hope watched him walk away, she further expressed her displeasure by writing a message of protest on his windshield with her damp nose, which by June had lost its winter pink.

Will approached a pretty woman in jeans and a white sweater. Her dark hair puffed out from her head like a cloud. She was pinning a flier onto the bulletin board, and he read over her shoulder, CATS NEED YOUR HELP. His curiosity piqued, he glanced at a photo of a blue-eyed, buck-fanged cat, staring out at him like someone in a mug shot. *Why would cats need my help?*

Stepping near enough to read the flier's text required moving closer to the woman. He didn't want to sneak up on her, so he said, "Excuse me."

She whirled around and looked at him as if he were a would-be murderer brandishing a box cutter.

"I didn't mean to frighten you." *Are you afraid of everybody or just me?* "I was trying to read your flier."

"Oh." She exhaled a shaky breath. "My cats need a home. If I can't find one by tomorrow, Animal Control is going to euthanize them."

"Why?"

"Because they're considered strays, even though I've been feeding them for years. My neighbors have suddenly complained."

"How many cats?"

"Seven. They're feral, but they're really sweet. I mean, they wouldn't attack you or anything."

"No worries. My vet keeps my rabies and distemper shots up to date." Will's full lips parted in a smile.

But his joke fell face-down on the sidewalk between them. So now he knew this woman's strong suit was not a sense of humor. Or maybe she was just uptight.

"I've tried everything to find them homes, but I've run out of time. It breaks my heart."

"I can see that." Desolation was scrunched into lines around her eyes. He glanced at the flier again.

The cat looked like a ruffian. If the others were as tough, they could patrol Will's barn and take care of the rats. Normally, he'd never jump into something that was none of his business, but the woman looked downtrodden, and he could use some help. It would be a simple *quid pro quo*, a win–win. And what the hell? She wouldn't have his house key, and there was nothing of value in the barn.

"How would you feel about a temporary arrangement?" Will asked.

The woman's unhappy eyes brightened. "Temporary would be a godsend."

"Would the cats be okay in a barn?"

"They would love a barn as long as they could go in and out."

"I could prop open the door and some windows," Will said. "While you look for a permanent home, the cats could take care of my rat infestation."

"They're good hunters. Before they came to me, they were living on their own."

"You'd take care of food and water? I'm too busy for that."

"I'd feed them twice a day. You wouldn't have to do a thing."

"Great." She could come and go, and he'd never see her. Will ripped Tessa's phone number off the flier and typed it into his cell phone contacts. "Your name?"

She hesitated for a beat, and Will wondered if he'd have to call her "cat lady." "I'm Tessa Jordan."

Gulp. You're kidding.

The island was small. He shouldn't be surprised to meet

Tessa Jordan like this. But still, of all people. And he'd already agreed to keep her cats, for heaven's sake.

It was too late to back out, and he didn't really want to because the cool fall weather would be coming before he knew it, and the rats would be looking for a cozy home. Besides, he told himself, there was no ethics problem because as much as he'd wanted to take Nick Payne to court, it would surely never happen. Since Will couldn't get justice for Tessa, giving her a hand with her cats was the least he could do.

"I'm Will Armstrong." He did not mention the thorny fact that he was the prosecutor who'd turned down her case. Nor did he give her a business card, on which was printed his title. "I'm at 444 Old Post Road. First driveway on the right after you cross Ferncliff. Why don't you come by tomorrow morning and check out my barn? If it's suitable, you can start rounding up the cats."

"Okay."

So she is *capable of smiling. Lovely.* Light seemed to shine from her face.

CHAPTER 29

"What if Will Armstrong was putting me on?" Tessa asked Emma, who'd had no time for breakfast and was crunching on a granola bar.

"Why would he do that?" Emma asked.

"To harass me. You know how men are."

"A few decent men still exist in the world. Will Armstrong could be one of them."

"I'm scared he's not." As Tessa drove along his driveway, which cut through a grassy field, a dust cloud rose behind her Beetle. "He may have wanted to lure me to his house. Nick Payne redux."

"Don't worry. I'm here."

Emma wadded up her granola bar's wrapper and tossed it into the Beetle's garbage bag. She leaned forward and peered out the windshield at a barn that hadn't seen paint in fifty years. The tin roof was on the rusty side, and the walls were lucky not to have collapsed. In a shed attached to one of them, an ancient Jeep was parked.

Next to the barn at a water spigot, Will was washing out two metal bowls. In jeans and a blue chambray work shirt, he nodded hello when Tessa pulled up. He wasn't especially friendly, but that was okay with her.

"Wow, Tess! You didn't mention he's a hunk," Emma whispered.

"That's the last thing on my mind."

"The first on mine." Emma checked her face in the visor's mirror. "Wish I'd put on makeup. I look like one of your cats dragged me in."

"You're fine."

Tessa and Emma emerged from the Beetle. Before they could say hello to Will, a yellow Lab streaked toward them from the field. The dog threw herself at Tessa like she was her long-lost BFF. Her panting shouted, *Whoopee! You're here!*

Confused, Tessa squatted down and greeted her. As Will walked toward them, she asked, "Is this Hope?"

"Um . . . sure is." He introduced himself to Emma, who gave him a radiant smile.

"What's Hope doing here?" Tessa asked.

"She lives with me."

"I don't understand. I've met her with Sandy and Louann."

"They're two of her handlers. I'm the primary one."

"Do you work together?"

"Yes."

Tessa's brain jumped through hoops of mental calculation. "They're in the prosecutor's office."

"Yes, they are," Will said.

"You are too?"

"Are we playing Twenty Questions here?" Emma asked.

"I'm surprised to see Hope. I'm trying to understand the connections." Tessa felt like she was dragging information out of Will. "What do you do?"

He looked like he wasn't eager to answer. "I'm a lawyer."

Tessa gaped at him as if he had twelve eyes and vermilion skin. She didn't have to ask if he was the prosecutor who'd turned down her case. She could tell that he was because of his hesitance to reveal his identity. She shrank back and blanched—she despised him! As Hope circled her legs and wagged her tail, Tessa couldn't think of anything to say.

Emma jumped in to rescue the lagging conversation. "Your barn is so authentic! It belongs in an Andrew Wyeth painting! How old is it?"

"I don't know the age for sure," Will said. "A hundred years, maybe. About the same as my house."

Tessa noticed his Victorian farmhouse, off by itself in an apple orchard. The ramshackle place matched his car. With a little loving care, the house could be charming, but it begged for a fresh coat of sage green paint and a few shingles to replace those that had blown off the roof. The front porch sagged; in the last hundred years, the worn steps up to it had seen thousands of feet. Too bad Will neglected the house. He must be as indifferent to it as to the women who needed him to go after their assailants.

Will and Emma chatted about the coming rain, but Tessa's mind went into overdrive. What was she supposed to do? She wanted to call him contemptible for turning down her case, get into her car, and leave. But what about her cats? She had to save her cats.

"You want to see inside the barn?" Will asked.

"Yes!" Emma sounded like they were about to take a magic carpet ride.

"Okay." Tessa sounded like she was about to write a check for a parking ticket.

Will and Hope led them past his Jeep into the barn's enclosed space—he must not have swept the concrete floor in months. He hadn't washed the windows, either. He pointed out a pile of old blankets he'd set in a corner for the cats' beds, and a rat-proof metal container Tessa could use for a kibble vat.

"The garbage can's out back. Feel free to use it. I left two bowls for the cats to drink from under the water faucet.

They'll like roaming my woods and field," Will said. "Is there anything else you need?"

Yes, a prosecutor with a heart. "No, nothing else. Thank you," Tessa said politely, though prickles spiked from her words.

"You've been so kind! The cats will be happy here!" Emma raved.

"I'm glad I could help," Will said. "I'm counting on the cats to live up to their part of the bargain."

"Oh, they will!" Emma said.

On the drive back to Tessa's cottage, Emma praised Will's virtues. He was handsome, kind, generous, and, by the way, had she mentioned handsome?

"Don't you realize who he *is*?" Tessa asked.

"A lawyer. I didn't see a wedding ring, did you?"

"I didn't look," Tessa said. "He's the prosecutor who sold me down the river. I don't want anything to do with him. I'd have left in a minute if there'd been any other way to save my cats."

"You don't know what kind of pressure he's under, Tess. He must have had good reason not to go after Nick Payne."

"It's so obvious Nick's a criminal. Anyone can see he belongs in prison."

"Juries aren't just anyone. Will's job is more complicated. He has to follow all kinds of rules in court."

"I still can't stand him."

"Go ahead, but he's doing you a big favor," Emma said. "And you're forgetting another bonus."

"What's that?"

"If he's a prosecutor, he's hardly going to assault you. You can feel safe going over there to feed your cats."

Hmmpf. Tessa hurried home to call Officer Bishop before Animal Control showed up.

CHAPTER 30

As soon as Will took Hope's brush from his kitchen drawer, she turned into a rampant hedonist. One look at the rubber bristles, and without a nudge of coercion, she plopped at his feet and presented her fur. While he worked his way from her shoulders to her tail, she half closed her eyes in ecstasy and surrendered to the pleasure. Then he moved on to her chest, her favorite petting spot, and she rolled onto her back and flopped out her legs to give him better access.

As she enjoyed her chest brushing, a car pulled up outside. *That would be Tessa,* Will thought. Since she'd come to inspect the barn four days ago, he'd not seen her, but he'd known from cat food cans stacked on his workbench that she'd been there and dropped off two ultra-spooked colony members. They tore out of the barn and raced across the field if Will merely stepped outside his house.

"Sorry, but we're done here," Will told Hope. "I can't brush you all night."

When she got to her paws, her slump muttered, *Bummer!* He put away her brush. She'd clearly heard the car outside because she went to the back door and peered through the glass at the visitor.

From the window above his kitchen sink, Will watched

Tessa lift an extra-large have-a-heart trap from her Beetle's passenger seat. *Three cats now. Four to go.*

She looked pale, and her face seemed set with stress. Certainly, trapping and transplanting wild, unruly cats could wear her down, but Will would bet that Nick Payne was responsible for the trouble etched into her forehead. Will had learned from Maria that a sexual assault was an assault on more than her body; it was on her mind and spirit, too. It left an indelible mark on every facet of her being—her physical appearance, her thoughts, her attitude. It was all-encompassing, and the effects could last for years.

Will stuffed his hands into his jeans' back pockets and watched Tessa open the trap's door. The cat must have been too frightened to shoot out into an unfamiliar place, so Tessa got down on her knees, peered inside, and coaxed. Though Will didn't pity Tessa—she seemed too strong and proud for that—he was sorry she'd gotten traumatized, like that cat. Of course, Nick Payne had done it, but Will knew he'd added to it by not taking her case.

Tessa deserved an explanation, and yet he believed that he should keep a businesslike distance from her. Talking with her about Nick Payne would only complicate matters, and Will could be opening himself up to familiarity that could be unwise. Nevertheless, one look at her face, and he knew that he should explain the limits of his job. He needed to let her know that his decision to drop her case had not been personal. He'd had no choice. He could not bend judicial rules.

As he kept watching Tessa and the cat, still huddled in the trap, he kept trying to decide what to do. Finally, his decency won out over his better judgment. "Come on, Hope," he said. He opened the kitchen door for her and started toward the barn. Freshly brushed and excited about a visitor, she pranced beside him. Her paws skimming over the grass shouted, *Company! Hurrah!*

When she saw that the company was Tessa, she ran, whimpering and wagging her tail. But then she recognized the trap's mystery occupant. *A cat! A CAT!* Hope aimed her nose to sniff through the open end. When Tessa blocked her, she sniffed between the metal bars along the side instead. Hope acted like she intended to inhale the cat. Her body quivered at the prospect.

Bronte responded as loud as a trumpet blast, #$%%@&*!!

Her hisses and snarls did not dampen Hope's enthusiasm. She whined and wagged her tail in a joyful circle—her sign of greatest exuberance, reserved for her biggest thrills.

"Don't terrorize Bronte," Tessa warned Hope.

"You don't need to worry," Will said as he caught up to her. "She was raised on a farm with plenty of cats. She loves them."

"Bronte doesn't love *her*," Tessa countered.

As if to stress that point, Bronte yowled, ^%$%&!=&$!

"Want me to put Hope back in the house?" Will asked.

"Doesn't matter. Bronte won't come out till we all leave anyway." To protect her for now from Hope's well-meant sniffs, Tessa closed the trap. "Bronte's named after Emily Bronte. She's a ladylike cat, but now she's outraged. She protested all the way over here."

"Once she sees the other cats, she'll know she's in a good place," Will said.

"I've caught the three tamest. The others are going to take a while."

"At least you're off to a good start."

When Tessa didn't respond, silence reared its head, and Emma wasn't there to iron out the awkwardness. He considered saying goodbye and going back into the house, but he'd come out here to talk with Tessa, and it was time.

Where to begin? Perhaps he should have thought this through a little more. "Tessa, when we first met, I didn't realize who you were. By the time I did, I'd already offered you the barn, and it didn't seem right to back out."

He paused. Talking to a jury was easier than this, but at least Tessa seemed to listen. "I didn't think the case would come up in relation to the cats. I forgot you knew Hope. I should have explained our connection."

"You'd have saved me a shock."

"I apologize," Will said. "And I expect you're annoyed with me for not filing charges."

"You bet I'm annoyed." Tessa's flash of anger emphasized that point. Picking up that she might need soothing, Hope moved over beside her.

"I wanted to take your case, but I couldn't without proof," Will said. "In court, I'd have to demonstrate with physical evidence beyond a reasonable doubt that Nick Payne forcibly assaulted you—and he intended to do it, and he knew it was a crime."

"Why else would he have drugged me if he didn't intend to assault me, and he didn't know it was wrong? It's a no-brainer," Tessa fumed.

"The drug is the problem. When you went for the exam, you didn't have any drug in your system. That's the evidence we needed," Will said. "Nick probably gave you something that left your body quickly. He knew what he was doing."

"It's not fair," Tessa said.

"I know. I wish *life* was fair. Unfortunately, this kind of thing happens too often."

"Doesn't my side of the story count for *any*thing?" Tessa demanded.

"It would be your testimony, not physical evidence. There's a difference. We have to have proof."

"There are photos of my bruises."

"They help, but Nick claims you wanted . . . well, rough sex. That casts doubt."

"He's a liar!"

"Yes," Will agreed. "The thing is, all these cases come down to consent. You say you were drugged and didn't consent. He claims you did. In court, a verdict would depend on which of you the jury believes, and I have to tell you, rotten as it is, juries are often biased against the victim. They could blame *you*. They could think you asked for it, or you were naïve to go to the house of a man you hardly knew, or you didn't fight hard enough to stop Nick."

"I couldn't fight! I was unconscious!" Tessa glared at Will.

"But there was no evidence of a drug," Will said calmly. "I'd have to prove that he assaulted you—and remember, *beyond a reasonable doubt*. That's a high bar. All his attorney would have to do is punch holes in my case. Bed of roses for him. The process is stacked against me. Without evidence, I don't have a legal leg to stand on."

"That's outrageous!"

She didn't have to tell Will. He could see the anger in her narrowed eyes. "Trust me, I hated seeing this happen to you," he said.

Tessa's disapproving frown and raised eyebrows told him that she doubted he hated it at all. "You say a jury could believe I didn't fight hard enough. I say *you* didn't fight hard enough to help me. It's totally obvious what Nick did."

He paused to take a breath before answering. "It's obvious that he had sex with you. We have solid physical evidence for that. But not for your inability to consent." Will chose not to challenge her belief that he hadn't fought hard enough for her. It was etched into her stubborn brain, and she seemed in no mind to change her opinion.

To appease her, he added, sincerely, "I understand your resentment."

"I don't think you do."

Arguing about my empathy would be a waste of time. And Will was getting rather resentful himself. He'd come out here to try and help her feel better, but she'd not listened to a word he'd said. He'd have had more success talking with Bronte.

But then Will remembered Maria's fury. It had seemed to rule their family's life for months—when she wouldn't eat anything but toast, and they found her crying in her room all the time. By not reporting her assault, she'd not even dipped her toe into the judicial process, but Tessa had jumped right in and swum upstream by going to the police and cooperating for interviews and medical tests. Maria had not gone an inch to get justice for herself, but Tessa had gone a miserable mile. She had earned her anger.

"These disappointments happen more often than not," Will said.

"It's a lot more than disappointment. It's devastation. It shouldn't have happened to me."

Will said nothing, just shook his head slowly. *It shouldn't happen to anyone,* he thought sadly.

Only then did he realize that Hope was sitting between him and Tessa. Hope's eyes went from one to the other, as if she weren't sure who needed soothing most. *I am here for you. I want to make it better.*

CHAPTER 31

On the evening of July Fourth, Tessa went to Will's barn. So far, she'd trapped and transported six cats—only Dickens was missing. She'd called Officer Bishop and begged for more time before Animal Control would hunt him down. "Hurry and get him," Bishop had warned. As if Tessa weren't already worried enough. As if she hadn't been baiting the traps with fresh liver to convince Dickens to step into them.

The six cats now living in Will's barn had let her know that being moved was an appalling imposition. They'd gone on strike about grooming themselves, and she'd seen resentment in their disheveled fur. Bristling distrust, they also refused to run toward her when she came with food, as they used to do. Tonight their disappearance let her know that they were still holding a grudge. *We trust you as far as we can throw you.* Meaning not a single inch.

Tessa checked around the barn. She peered under Will's workbench and around paint cans stored on his shelves. She climbed the ladder to his loft and shone her flashlight on his chairs and trunk, and she sifted through the cats' blankets. No kitties. Not a whisker or a telltale tip of a tail sticking out anywhere.

After Tessa looked under Will's Jeep and found no cats,

she walked out into the field and called, "Here, kitties!" No yellow eyes reflected her flashlight beam. She heard no swish of grass or crackle of leaves under stalking paws.

She mostly heard sporadic fireworks. In the dark sky, distant Roman candles shot stars of yellow, green, and red. Tessa understood that her cats were not just huffy about being moved; they were also scared of the flashes of light and noise. All day, the cats had endured explosions, set off by thoughtless people. Like every wild animal on San Julian Island, the cats had run for their lives.

If Tessa could, she'd banish booths selling fireworks along Highway 29. Since there were no laws against *them,* laws against stray cats seemed all the more heartless. Fireworks disturbed the peace far more than any feral cat did. As Will had recently pointed out, life often wasn't fair.

That was as true for cats as for victims of assault. Tessa had been fretting over Will's insistence on physical evidence, as if it were more important than the truth she was willing to swear to in court. It seemed to her that the legal requirements for a trial were stacked against victims instead of their assailants. How could Nick's rights be protected, and Tessa's were not? How could Will have so little regard for her feelings and not see her point of view? He didn't care what Nick had done. He'd doled out false sincerity while turning his back on her.

Irritated all over again, she went back to the barn, ran fresh water into the cats' bowls, and washed the aluminum pie tins. As she spooned Turkey Delight into them, she mentally begged the cats, *Please, come back for dinner. I know you're upset, but hunger won't solve anything.* Though no kitty ears were around to hear, she said out loud, "I'll be back in the morning. You be safe." She pulled her car keys from her jeans' pocket and climbed into her Beetle.

As she set out for home, she glanced back at Will's house. Light shining from the windows made it look warm and inviting, but that impression was false. Will Armstrong was neither of those things—his kindness to her cats had been born from self-interest, not from compassion. Justice for women meant nothing to him. Tonight he'd been home, but he'd obviously avoided her.

Good. The less of him, the better.

CHAPTER 32

"Hope, it's bath time again." Standing by the doorway between his bedroom and bathroom, Will pointed toward the dreaded shower stall.

Hope could not bring herself to turn and look at it directly; she glanced at it from the corner of her eye. She knew what Will was asking, but her toenails digging into the bedroom carpet straightforwardly announced, *No way am I going into that torturous place. There's water in there.*

As a retriever, Hope was supposed to love water. Just about every other member of her breed on earth leapt into it and paddled around with joy. But not Hope. Tracy Engels had told Will that as a puppy, she'd fallen into a pool and had to be rescued. She remembered. To this day, water was her enemy. She acted like she'd had aversion therapy for it.

To get her to step into the shower stall, Will had tried trickery. He'd dried the tile until not a single threatening water drop clung to it, and he'd propped her yellow duck in the corner to make it look like a happy place. For days, in the stall he gave her treats, fed her dinner, and even brushed her teeth so she could slurp her beloved ham-flavored toothpaste there. After sweet talk and coaxing, she no longer wriggled under the bed to hide when he mentioned "bath." But she always stood her ground to resist.

As she did now.

It was Friday night, and Will was tired and wanted to go to bed. But he had to get her ready for Maria's birthday barbecue for Uncle George tomorrow. "Okay, Hope. We've got to gussy you up. No more procrastinating."

Huff. Refusing to wag, her tail lay on the carpet like rope from a hangman's noose.

"It's been a while since your last bath. You can't go there dirty. You know Uncle George is a germophobe, and you've got to be clean for work."

Though Hope hated water, Will could count on her to listen to reason. When he grabbed her collar and tugged her to the bathroom, she relented, sort of, so her opposition became half-hearted. He closed the door behind them so she could not escape, and gave her a dog biscuit to distract her while he set shampoo, towels, and a hair dryer on the counter by his sink. Then he nudged her into the stall, took the showerhead off its holder, and turned on the water.

Hope may have relented, but that didn't mean she approved. As water hit her fur, she stared at the tile, avoiding his face. Will wet her down quickly, then lathered her up. Once the shampoo looked like slightly gray whipped cream, he rinsed her. The cloudy water gurgling down the drain testified to her recent forays into his dusty field.

"See, Hope. You needed a bath."

I liked the way I was.

"You're going to be gorgeous. Everyone will want to pet you."

Phooey.

Will rubbed her down with towels, then flicked on the hair dryer, whose whine disturbed Hope's sensitive ears. She

flattened them back as she endured the final indignity of being dried and fluffed and denied her doggy smell. As Will was
moving the dryer toward her paws, her most sensitive spot,
the phone rang.

"You wait," he told her. Because she was a flight risk, he
closed the door behind him and checked to make sure she
couldn't nose it open and make a run for it.

"Will, am I calling at a bad time?" Sandy asked.

"I was bathing Hope."

"Sorry to interrupt. I'm calling from my car. I just got out
of a meeting with my team."

Will knew that meant the Nisqually County detectives,
psychologists, medical staff, and law enforcement officers she
met with on the first Friday evening of every month. They
discussed their assault cases and supported each other. "Anything interesting?" Will asked.

"Possibly. Mason Harbor P.D.'s detective was venting
about a dead-end case. In June, a man drugged and sexually
assaulted a woman in her home. She could provide a description of him, but she never learned or could remember his last
name."

Great. Once again, luck is on the pervert's side. "No way to
follow up, then."

"Right."

"So?"

"So his first name was Nick."

That got Will's attention. It shook him out of his end-of-
the-week fatigue. "You think he's Nick Payne?"

"Could be. The victim said he was a white male, about
forty-five, brown hair."

"The description's on target, but it's too general."

"Yeah. That's what I thought. It's a stretch," Sandy said.
"But you never know. It could be Nick Payne."

"It could." *I wish.* Tessa's stricken eyes appeared in Will's mind. Her stubbornness may have exasperated him, but it would be nice to wipe the sadness off her face—and to see Nick Payne get what he deserved.

"Want me to follow up?" Sandy asked.

"Absolutely."

"I'll get back to you in a few days."

"Amazing," Will mumbled under his breath as he hung up the phone.

On his way back to the bathroom, he warned himself, *Easy, easy.* He had to stand back and let this play out. Excitement or any other emotional investment would only make it difficult for him down the road. Still, he could always hope.

CHAPTER 33

One morning in the back of Howard, Tessa worked on a bulletin board about the beginnings of famous novels. At the top, she pinned a sign, INTRIGUED BY THE FIRST LINE? At the bottom, another sign, CHECK IT OUT. Between them, she began posting first lines written on index cards. Her patrons could figure out what book the quote started, and she'd provide hints, if needed.

The first card started Leo Tolstoy's *Anna Karenina*: "Happy families are all alike; every unhappy family is unhappy in its own way." Tessa wondered what Nick's family was like, and she concluded that it must have been miserable. Otherwise, he'd not have turned out as loathsome as he was. But a crummy family was no excuse.

She pushed a pin into the second card, compliments of Jane Austen's *Pride and Prejudice*: "It is a truth universally acknowledged that a single man in possession of a good fortune must be in want of a wife." *Except for perverts like Nick Payne. They don't want a wife; they want a victim,* Tessa thought.

The third card, from *A Tale of Two Cities*: "It was the best of times, it was the worst of times . . . it was the spring of hope, it was the winter of despair." *No question about it, Charles Dickens. Thanks to Nick Payne, I'm in the winter of despair. It may be July, but snow is piling up around me, and wind is howling in my trees.*

As Tessa was about to pin the last card, she stopped and stared at it: "I am a sick man . . . I am an angry man." It occurred to her that in *Notes from Underground,* Dostoevsky's narrator could have been speaking for Nick and his sick mind. But was he also angry? At women? Did he hate them? Was that his problem? Mary O'Malley had said that Nick had been after power, but maybe hate had been driving him, too.

Tessa sat at her desk and closed her eyes. "You're doing it again. You know that, don't you? You're obsessing," she mumbled to herself.

What was *wrong* with her? Nick, the pervert, didn't deserve a second of her thoughts, and yet he'd been constantly on her mind—*again.* Allowing him to color her outlook was a self-destructive waste of time. She had to think about something else.

To pry him out of her thoughts while she waited for her people to stream through Howard, Tessa opened the *San Julian Review* she'd brought that morning from the library's main branch.

On the front page, she read that the Rotary Auction had collected two hundred thousand dollars, which would be used for pipes to carry clean water to remote villages in Chad. The San Julian Women's Club had opened a new thrift shop next to City Hall, and volunteers were needed to help with displays and sales.

Page two contained the police log. A woman had dug up her vegetable garden and found a suspicious knuckle, which turned out to be the bone of an unfortunate raccoon. Two police officers had been called to break up a fight at Rainier House, a memory care facility, but when they arrived, the male residents could not remember what they'd argued about.

Tessa turned to page three, and a headline jumped out and

startled her. "Nick Payne is Setting Things Right for Moms and Kids." Seeing his name in print was bad enough, but worse was his photo. His self-satisfied smirk seemed to shout at her, *See? I got away with it.* How could a man like him be setting *anything* right for *anyone?*

The image revolted Tessa. Yet she couldn't stop herself from reading on. Below Nick's picture was a Q&A. Asking the Qs was the *Review*'s feature editor, an attractive woman about Tessa's age. Last year, they'd met at a library fundraiser.

Q: I'm impressed that you're raising money to fund an after-school club for kids of single working moms. Those women must be thrilled! Why have you put your time and energy into a project like that?

A: I really care about the club, and I want to help those children. When I was four, my father left my mother and me and my older brother, and we never saw him again. My mother worked long, hard hours at Walmart, and my older brother Alex bagged groceries after school. For me, it was tough coming home every day to an empty house.

Q: So you were a latchkey kid?

A: Yes. A lonely one. I don't want other kids to feel that way. I want them to have the support I didn't.

Q: That's so kind of you, Nick. You've turned your own hardship into something beautiful. Most people don't do that.

A: I try. It means a lot to me to feel I'm helping others. That goal gets me out of bed in the morning.

Q: That's why you're running for City Council?

A: Exactly. There's so much to be done for our town. The after-school club is an example. It will improve the lives of kids *and* their mothers—and those women need a hand. I'd also like to work for affordable housing on our island and lead a campaign for more nutritious lunches in our schools.

Q: So you've got a big heart! No wonder you're ahead in the polls.

A: I've been truly humbled by the numbers . . .

Tessa could not read another word of Nick's self-serving pap. If he had half a chance, he'd drug and rape that fawning interviewer and all those mothers he supposedly cared about so much. If Tessa had been able to take him to court, people would know the truth. At least her survivors' group knew it.

In a fury, Tessa got up, stomped down Howard's aisle, and shoved the *San Julian Review* into the trash can at his entrance. How she hated Nick Payne! If she could leave the bookmobile during regular hours, she'd take the paper outside and burn it, or bury it, or drown it in Puget Sound. Too bad she couldn't do something equally destructive to that wretched man!

CHAPTER 34

"Knock, knock." Sandy rapped an imaginary door as she breezed into Will's office wearing black pants and a black linen blouse that she must not have had time to iron. Today's color of shadow on her exposed eyelid leaned toward an eggplant's dark purple.

Will looked up from his desk. Papers covering its writing surface testified to how busy he was. He turned his swivel chair toward Sandy. "Hey. Good to see you. Have a seat."

Hope, always on the lookout for potential bliss providers, raised a hind leg, exposing her stomach, and let be known her wish for a belly rub.

When Sandy squatted down and rubbed, Hope closed her eyes. She thumped her tail against the carpet and urged Sandy, *Don't stop!*

"My bum knee only lets me squat for a minute, Hope," Sandy said.

"So what's going on?" Will asked.

"Lots." Sandy's knee made a cracking sound when she rose to her feet and left Hope disappointed that her rapture had ended. "You know the Mason Harbor assault I told you about?"

"Yep." It had been on Will's mind the last four days.

"Yesterday I interviewed the vic, Abbey Greenwood. I showed her a photo lineup, and she identified Nick Payne as the perp."

"Yes!" Will slapped his fingers against the desktop. "Great work!"

"Looks like we've got him this time, and there's more."

Will leaned forward and listened as if his whole body were covered with ears.

"Abbey met him at the Nisqually Food and Wine Festival. He told her he had a great bottle of wine he wanted her to try. That's the same line he gave Tessa."

"So the MOs link."

"Right. And Abbey agreed to let him follow her home."

Will shook his head, dismayed. "Why do women do these things?"

"She said she knew it was stupid, but she was a little bombed, and he seemed nice."

"A nice wolf in sheep's clothing."

"Unfortunately." Sandy crossed her leg and grimaced as if her knee gave her extra pain today. "After a couple of glasses of wine, like Tessa, Abbey passed out. Nick was gone the next morning when she came to. I think we've got a second verse of the same song here."

"Sex?"

"His DNA inside her."

"What about consent?"

"I'm glad for once to be the bearer of good news," Sandy said. "Abbey got to the forensic exam sooner than Tessa did. Ambien was still in her body. It could be proof she was drugged."

Will's smile had a touch of glee. The drug test was the proof they needed. In his line of work, this kind of positive development didn't happen every day. "Looks like we may have a predator and a pattern here."

"Seems like a breakthrough to me."

Will was experienced enough not to celebrate; as he knew well, cases fell through for countless reasons. At this early stage, he would be naïve to assume that a successful prosecution lay ahead. But his intuition told him that he and Sandy might have a chance of catching Nick this time. Will allowed himself to feel guarded confidence that he could get this case to court.

"You have Abbey Greenwood's number?" he asked.

"Right here. Work and home." From her backpack, Sandy handed Will an index card. "It's got her home and email addresses, too."

The instant Sandy left Will's office, he picked up the phone and dialed Abbey's numbers. When she didn't answer, he left his own, office and cell, and he explained that he was calling from the County Prosecutor's office. He said, "I'd like to talk with you as soon as possible."

CHAPTER 35

While Hope was visiting her friend Lucy, the receptionist, Will went to the staff lounge for a cup of coffee. He needed a jolt of caffeine. In the middle of the night, he'd woken up, stared at the ceiling, and worried that Abbey Greenwood had not returned his calls. She'd had two days. Though she might be out of town, Will suspected she was avoiding him. For hours, he lay there and stewed.

Prosecutors often faced reluctant witnesses, but he'd expected Abbey to cooperate. Like Tessa, she'd gone to the police and had the forensic exam. She'd agreed to talk with Sandy. Abbey must want Nick punished, but why hadn't she gotten back to Will?

Why? he asked himself again as he worked a paper cup off the upside-down stack by the coffee urn. Bret Bailey, his boss and the elected county prosecutor, threw open the door and came into the lounge. Usually a force of nature, like a hurricane, today he slumped as if he hadn't had much sleep himself. His eyes looked dull; his cheeks, pasty.

"Sometimes kids are more trouble than you bargain for," he told Will while filling his cup. "Ever clean vomit off a mattress? Three times in one night?"

"Can't say I have," Will said.

"My son sneaked half a box of his grandmother's chocolates. I'll tell you, if I hadn't felt so sorry for him, I'd have wrung his neck." Bailey poured a packet of sugar into his cup and stirred with a wooden stick. "Things okay with you?"

"Good enough." Will wondered if he should tell Bailey about Abbey Greenwood. Will's motto was usually "If in doubt, don't," especially when his ducks for a case were not yet in a row. But he was impatient to talk with Bailey about Nick Payne. The case could be sensational, and Will wanted Bailey's approval from the get-go.

"Something's just come up." Will's slug of coffee burned a path down his gullet. "A couple of months ago, a San Julian woman claimed she was sexually assaulted, but she waited too long for the forensic exam. We couldn't prove she'd been drugged, so we had to drop the case. Last week, Sandy stumbled on another of the same man's vics, and *her* blood test showed Ambien. Right now I'm trying to reach her."

"You're sure it's the same man? The cases are linked?"

"His DNA on both women. Same MO."

"Just because he drugged the second woman doesn't mean he drugged the first."

"The first is ready to testify he did."

Bailey scoffed. "Testimony's not proof, and the defense will claim the second woman took Ambien just to go to sleep that night. You know how it goes." Bailey blew at steam billowing off his coffee. "You don't have a smoking gun."

Will took a labored breath. This morning, the usually supportive Bailey had turned grumpy and contrary. Will had had the bad luck—and poor judgment—to bring up this case on the wrong day. He took another slug of the damned coffee, felt his esophagus burn again. "Look, I think you should know who the perp is."

"Okay, who?"

"Nick Payne."

"Oh." Bailey's lips froze in a circle like he was blowing smoke rings. He seemed to recalibrate his stand. "Payne makes this case more risky. The press would be all over it. To go after him, you'd need air-tight evidence—which you don't have."

"I've got enough to try."

A vein bulged in Bailey's temple. "You're reaching. Those women might go through hell in court for nothing. If you lose, you'll make us look like a pack of fools."

"Nick Payne deserves to be tried and punished, and any woman brave enough to come forward deserves to be heard," Will said. "I've got the Ambien to argue that consent was impossible for at least one victim. Maybe if we dig, we'll find more evidence."

"To hell with it. Dig if you want." When Bailey waved his hand dismissively, he let Will know that cleaning up after his son all night had worn down his usual bulldog stance about the law. He did pin Will to the wall with his eyes, however. "You remember one thing. This case is on you. If you want to go ahead, you take the heat. And if you make this department look like a bunch of buffoons, I'll make sure traffic violations will be all you'll prosecute for the rest of your life."

Back in his office, Will picked up the phone. He'd been wrong to tell Bailey about Nick Payne's alleged assaults before he could present them in a tidy package, ready to go to court. He'd let his zeal run away with him. Now the pressure was on him big time, and he was out on a limb. He suddenly knew how a climber felt, dangling by a frayed rope from the rock face of El Capitan.

But chastising himself for his mistake would do no good. Better to put his energy into filing charges and winning in court. At least Bailey wouldn't stand in his way. If only he could persuade Abbey Greenwood to join the fight. Without her, he had no case.

Will dialed her work number. It rang and rang. *Damn!* His eyelid twitched.

Her voicemail clicked on. "I'm either out of the office or away from my desk . . ."

Yes, I know, Abbey. Too bad there was such a thing as caller ID.

With humility that was almost too close to kissing her ass, Will introduced himself again in case she'd forgotten who he was, and he left his home and cell numbers in case she'd misplaced them. *Fat chance.* Then he called her home. No Abbey. In his message, he didn't quite grovel, but he did become an obsequious lackey. Sure, witnesses slipped through his fingers sometimes, and he'd learned to roll with the punches, but he needed her!

Trying not to sound desperate, he said, "Call me day or night. It's important."

CHAPTER 36

"Welcome back, Tessa." Louann handed her a box of peanut butter cookies. Into each one, she'd pressed a fork's tines, like a prison cell's bars. Tonight, Carmen had also brought a paper plate of Mexican wedding cookies, rolled in powdered sugar. Tessa took one of each and set them on a red cocktail napkin from the pile in the table's center.

"We missed you last meeting," LaKeisha told Tessa.

"I was rounding up my last feral cat," she said.

"Did you get it to the barn?" Gail asked.

"Finally. It took weeks." Tessa bit into a wedding cookie, loving the sugar that dissolved on her tongue. "I still can't believe my cats are living on the property of the horrible prosecutor who wouldn't take my case." She looked over at Louann. "Sorry. I know you work with Will Armstrong, but I still think he's a jerk."

"Everyone's entitled to her own opinion, Tessa," Louann said. "Maybe you'll forgive him someday."

"She has a right to be angry at him," Sam said.

"Of course, she does. We all have a right to our feelings," Louann said.

"Just because the prosecutor won't get justice for you, Tessa, it doesn't mean you can't heal," Sam said. "I've been thinking we have to heal our*selves*. It's up to us—an internal thing, you know what I mean?"

Nods of understanding all around the table. Sam, who'd begun knitting a baby afghan for her pregnant sister, turned her needles and started a new row.

"Do you think you can heal without seeing your assailant punished, Tessa?" Louann asked.

"Maybe in five hundred years. For now I'm still nursing my grudges." Tessa brushed the last powdered sugar off her fingertips. "I don't know what to do with my anger. I go along okay for a while, and then all of a sudden it leaps out and sets me into a fury." Tessa explained last week's Q&A with Nick. "The hypocrisy! It took me days to calm down."

"I expect everybody in here is as angry as Tessa, right?" Louann asked.

"More than angry. Infuriated," LaKeisha said.

"Let's talk about anger. None of us wants to spend our days calming down," said Louann.

"How do we keep from getting so mad?" Gail asked.

"Well, first you need to understand triggers. They resurrect memories or flashbacks of your assault, and they can bring on all sorts of bad feelings. Anger is one of the most common," Louann said.

"What are some triggers?" Sam asked.

"A good question to ask yourselves. Everybody's are different," Louann said. "Anyone want to share what can set you off?"

"Trains passed behind the warehouse where my car was parked when I got raped. Now every time I hear a train, I want to scream. I feel like I'm going crazy," Gail said.

"What about my boss's disgusting cologne? If I smell anything like it, I almost get sick," LaKeisha said.

"Good examples of triggers. Smells and sounds can send

you right back to the assault," Louann said. "What about places and people?"

"I wouldn't drive by Nick Payne's house for a million dollars. I can't even stand thinking about it. And you already know what reading his quotes did to me," Tessa said.

"Understandable," Louann said. "So you've all got the concept. Once you're aware of your triggers, you can avoid them as Tessa does the house. Or if one crops up that you can't or didn't avoid, like a distant train whistle, you can take a moment to recognize what's going on, and you can often keep from flying into a fury by beginning one of the grounding techniques we've discussed."

Carmen screwed up her face like she was feeling physical pain. Her eyes looked sadder than usual. "Do you mind listening to what happened to me at Safeway last night?"

"We'll listen to anything," Louann said.

"There was no way I could have anticipated what happened. I reacted before I even realized what was going on," Carmen said.

"How so?" Gail asked.

"I was standing in the aisle looking at canned tomatoes, and some man brushed against me. Looking back, I don't think he meant to—the aisle was narrow, and he was trying to get his shopping cart past mine. But I just about jumped out of my skin. I was right back to being hauled behind the bushes—I could even smell my attacker's sweat—and that led to a major panic attack. I could hardly breathe."

Carmen wrung her hands. "On the way to my car, I got so angry it scared me. I had to deal with all these emotions just because that man accidentally touched me. I realized how serious my anger is."

"Did you breathe in through your nose and out through your mouth to ground yourself like we're supposed to?" LaKeisha asked.

"It didn't help. I sat in my car and said 'peace' about three hundred times, but I was too freaked out. I got to thinking I'll never get over being raped. It's like that man did more than assault me. He ruined my life. I swear to God, if I could get away with killing him, I'd do it."

Exactly how I felt last week, Tessa thought.

As Carmen began to weep, Hope rose from her pillow in the corner, came to her, and rested her head in her lap. Hope looked up at her, and her soulful eyes spoke whole volumes of reassurance: *I know you're distressed. Go ahead and cry. I'm here for you. I love you. I want you to be all right.*

When Carmen put her arms around Hope's neck and cried into her fur, a hush fell over the table. Tessa would have reached over and hugged Carmen if she'd been sitting next to her, but Gail did it for the whole group. Carmen pulled a tissue out of the box. After blowing her nose, she kissed Hope, leaving a lipstick print on her forehead, and straightened up again. "I'm sorry."

"Nothing to apologize for, Carmen. Everyone in here has had triggers like that and been outraged. And tears are good," Louann said gently. "It's important for us to remember that sometimes a trigger comes like a bolt out of the blue. We're unprepared for it, and it can flatten us and bring on a whole cascade of overwhelming feelings we need time to sort out."

"Agreed," Sam said, and everybody nodded.

Tessa passed Louann's cookies to Carmen. When she took one, Hope must have felt that Carmen's storm had passed. But she curled up under the table at Carmen's feet, close enough for further comforting, if needed.

"You know, when we have these inevitable emotional storms, we can turn them around to help us," Louann said.

"Impossible," LaKeisha said.

"No, it's true. You can get helpful insights. Take the anger like Carmen felt on the way to her car. It might show her something," Louann said.

"Like what? Never go into a store with narrow aisles?" LaKeisha asked, and everybody chuckled.

"Well, Carmen does realize now that being accidentally touched by a stranger can upset her, and that's something to be aware of when in close quarters with strangers. But I'm talking about something different," Louann said. "When anger overwhelms you, it's important to stop and think about it and try to understand if any other feelings might be behind it. Sometimes people make themselves angry so they don't have to feel pain. I mean, it feels better to be mad than to suffer something deeper."

That seemed to pique everyone's interest. You could have heard an ant crawl across the table. Every eye was riveted on Louann.

"Does that ring true for any of you? That anger could be masking something that hurts more?"

"Yes. Definitely, there's pain in here." Sam patted her heart. "I've wondered if some of my rage at my ex-boyfriend has to do with how hurt I am that he thought so little of me as to assault me. Talk about betrayal. Even if we're not a couple anymore, I wish he still respected me."

"That's exactly the kind of thing I'm talking about, Sam," Louann said. "I'm wondering, Carmen, if you could have gotten angry because deep inside you felt terrified. Not just of your assailant, but also of the world. It can seem like a scary place after a sexual assault. Anger can cover up the terror and give us something else to focus on. And it can make us feel more powerful."

Carmen nodded. "No doubt about it, I was terrified in the Safeway. I didn't make the connection to anger, but you're right."

"Anger can mask all kinds of things. It can cover up anxiety or shame or guilt. Even helplessness and grief—almost anything we feel we can't handle at the moment and we need to hide even from ourselves," Louann said.

"So you're saying we should go deeper, figure out if there's something more under the anger?" Gail asked.

"Right. Sometimes anger is all there is, but sometimes there's more to it." Louann picked up a peanut butter cookie and took a bite.

"Isn't anger a big problem for women anyway?" Gail asked.

"Yes, and especially for assault survivors," Louann said. "The problem is that women are taught from childhood that anger is bad, and we shouldn't feel it. When we do, we feel guilty, or it hurts us physically. We sweat and shake, or we get headaches, or our faces break out. I'm sure you all know what I mean."

Nods all around the table.

"I want to encourage you to bring your anger here so we can keep talking about it. Don't hold it in. If you don't acknowledge it, it can turn inward and cause you to get depressed," Louann said. "And I want you to remember that anger can be positive. It's not your enemy. If you accept it, it can motivate you."

"To do what? Commit murder?" Tessa asked.

"No." Louann's smile radiated kindness. "But anger can motivate you to take some kind of constructive action."

"Such as?" Sam asked.

"Such as when someone makes you mad, you can state your grievance and make clear what you want the person to do to set things right."

"I can't do that when I don't even know who raped me," Carmen said.

"That's true," Louann acknowledged. "For lots of reasons, assault survivors often can't confront their assailants, but they can write a letter."

"I wouldn't know where to send it," Carmen said.

"You wouldn't need to. The point is to express your feelings. Don't hold them back. There's a saying among psychologists, *What you feel, you can heal.* Just writing or saying it out loud can help," Louann said.

"If I wrote my boss, he'd fire me," LaKeisha said.

"Only if you showed him the letter. Remember, you don't have to. You mostly write it for yourself," Louann said.

Suddenly, Hope stood up from her spot at Carmen's feet and shuffled over to Tessa, who hadn't realized that she'd slumped in her chair. "Are you all right, Tessa?" Louann asked as Hope rested her chin in Tessa's lap.

"I keep thinking about my rage at Nick Payne. It's a general fury. It's free-floating, overpowering. It's like it's made me sick, and I can't get well."

"I know what you mean," Gail said.

"Tessa, can you think of a feeling you haven't wanted to deal with yet? The anger could be protecting you till you're ready to face it," Louann said.

Tessa rubbed her forehead, looked down at the puppy-dog eyes looking back at her. *It's okay. I am here.* The feeling that occurred to Tessa was a terror so stark it could shake her to the core. "Maybe I don't want to think about feeling helpless," she said. "Since I was too trusting, I ended up at the mercy of a totally sick man. I couldn't escape. By most women's standards, being that vulnerable is about as scary as life gets."

"It's like we've all starred in a horror movie," Sam said.

Tessa thought of Alfred Hitchcock's *Psycho*, which she'd ordered for a patron last week. Tessa knew the panic of Janet

Leigh, standing naked in the shower when psycho Anthony Perkins yanked back the curtain. A woman couldn't feel more vulnerable than that.

Nick Payne may have drugged Tessa so she didn't know exactly what he'd done to her. But the terror of being helpless in the hands of a pervert like him—yes, anger was easier to feel than that.

CHAPTER 37

At nearly seven in the evening, almost everyone in the office had gone home. Sitting on her denim bed, Hope was watching Will with her usual I-am-about-to-collapse-from-hunger expression. Her pleading eyes warned him, *I am malnourished! I might faint!*

"Okay, girl. In a minute," Will said as he piled folders into his battered messenger bag. He picked up his phone to check his voicemail one last time, and, of course, Abbey Greenwood had not gotten back to him. He'd left her as many messages as were allowed without seeming like a stalker. Finally, unwilling to grovel on his hands and knees for a return call, in the last few days he'd stopped phoning.

He'd like to think she was on vacation, but he knew better. As a prosecutor, he was familiar with the effort required to corral recalcitrant witnesses, though Abbey had been more obstinate than most. As humiliating as trying her one more time might be, he could not give up. Expecting her answering machine again, he punched her number into his phone.

"Hello?" A woman's slightly reedy voice.

Though it was what he'd hoped to hear, she caught him off guard. "This is . . . um . . . Will Armstrong in the prosecutor's office." *But of course, she knows that from the caller ID.*

Her thunderous sigh made it quite plain that she was not pleased to hear from him—again.

"Yes?"

"Last week, when you talked with our detective, Sandy Johnson, did she tell you we have another of Nick Payne's victims?"

"Yes."

"We might file charges against him. Could I meet with you to discuss it?"

"No."

The door slammed in Will's face was abrupt enough to break his nose. Her one-syllable responses didn't give him much to work with. "May I ask why?"

"I've decided I don't want to get involved."

"Because you're afraid?"

"Because these last months have been hell. Only lately have I felt like *maybe* I can get my life together someday. I refuse to go back and revisit the trauma. If I faced Nick Payne in a courtroom, psychologically I'd have to start over at square one."

"We'd be there to help you. We've got an assault advocate and a psychologist who could see you through the legal process."

"Yes, and a defense attorney who could rip me to pieces. No thanks. It's been nice talking with you."

Click.

Will's phone in his hand, hanging by his side, he stared at the files stacked in front of him. His dander was up. Rigid cords stood out on his neck. *Damn it!*

Hope bounded over to him and pressed against his leg. As he stroked her ears, he thought what a fine line he had to walk with potential witnesses like Abbey Greenwood. He was sensitive to what she'd gone through, and reluctant to push her too hard. Still, he needed her cooperation. The least she could do was talk with him! She wasn't giving him a chance to explain why her testimony was so important.

He slammed the phone back into its cradle. *So there went that.* Just as he'd thought he was closing in on Nick, he'd wrangled free. Again.

After Will fed Hope and scrounged canned minestrone from his nearly empty pantry, he sank into his wingback chair, which was as tattered as his messenger bag. Upholstery stuffing peeped out from a small tear in the seat. Where he'd rested his hands on the arms, he'd worn the blue-gray fabric thin. For years, Will had sat in the chair and read, watched TV across the room, mused about life, and mulled over problems.

Tonight, he was fretting about the problem of Abbey Greenwood not cooperating. He felt as beaten down as his chair. *Why does everything have to be so hard?* Nothing—and he meant absolutely nothing, not one tiny speck of life—was ever easy. Nobody handed you success on a platter. Lucky breaks were scarce. Will felt like he was sitting in his Jeep, looking at a downed tree blocking the road ahead, and he had no chain saw to cut through it.

When a paw thumped his knee, he returned from the Land of Rumination to his living room's here and now. Hope was staring at him, her head cocked like she was trying to read his every signal. On her face was the concerned expression he'd seen her give to many a troubled person in court.

Suddenly, she darted upstairs to the bedroom. He heard her rooting around in her wicker basket, and then she ran back down. Into his lap she dropped her ratty yellow duck. It looked as if a pirate had slashed it in a swordfight, but the duck was Hope's greatest treasure, the best gift she had to offer.

Will picked him up, fussed over him, and acted like he'd

been waiting for weeks for a chance to hold him, stiff as he was from Hope's drool. Though Abbey Greenwood still rankled him, Hope's beloved duck did make him feel better.

"Thank you, Hope." When he reached down and hugged her, she nuzzled his ear.

CHAPTER 38

Every July, Will was required to bring Hope to the Washington Facility Dogs campus and prove to Tracy Engels, the director and her former trainer, that he was upholding her obedience standards. Most of the time, and especially when Hope was wearing her vest, he could count on her to do as she was told. But once in a while, her hooligan streak emerged, and she acted like any other naughty dog.

Knowing she was obedient but not perfect gave Will pause as he let her out of his Jeep and walked her to the campus's barn. Adding pressure was the contract he'd signed, in which was a clause that Washington Facility Dogs could take back Hope if Will did not live up to his part of the agreement. Among other things, he'd agreed to maintain established rules of her behavior. So if Hope didn't perform today, Tracy Engels could legally reclaim her.

But Hope tried hard to do the right thing. Will's confidence in her was tinged with only a sliver of concern. It must have been too slight for Hope to sense because, with joy, she hurled herself at Tracy and danced around her pipe-stem legs.

Tracy was a Millennial sylph who looked like a gust of wind could knock her flat, but her appearance was deceiving.

She spoke with the authority of a lion tamer. From her slight body, commands emerged like a Great Dane's barks.

"Welcome, Hope!" Tracy stooped down and patted her. "And you, too, Will."

"You can see she's missed you." He and Hope stepped into the bright, airy barn.

It was as big as a basketball court, and in the middle was a rubber mat. Around the perimeter were dog beds, benches, and tables. The room smelled of fresh paint, being applied by Tracy's husband, Joe, to a window frame. He waved to Will from a ladder.

After a few pleasantries, Tracy got down to business. She ordered Will and Hope to the center of the barn and sat on a sideline bench. "Let's start with the basics," she said. "You know the drill. No leash. Come, sit, down, stay."

Will unfastened Hope's leash and draped it around his neck. He backed up fifteen feet and said, "Hope, come."

Hope shot toward him like a bullet to its target and sat perfectly in front of his toes.

"Good girl." He got her to stand. "Now sit."

Kerplop went Hope's bottom onto the rubber mat.

On a "down" and "stay," she assumed her most impeccable library lion position and kept her eyes on Will.

"Excellent," Tracy called to them. "Now come by me. Let's have a comforting session."

Staying close to Will, Hope dutifully padded across the barn and sat at his feet. When he said, "Visit Tracy," Hope set her chin on Tracy's knee and looked up at her with adoring eyes. When he said, "Kiss Tracy," Hope jumped up onto the bench, pushed her damp nose against Tracy's neck, and gave her a fervent nuzzle. At "Snuggle," Hope's favorite command, she lay down next to Tracy and placed her head on her lap.

"Outstanding," Tracy said. "Hope has a big heart."

So far, so good.

Tracy stood, called Hope off the bench, and unzipped a pouch she always wore around her waist. Hope stared at it with a laser beam's focus; from her training days, she knew that treats were hidden inside. When Tracy removed a piece of turkey, Hope's eyes followed it as a compass needle follows north. She acted like she'd just been released, starving, from the Gulag. A drop of drool appeared on her pink tongue.

Tracy commanded Hope to sit, and she set the turkey in front of her. "Leave it," Tracy ordered in her most commanding voice.

Will held his breath. If only it were not almost lunchtime, when he always gave Hope a biscuit. If only Tracy had set the turkey farther away. If only Hope were not a closet glutton. *Please, Hope, be good!*

Hope unglued her gaze from the turkey for a glance, as quick as a finger snap, at Tracy. She seemed to check that Tracy had given the order to her and not to some invisible dog in the barn. Back went Hope's eyes to the turkey. It smelled good. It would be delicious. Hope licked her mouth with such zeal that her tongue covered her nose. She marched her front paws in place and quivered with anticipation. She sniffed the turkey as closely as she dared.

"Nooooo," Tracy growled.

Hope's innocent expression suggested that Tracy misjudged her, and her lack of trust hurt. But then darkness flickered on Hope's face. She lunged at the turkey.

Will leapt out of his chair. "Drop it!"

He tried to wrench the turkey from her gritted teeth. But he was too late. She swallowed it whole.

"I'm sorry," Will said. "She's usually law-abiding. All her handlers love her."

"That may be true, but her behavior is unacceptable," Tracy said.

She didn't have to tell Will. He knew that mistakes like

this were not allowed, especially since Hope was wearing her vest. What if she were working, and she snatched a sandwich out of a child's hand? Will had to have her under control.

Hope knew that she'd done wrong. She flattened back her ears and looked at the floor. Clearly regretting the turkey of doom, she couldn't seem to rest her guilty gaze on Will or Tracy—or even Joe, across the barn.

"You want to try again?" This time, Tracy handed the turkey to Will.

Thinking again of the contract he'd signed, he placed the lure in front of Hope and said, "Leave it." He silently begged her, *Please.*

Hope cast a withering glance at the turkey as if it radiated evil. She acted like she wouldn't touch it even if Will said she could. Time slowed. A minute crawled by. Will held his breath.

Finally, Tracy said, "Tell her 'that's better,' so she knows she's made up for her mistake."

"That's better." Will sank to his knees. "Come here!" He opened his arms, and Hope, now redeemed, threw herself into them. Will finally gave her the turkey, which disappeared in one lusty gulp.

On the long drive home, Hope was quick to forgive and forget. In the Pointillist style of Georges Seurat, she applied periods and decimal points to the windshield with her damp nose. She took note of passing buses and trucks. At a stoplight, she watched a van lined up at a car wash and gulls circling overhead.

Will hashed over the afternoon with Tracy. When they'd been about to leave, she'd given him a lecture on the importance of obedience training. "It's like a musician practicing scales," she'd said. "You have to keep doing it forever. You can't give up."

For years, "you can't give up" had been Will's mantra. He'd started saying it to himself at the University of Washington. As the first in his family to go to college, intellectually he'd had to leave his parents behind, and financially he'd had to make it on his own. He went to classes during the day and, to support himself, he worked as a warehouse guard at night. He lived on canned tuna, hot dogs, and coffee—and studied and scrapped and clawed from the first day of his undergraduate freshman year to the last day of law school. Will's dogged fight for his degrees taught him that he could accomplish monumental tasks if he worked hard and persevered. Since then, he'd told himself hundreds of times, *You can't give up.*

As he turned into his drive and started through his field, he looked with satisfaction at his homestead up ahead. Though his barn was rickety, and his porch would sag till he got around to shoring it up, his property belonged to him, and it was testimony to what hard work and not giving up could get you. He couldn't give up on Hope's obedience training, either—and, as he pulled into his parking spot, it struck him that he also couldn't give up on prosecuting Nick Payne.

Will could now identify two women Nick had assaulted; who knew how many more of his victims had never come forward? Will had to stop him. Though Will may have wavered, discouraged, the last few days, he was still determined to put Nick Payne behind bars.

You can't give up.

He hurried to his kitchen and fed Hope, then changed into his Sons of Pitches uniform. Before leaving for the game, he buttressed himself with two chocolate chip cookies from Mel's Market and called Abbey Greenwood one more time. She picked up the phone.

CHAPTER 39

Stirred up after another survivors' meeting, Tessa headed home. This time, the group had discussed PTSD symptoms, such as anxiety attacks and nightmares, and some of the women had also reported on letters they'd written but not sent to their assailants. Tessa had stayed silent for that part of the discussion. Though she'd tried to write Nick, she had not felt free enough to speak her mind, and her reticence bothered her. She thought about it all the way home.

Tessa found Emma waiting on her front porch. Rocking in the wicker chair at a faster speed than usual, she looked like she was taking out aggressions on the rough-hewn plank floor.

"I'm so mad!" Emma tugged at her T-shirt's sleeve as if she were trying to get her own attention.

"You should visit my survivors' group—we're all mad," Tessa said. "What's happened?"

"My boss. Today for my annual evaluation, we were supposed to talk about what was going well and what needed to be improved," Emma said. "After all my hard work, I expected at least a *few* kudos, but on a scale of one to ten, he rated my overall performance a three." Emma pursed her lips like she wanted to spit on him. "Can you *believe* that?"

"He's been lusting after you. He's paying you back for not giving in."

"But I've put in endless hours on our loyalty program. I'm the one who's thought up new ways to connect to our customers, and he's sat back and taken the credit." Emma rocked so fast, the floorboards squeaked.

"Can't you complain to his boss?"

"And be reassigned to sweeping the parking lot?"

"What are you going to do?"

"I'll kill him."

"Not a good idea." *How do these horrible men get away with what they do?* Tessa extended her hand and pulled Emma to her feet. "I baked an apple pie last night. Come in and have a piece."

"Or two or three," Emma said.

Tessa led Emma into the cottage, and the screen door slammed behind them. Over the years, they'd shared many a woe-fostered pig-out. While Tessa cut up the pie, Emma poured boiling water over three decaf English Afternoon tea bags in Tessa's blue ceramic pot and set placemats, napkins, forks, and spoons on her butcher-block table.

"You up for à la mode?" Tessa asked.

"The more calories, the more comfort."

Tessa spooned ice cream on each slice, and they dug in for the first bite. "Can't you talk with your boss?" she asked, but then, she'd been too intimidated to *write* to Nick.

"And say what? If I go to bed with you, will you change my three to a ten?"

"You could ask what you've done to deserve the low rating."

"He'd make up some ridiculous reason."

Tessa and Emma took more giant bites and quietly chewed. When Tessa had eaten her way past her crust's flutes, she asked, "Want another piece?"

"Of course."

"We're eating to compensate for anger and frustration. You know that, don't you?"

"Compensation. Bring it on," Emma said.

Tessa got up and went to her kitchen counter a few feet away. *Why get up between pieces?* She brought the whole pie back to the table.

CHAPTER 40

On a Friday afternoon, every seat in Starbucks was taken. Disgruntled new arrivals stood around, scowling at those who had a table and waiting for one of their own. Animated conversations seemed to thicken the air, like a haze. A run-ragged barista handed Will two iced mocha coffees.

He gave one to Abbey Greenwood. "Want to go to the park across the street?"

"May as well." Her voice could not claim eagerness. A hint of scorn rested in the crow's feet at the edges of her almond-shaped eyes. She was slight, a dishwater blonde, a little on the mousy side. Will had guessed she was about his age, but her annoyance made her look older. When they'd met here, as agreed, she'd shaken his hand but refused to smile.

At least I managed to get her here, he thought as he stirred sugar into his coffee. He pulled a wad of napkins from the dispenser and opened the door for her. Waiting in his Jeep, Hope saw him coming, rose to her paws, and whimpered. He attached her leash to her collar, and she jumped to the street.

"This is Hope," he said.

For one brief moment, Abbey's disdain seemed to melt. In her slacks and blazer, she squatted down and patted Hope's chest.

"Do you have a dog?" Will asked.

"A Giant Schnauzer. Winston. When I get home, he'll smell Hope, and I'll have to confess I've been unfaithful." Abbey kissed Hope's forehead. "Why is she wearing this vest?"

"It's her work uniform. Her job is comforting people. She's a courthouse facility dog."

At *courthouse*, Abbey's disdain refroze. In their phone conversation, Will had explained the purpose of their meeting, and she'd agreed to it, but she'd made no secret of her reluctance. She stopped petting Hope, straightened up. "Let's get this conversation over with," she said as sharp and flinty as an arrowhead.

When she strode across the street to Waterfront Park, Will had to interrupt Hope's sidewalk sniffing and hurry her along. Abbey went to a bench and sat as close to the edge as she could get without falling off, far out of Will's reach on the opposite side—not that he had plans to touch her. Between them on the ground, Hope assumed her sphinx position and kept her eyes on Abbey, a possible candidate for soothing. Abbey seemed mentally to retreat to a distant place.

Will watched her sip her mocha coffee. So much was riding on this meeting, and he had to be careful. He didn't want to scare her off. As children shrieked on nearby swings, Will faced her straight on. "I appreciate you coming here today."

"I agreed to talk with you just to get you to leave me alone."

"So I figured."

"You haven't respected my decision about appearing in court. It's not going to happen. I want you to quit bothering me."

"Why are you so hell-bent on not getting involved?"

"People in Nisqually County know me from my newspaper columns. There's no way I'm going to lay out the most harrowing experience of my life for public consumption, and I refuse to become an object of pity."

"Nobody will know who you are. Your name will never appear in newspapers. The trial will be in Port Richmond, far from your hometown," Will said. "We'll make every effort to keep you anonymous."

"Anyone can nose around and find a victim's name. A salacious story like mine always gets out. I'm not taking that risk." Abbey paused as if she wanted the full effect of her determination to sink into Will. "I don't intend to relive what happened. Not for anybody. Ever again."

Will set his coffee cup on the bench, rested his forearms on his thighs. "Are you afraid of meeting Nick Payne in court?"

"I told you on the phone—one glimpse of him, and my recovery zooms back to square one. Sayonara to my tiny bit of progress."

"You think people will judge you?"

"I don't *think* they'll judge me . . . I *know* they will. After I told my sister what happened, my brother-in-law railed at me like I was a slutty teenager." Abbey dug a thumbnail into her cardboard cup. "You should hear what people say about a rape victim."

"I've heard it all. I understand how you feel."

"You don't. You're a man. You can't possibly understand."

"Well, maybe not perfectly. But I try." He took a breath. "Why should you care what some callous person thinks, anyway? You're tough, or you'd never be in the newspaper business. So some loser belittles you? You can take the heat."

"I don't want to subject myself to it. It's not worth it. I have nothing to gain." Abbey looked across the park at the harbor. Wind ruffled the water. "You don't underst—" Her voice cracked. She pressed a fist against her lips, bit into a knuckle. "See what you've done? Can't you leave me alone?"

Hope got up, pressed herself against Abbey's knees, and rested her head in her lap. Hope's eyes assured Abbey, *I know you're hurting. I understand. I'm right here. I care.*

Weeping silently, Abbey bent down, wrapped her arms around Hope's neck, and pressed her cheek against her ear. Scarcely breathing, Hope didn't move a muscle. Time seemed to stop.

Will waited till Abbey seemed calmer, then said as gently as he could, "I'm sorry you're hurting. It's going to take you time to process all that's happened to you. I've seen women go through this again and again."

A child in the sandbox yelled to his friend, "You can't do that! It's not fair." A helicopter's blades *whap-whap-whapped* as it headed across Puget Sound to Saint Francis Hospital.

"You told me just now that you had nothing to gain. But don't you think helping put a sick man in prison would give you satisfaction?" Will asked.

"Why can't his other victim do it? You don't need me," Abbey mumbled into Hope's fur.

"I need you to prove he sexually assaulted *her*. Without your testimony, that's not possible. Your cases are linked. She's longing to see Nick punished."

When Abbey sat up and wiped tears off her cheeks with the back of her hand, Hope stuck to her like lint. "I'm sorry for her, but I've been through enough. I can't take anymore."

Will felt like Sisyphus, almost to the top of the mountain with his huge rock, but knowing it would soon roll back down. He was losing this argument. Abbey had an iron will, and he was running out of Hail Mary passes. *You can't give up!*

Will finally said, "There's something bigger than either of us at stake here."

"What do you mean?"

"We need to lock up Nick so he can't assault anybody else. Wouldn't it make you feel better to keep women safe from

him? They need you to help put him away." Will finished
his coffee and tossed his cup into a wire trash basket by the
bench. "Won't you reconsider?"

Abbey hunched her shoulders. She seemed to pull back
into herself again.

You can't give up. You can't give up. "Won't you reconsider?"
Will repeated.

Abbey nodded vaguely.

"May I take that as a yes?" he asked softly.

She nodded again.

CHAPTER 41

Tessa drove Howard to Upton Gap, a small town, where five o'clock traffic meant three cars and a motorcycle on Main Street at the same time. She parked near the only grocery store. In the quiet before her people began to appear, she worked on her Book-in-a-Jar Contest. Last weekend, she'd shredded *The Hunger Games* into thousands of paper strips and squashed them into a glass cookie jar. Onto it, she'd glued a man's Halloween nose and eyeglasses and drawn Groucho Marx brows and a moustache on the glass with a black felt-tipped pen. Now she set him on her desk and printed a sign for her teen readers, though adults were welcome to enter the contest, too: *GUESS WHAT BOOK THIS IS! The first person with the correct title will win a twenty-five-dollar gift card.*

Imagining her people shaking the jar to see characters' names or read dialogue snippets, Tessa arranged the sign just so in front of the face. She was thinking, *Let the contest begin!*— when Sandy climbed into Howard in gray slacks and a light blue T-shirt. Her exposed eyelid was shaded cornflower blue.

After Tessa's last dismal conversation with Sandy, she was surprised to see her. In fact, she'd been sure she'd never see Sandy again. Certainly, she'd lost hope that Nick Payne would ever be punished.

As Sandy made her way down Howard's aisle, Tessa rose from her chair and rested her palms on her desk. "Hello," she said.

"I've got good news," Sandy said.

Out of the question. Weeks ago, Tessa had given up on good news.

"Nick Payne's been arrested."

"Oh . . ." Stunned, Tessa fell back into her desk chair, but joy quickly elbowed her shock out of the way. She clapped her hands and laughed out loud. She could hardly wait to tell her survivors' group! "So Will Armstrong finally believed me?"

"He always did, but he needed more proof, and now we have it," Sandy said. "We just found another woman Nick assaulted. We've got solid evidence he drugged her."

"So that shows what he did to me, too?"

"No guarantees, but it's what Will's going to argue. He's taking both your cases to court."

Tessa's brain buzzed at this glorious revelation. As quick as a camera click, everything had changed. Maybe Will's reasons for not taking her case before had been valid. Maybe she'd judged him too soon. Her opinion of him rose from indifferent jerk to decent man. "I can't believe it," she said.

"It's true. You should have seen the police grip Nick's arms and walk him to the van. His pathetic lip was quivering." Sandy's smile revealed delight in her job well done. "I wish he'd resisted so we could have had the pleasure of escorting him to the ground."

"Where is he now?"

"In the nick!" Sandy chuckled. "He'll cool his heels in the P.D.'s Hilton till the arraignment. Probably Monday. The grimy mattress and flies smushed on the walls will make him wish he'd behaved."

"Will he get out on bail?"

"I expect so."

The hands Tessa had just clapped in triumph stilled with apprehension. Her eyes went wide. "What if he comes after me?"

"He won't. He'll leave custody with conditions. One will be that he can't contact you. If he dares, he'll go back to the slammer."

"If he hates me, he won't care. He's arrogant enough to think he can get away with anything."

"Maybe he's learning a little humility," Sandy said.

Tessa doubted it. She ran her index fingertip over the bulbous nose glued to the contest jar. "Is Nick's other victim okay?"

"Like you, she's had a hard time, but she's trying to put her life back together. She's eager to get the trial behind her."

"When does it begin?"

"Don't know yet. We have some hoops to jump through first. The arraignment, legal skirmishes, pretrial hearings, motions, red tape. Maybe Nick will plead out and avoid a trial." Sandy rested her fist against her hip in a badass stance that matched her punk haircut. "If I have anything to say about it, we'll get him. But we have to take this one step at a time."

For Tessa, the stakes were high. Justice and hope glimmered in the distance, but they might be like the pot of gold at the end of a rainbow—the closer you got, the more the rainbow faded away. "I can't take getting my hopes dashed again."

"We'll do our best," Sandy said.

"Nick Payne *has* to get what's coming to him," Tessa insisted. She wanted a promise that he would.

But Sandy only said, "You can be sure we'll try."

CHAPTER 42

When there was a lull in her workday, Tessa booted up her computer. Though the *San Julian Review* came out in print on Fridays, important stories sometimes appeared sooner online. She was curious if there was any word about Nick Payne's arrest. The very thought of it made her gleeful. At last he'd get what he deserved.

Since yesterday, she'd imagined him, worried and bored, pacing his cell, scared of what might be in store for him. He'd get a sick feeling in the pit of his stomach, and thoughts of his future would shake him. At night he'd try to find a comfortable position on a lumpy, greasy mattress while keeping his arms from brushing against the filthy wall. Perhaps it was wrong to gloat, but the image gave Tessa pleasure. Maybe what goes around really does come around, and he was receiving some of the misery he'd inflicted on others.

Tessa Googled the *Review*'s website and scrolled down for the latest news. Nick stared at her from a professional headshot that a reporter must have gotten from Rainier College. In a button-down shirt, paisley tie, and blazer, he looked respectable. Behind his glasses, his earnest gaze could have won anybody's trust. No one would peg him for a rapist, and that was the problem. In a trial, his lawyer would paint him as Nisqually County's most sainted professor.

The accompanying article reported that at seven-thirty yesterday morning, the police had taken Nick from his home and booked him for two alleged sexual assaults. An investigation was ongoing, and the police chief would keep the public informed.

So far, three of seven San Julian City Council members had urged Nick to step down from the election. The Central Ward's representative, a woman attorney, had told the reporter, "We can't allow Nick Payne on the Council when his morality is in question. But we will welcome him to run again later if the allegations against him prove false."

The allegations are true. Nick Payne is beyond immoral—he's criminal! He should never run again! Tessa scrolled down to a statement from Nick's attorney, Justin Warfield:

"Nick Payne's arrest is preposterous. He's done nothing wrong, and let me make this perfectly clear—he refuses to quit the City Council race. Groundless accusations will never stop him from going ahead with his campaign. Nothing will change his commitment to this community."

Tessa straightened up as if a steel rod had been rammed up her spine. Nick could portray himself as a virtuous citizen forever, but her and his other victim's testimonies would show he was scum. He couldn't escape that truth. It was irrefutable, chiseled into stone.

As Tessa turned off her computer, Mona Upton waltzed into Howard wearing a delicate whisper of a gold tennis bracelet and dazzling white tennis togs that showed off her tan legs. Her ponytail bounced as she made her way down the aisle. Tessa pushed Nick out of her mind and took on her professional mode as she might wrap a cloak around her shoulders.

"Did you get *To Kill a Mockingbird* for me?" Mona asked.

"Sure did." Tessa got up, went to her on-hold shelf, and handed the book to Mona.

"It's for my daughter, Valerie. She'll be in ninth grade next year. Do you think she's too young for it?"

"You haven't read it?"

"No. Last year Val's English teacher suggested it for the summer."

"Hmmm." Tessa thought for a moment. "I think she's old enough, but you should know it's about sexual assault." Tessa forced herself to squelch her aversion to the thought and stay detached.

"Good Lord! You mean rape?" Mona's tennis bracelet slid down her arm as she placed her hand, like a giant asterisk, over her heart. "Have you heard about Nick Payne? I can't believe what people are saying about him."

Tessa should have prepared herself for a conversation like this, but she'd been trying to digest the news of his arrest herself. "I just read the story online."

"My neighbor says his rivals are trying to ruin his campaign before he's ever had a chance. I mean, why would an accusation like that come up *now* when he's ahead in the polls? I think people are trying to force him out of the race."

"Some . . . would say." A non-committal response.

"San Julian politics have always been cutthroat, but this is outrageous," Mona said. "Who do you think Nick's supposed victims are?"

"I only know what I've read online." A lie, but there it was. Needing space, Tessa returned to her desk.

"My husband's sure somebody's paid those women to make up their stories. It's all rigged. Anybody can see what's going on," Mona said. "I mean, I met Nick Payne at a neighborhood party. He's a fine man. He's got integrity. All he cares about is other people."

If you only knew how much he cared about me.

As Mona railed on, Tessa's vindication at Nick's arrest seemed tarnished. She felt queasy, as if goldfish were brushing their fins against her stomach lining. She didn't have the courage to tell Mona that, indeed, she was one of the women who'd accused Nick Payne, and she considered him a monster. If there were any fairness in the world, she'd get her greatest wish—and he'd rot in prison for a good long time.

When Mona left, Tessa sank into her desk chair, sapped of color and strength.

How has Nick Payne fooled everybody? she asked herself.

The painful answer: *The same way he fooled you.*

CHAPTER 43

Early on a sunny morning, Will found a parking space across the street from the Nisqually County Courthouse, where Nick Payne was about to be arraigned. The building was a two-story nineteen-fifties concrete cube that could have passed for a department store. The only hint that judicial proceedings took place inside was THE LAW HATES WRONG molded into the plaster above the entrance's glass doors.

Will climbed the steps to the entrance and walked into the lobby, where a buzz of conversations rose from the employees hurrying to work. He went through the turnstile and handed his messenger bag to an armed security officer, who rifled through it, looking bored. After going through the metal detector, Will passed the offices of the county clerk, tax assessor, and probate judge.

After taking the elevator to the second floor, he made his way into the cavernous courtroom and down its blue-carpeted center aisle, which looked like a river flowing to the judge's raised bench at the end. The room shouted *mahogany*. The walls were paneled with it, and the judge's bench was made of it. The empty jury box to the right, the witness stand to the left, and the attorney's tables in front of the bench shone the same polished brown.

Will set his papers in tidy stacks on the prosecutor's table. Nick was across the aisle at the defense's table with his attorney, Justin Warfield. Three days in San Julian's jail had changed Nick—at least for now. Gone was the smug professor whose world had shimmered with promise. The glad-handing Nick who'd grinned on campaign posters was stooped in his courtroom chair, his head in his hands, staring at the blue-carpeted floor.

Will had heard that Nick was persuaded to drop out of the City Council race; defeat, plus the shock of arrest, clearly did not sit well with him. You could see it in the slump of his shoulders and, when he raised his head, in his glassy eyes. Worry paled his skin. The change might be fleeting, and the arrogant Nick could fight his way back, but finding him psychologically beaten down this afternoon bolstered Will's resolve to send him to prison. What would Tessa and Abbey think if they saw their assailant now?

Snatches of conversations drifted toward Will from the mahogany benches in the gallery behind him. "I can't believe . . ." "Such a shame . . ." "Is he married . . . ?" Will had expected a few reporters, but other people had been unable to resist the prospect of a former City Council candidate's undoing, especially when it involved sex.

The talking stopped when a strapping bailiff stood akimbo in front of the United States and Washington State flags. In a deep, melodious voice, he announced, "All rise. The Court of Nisqually County is now in session, the Honorable Judge John Plodsker the Third presiding."

Judge John Plodsker trudged in, carrying a large binder, his black robe protruding over his stomach. There was something of a lethargic hippo about his bearing, and he had coarse features—a bulbous nose, bushy eyebrows, and fat earlobes. He set down his binder, worked his ample bottom into his seat, and leaned back against his chair's black leather headrest. Looming over the courtroom from his elevated bench, he grimaced at the spectators as if the sight of them caused him indigestion.

Judge Plodsker smoothed back his few remaining wisps of hair and yawned. Reading from the complaint, he told Nick Payne that he was charged with two counts of rape in the second degree, pursuant to section 9A.44.050 of the Revised Code of Washington.

"How do you plead?" Judge Plodsker asked.

"Not guilty," Nick said more softly than he should. Will could tell he was scared. *Excellent.*

Judge Plodsker rocked back in his swivel chair and asked Will, "What is the State's recommendation for bail?"

Will stood and set his hands like starfish on his papers. "Your Honor, the State recommends bail in the amount of five hundred thousand dollars. Mr. Payne is a flight risk. He's facing multiple serious charges and possible imprisonment that he doubtless wants to avoid. He gets a substantial salary from teaching at Rainier College and consulting for political candidates, so he has plenty of means to leave the county and go wherever he wants.

"On a personal level, he has no family to keep him here—no obligations, no ties. Fleeing would be easy for him. Furthermore, if he remains free pending trial and continues his pattern of drugging and raping innocent women, he would pose a risk to the community."

Justin Warfield popped up like a boxer from his corner of the ring, eager to get on with the fight. His muscled chest bulged beneath his tie. He looked like he had eaten twelve-penny nails for breakfast and his hobby was ripping Seattle phone books in half.

"Nick Payne is an upstanding man. For years, Rainier College administrators have entrusted hundreds of their students' education to him. If these spurious charges hadn't been levied against him, San Julian voters would be showing their confidence in his integrity by electing him to their City Council." Warfield puffed out his chest.

"Mr. Armstrong claims . . ."—Warfield glanced at Will as if he were a cockroach—"He *claims* my client has no ties to keep him here, but that's not true. Mr. Payne is greatly committed to his community, as evidenced by his candidacy for City Council. He has lived here for fourteen years, owns a home, and is well known."

"He doesn't want to *avoid* a trial! All he wants is to *have* a trial so he can clear his good name and get on with his life. His reputation and honor are supremely important to him. I ask you to release him on his own recognizance."

When mixed opinions about Nick's honor and release rippled through the gallery, Judge Plodsker thumped his gavel on the bench, an act seemingly born more from weariness than conviction. "Order in the court."

"Your honor," Will began again. "The charges against the defendant are serious. Two counts of second-degree rape, not shoplifting."

"But," Warfield insisted, "the charges are false. It's commonly accepted that Mr. Payne's political opponents have trumped them up to push him out of the City Council election. And my client has no past criminal history."

Judge Plodsker listened until the arguments became repetitive, and his eyelids sagged to half-mast. He waved his hand as if to signal, *Enough.* "My main concern is the severity of Mr. Payne's alleged crimes. They make him a more likely flight risk, and they require strict conditions for his release, if obtained. I'm setting bail at five hundred thousand dollars."

A collective gasp rose from the gallery. Will was careful to hide his pleasure in the triumph.

"Your honor, may I suggest fifty thousand?" Warfield asked.

"To post a bail bond for that amount costs only five thousand. That's pocket change for a man like Mr. Payne," Will said. *Besides, what could be more gratifying than Nick having to scrape together fifty grand to get out of jail?*

"As Mr. Armstrong said, we're not dealing with shoplifting. I'm leaving bail at five hundred thousand," Judge Plodsker said. "If Mr. Payne is able to post bail and be released from custody, I will require him to wear an ankle monitor. He will not be allowed to possess firearms. He will be subject to unannounced drug and alcohol tests conducted by law enforcement officers. Most important, Mr. Payne is prohibited from having any contact whatsoever with his alleged victims. If he fails to meet any of these conditions, he will be remanded into custody immediately."

Judge Plodsker let Warfield argue for another minute, then slammed his gavel with finality and announced, "Court is adjourned." He clumped out of the courtroom. Will gathered up his papers. Out of the corner of his eye, he saw Warfield give Nick a reassuring pat on the back as if to say, *Don't worry. Give us time. We'll show 'em.*

Warfield's confidence and superiority grated on Will. *Just wait.* He'd go after Nick like a battering ram.

CHAPTER 44

"Will, I know it's Friday night, but is this a bad time?" Sandy asked.

"It's a great time. I was washing dishes—interruptions welcome," Will said.

"Sounds like your life is as interesting as mine. I'm doing laundry."

"That comes after the dishes," Will said. "What's up?"

"Late this afternoon, I got a call from a woman who lives behind Nick Payne. Her sister just arrived from Boise and learned of his arrest. The last time she visited was when Nick assaulted Tessa."

Cradling the phone between his ear and shoulder, Will wiped his hands on a striped terry cloth dishtowel and tossed it onto his kitchen counter. "Anybody see anything?"

"The sister believes she saw Nick and Tessa drinking wine on his deck, and he carried her into his house. Tessa had passed out."

"Wow. You interviewed her?"

"Not yet."

"Go see her. Find out what else she knows," Will said.

"I'll stop by there tomorrow. I'll get back to you."

Will hung up the phone and returned to his dishes, where

he was greeted by a crust to be scraped off his chili pot. He picked up his copper scrubber, unleashed his elbow grease, and set to work. Once in a while, a useful witness came out of the woodwork, and, if he were lucky, she could make a difference. Otherwise, she could be a waste of time. He never knew which it was going to be.

Will was so busy wrestling his chili crust that he didn't notice Tessa's arrival. As he rinsed the pot for the last time, he looked out the window above his sink to check on Hope. She was wagging her tail in her most excited circle to greet Tessa, lifting a wicker basket from the passenger seat of her Beetle. Hope followed her into the barn. *I wonder what Tessa brought to feed her cats tonight.*

When she emerged with their pie tins, Hope accompanied her to the water faucet. Tessa had even brought a sponge and soap. As he watched her wash the tins, he thought that he'd hardly spoken to her in a month.

Since he'd tried to explain why he was not going to take her case to court, they'd kept a formal distance from each other. If Will saw her outside, he stayed inside. On rare occasions when he'd driven up to the barn and found her there, he'd said a stiff hello and gone into the house. Since Nick's arrest, Will had not seen her at all.

At times it seemed ridiculous to him that a woman he was barely speaking to had taken over his barn. Why should he offer refuge to cats whose person was hostile toward him? The answer was that he shouldn't, especially now that he'd not seen a trace of the rats for a couple of weeks. It was time to end this absurd arrangement, but truth be told, even though he had no idea why, it was nice to see her out there once in a while.

Now as he watched her, he also thought that circumstances between them would be taking a new turn. With her as a witness in Nick Payne's trial, they were going to have to work together, and that required being on civil terms. *Now is as good a time as any.* With no idea how she'd react to more than a formal hello, he stepped off his back porch, strode across his lawn, and walked toward the barn.

The warm August night was not quite dark at nearly nine o'clock. The stars had not yet shown themselves, and the air smelled of cedar and fir and dust from the road through Will's field. The crows, who loved to peck his apples, had shut down for the evening. Except for the squeaky chirp of Pacific tree frogs, it was peaceful, quiet.

When Will came into the barn, Hope hurried over to greet him, but the cats, as usual, were nowhere to be found. Tessa turned to see him and smiled. She looked pretty when her face was soft like that. No hard set of her eyes and jaw.

"What are you feeding the cats tonight?" he asked.

"Cod. It was on sale at Mel's Market."

"They eat better than I do."

"People tell me that," Tessa said. "Did you know that Hope and Bronte are friends now? I found them curled up together. I was amazed."

Will was amazed that they were having a normal conversation. He couldn't say he didn't like it, but he also couldn't get too friendly. He and Tessa had to stay on professional terms.

"Sandy said she talked with you the other day. So you know we're moving forward with the case," he said.

"I'm thrilled about it. Thank you for changing your mind."

"I didn't exactly change it. I always wanted to go after Nick Payne, but as I explained to you, I couldn't before."

"I'm glad you can now."

"Did you know that as of this afternoon, Nick's out on bail?" Will noted the stricken look that appeared on Tessa's face. "You don't have to worry. If he comes near you, he'll go back behind bars. I don't think he'd be so stupid."

"I'm still scared of him."

"We're assigning you an advocate. I'll have her call you on Monday," Will said. "She can talk with you about feeling safe."

"We've discussed it in my survivors' group, but I won't feel safe till Nick's locked up in prison. You've got to make that happen."

"Let's hope," Will said.

"What do you mean 'hope'? It has to be a done deal."

"Nothing in the law is a done deal. I'll do all I can, but you've got to go into this knowing the outcome isn't definite."

"It should be," Tessa insisted. "Nick did what he did. That's the truth."

Why does she have to argue every time we talk? "It may well be the truth, but that's not always how the law works. So many things can happen. You'll have a defense attorney attacking the truth and a jury questioning it. I can't control all the puzzle pieces."

"But the truth has to win!" Tessa said.

"It should, but we can't be sure what the jury will decide."

Tessa's sigh brought Hope to her, ready to assist. Will disliked seeing Tessa deflated, but she had to know that trials had no predictable outcome. Till the trial was over, no one could be sure of anything.

"When is the trial?" Tessa asked.

"No date yet, but I'd guess, if we're lucky, in about three months."

"That's November!"

"Believe me, that's pretty quick. In some counties, you have to wait a lot longer."

"It's not fair."

"I think I told you, I wish *life* was fair. You can't demand fairness. The law is more complicated than that," Will said.

"Then the law is wrong."

Well, sometimes you could look at it that way.

"The law should be about truth and honor," Tessa added.

"In an ideal world, yes. In a real one, the law is about argument and evidence and witnesses. It's about many things, Tessa."

"I hate thinking about it." She lifted a bowl from her picnic basket and spooned a fluffy green concoction into the pie tins to accompany the cod. She didn't look at Will.

He was sorry to see her worked up again. That's not what he'd wanted when he'd come out here. And it was all the worse after she'd just given him a glimpse of the warm person he believed—deep down, pre-Nick—she must be.

"Well." He hooked his thumbs on his jeans' pockets. "I'm off. I've got things to do."

"So do I."

CHAPTER 45

November 2014

Three months later, on the first Friday in November, Will arranged for Tessa to come to his conference room to prepare for meeting Justin Warfield and Nick Payne in court. He'd connected with Abbey Greenwood and other witnesses earlier in the week, and on Monday he'd begin jury selection. Then the trial would start.

While Will and Tessa had waited for it, they'd often said hello to each other, always in his barn and nearly always on the run. He took care to keep their relationship professional, but there was an undercurrent of something that he couldn't quite define. Their conversations could be pleasant, but then, as jumpy as her cats, she'd back away like she was afraid of him—and perhaps all men. It was disconcerting, but he understood what an assault could do to a woman.

Today when she arrived, he asked her to sit at an oak trestle table in his conference room, two walls of which were covered, floor to ceiling, with law books. He and Valentina Herrera, Tessa's assault advocate, took their places across from her, their backs to a window that looked out on a stand of firs.

Recently, Tessa had become acquainted with Valentina,

who was another of Hope's handlers—and Hope was also there today. During innocuous exchanges about the rainy season, Hope rested her chin on Tessa's feet and made her presence known in case she was needed.

Valentina, who was in her late fifties, had clearly once been a gorgeous woman. Though she may have put on twenty pounds in the last decades, her lips were voluptuous and her skin, perfect. Her hair shone in a sophisticated bun above her neck, and there was still plenty of fire in her dark, sultry eyes. In her youth, she might have Flamenco danced on tabletops. Now she had five grandchildren.

"How are you feeling about being a witness?" Valentina asked Tessa.

"I'm nervous," she said.

"Nearly everybody says that, and those who don't are lying," Valentina said.

"It's hard to be on stage when Warfield grills and attacks you," Will said. "I'd like for us to go over some of his possible questions. You'll feel more confident if we practice."

Tessa closed her eyes as if to collect herself, then opened them again. "Okay."

Will could tell that she was uncomfortable. "How about we start with some softball questions?" They'd be more than softball; till she relaxed, he'd make them like dandelion puffs. "Pretend I'm Warfield, Tessa. Tell me, where do you work?"

"All over the county. I drive the Nisqually County Library's bookmobile."

"Do you like your job?"

"I love it. It's always rewarding."

"Why rewarding?"

"Because I help people. Look up things for them. Find books for them to read. Get to know them." Tessa's face brightened, as if it were emitting sunshine.

Will noted that the jury would like her pleasure in serving. "Good going," he encouraged.

Switching gears to throw her off her stride, as Warfield would, Will lowered his brows to appear harder, tougher. He demanded, "Tell me, what were you wearing when you went to Nick Payne's house on the night of May fifth last year?"

Looking startled, Tessa's sunshine changed to rain. "What difference does it make what I was wearing?"

"You never answer a question with a question," Will said. "But I want to know."

"Warfield wants to hear about your clothes to see if he can make you look like you went there dressed provocatively and you were looking for sex."

"But I wasn't," Tessa said.

"I know that, but the jury doesn't," Will said. "Let's try again. What were you wearing?"

"I was dressed totally conservatively. I wasn't trying to hook up at all."

Will's eyes met Valentina's and returned to Tessa's. He told her, "You never argue your point like you just did. You answer the question as simply as you can, and you don't give your opinion or any extra information."

Tessa stared at the table, her folded fingers tangled together.

Valentina jumped in and said kindly, "Tessa, Will means you keep your answers simple. Succinct. You tell it like it is, just the facts, as honestly as you can. In this case, you'd say you were wearing a denim skirt and sweater or whatever. Period. You don't have to interpret or defend anything."

"And keep your eyes on the attorney who's questioning you. Don't look down at the table or around the courtroom, especially at Nick," Will added.

Tessa raised her head and fixed her eyes on him. "I don't want to look at you. I feel like you're picking on me."

"That's exactly what Warfield is going to do. He wants you to lose your cool," Will said. "If you feel yourself getting angry, pause for a moment. You can ask the judge for a short break if you need one. You have to keep your emotions in check."

"Fffooooooh." Tessa sounded like a pressure cooker releasing steam. Hope moved her chin from Tessa's feet to her lap and presented her ears: *Pet me. You'll feel calmer.*

"Let's try another question. When you arrived at Mr. Payne's house, did you expect his brother and sister-in-law to be there?" Will asked.

"Yes."

"When you heard they weren't coming for dinner, what was your response?"

Tessa shrugged. "He said they had to be in Ellensburg."

"Did that bother you?"

"No. Well, maybe I felt a little uncomfortable for a second."

"If you felt uncomfortable, why didn't you leave?"

Flustered, Tessa said, "I went out once with Nick . . . um . . . Mr. Payne . . . and I liked him . . ."

"So you admit you liked him. Did you hope to hook up at his house?"

"No, I did not." Tessa glared at Will. "I just wanted to get to know him."

"And you trusted going to the home of a man you *didn't* really know?"

"I am not some loose woman, if that's what you're implying. I had no idea he was going to drug and assault me."

Will groaned in exasperation. "Look, Tessa, you're arguing again, and you're saying way more than you need to, starting with mentioning that you felt uncomfortable. Do you see how, step-by-step, you gave Warfield rope to hang you?"

"*Hang* me?"

"It's just a manner of speech," Will said.

When Tessa screwed up her face, she looked scared and vulnerable—and something snipped at Will emotionally. He'd gone through trial prep with hundreds of witnesses, but this was the first time he wanted to protect one. Though as a prosecutor, he won cases for the state and not for victims, this time he'd like to win for Tessa, too.

"Look, I'm sorry if I've upset you," Will said. "The problem is that Warfield will do far worse. You need to get tough here. Let's start again." On a piece of paper from his yellow legal tablet, he printed in black ink five points to remember:

1. *Listen carefully to each question.*
2. *Think before answering. Take your time. If you don't understand, ask for clarification.*
3. *Answer only the question. Just the facts and nothing more. Don't volunteer anything.*
4. *Try to relax and be yourself.*
5. *NEVER SHOW ANGER.*

Tessa chewed her thumbnail as she studied the list. "All right. I get it."

"So what were you wearing when you went to the defendant's house?"

"Denim leggings and a T-shirt."

"Did he offer you wine?"

"Yes."

"How much did you drink?"

"A glass and a half."

So now we're getting somewhere.

Until evening, when Valentina had to turn on the overhead lights, Will asked questions, and Tessa answered them. Occasionally, Valentina stepped in to reassure her. Hope never left her.

Finally, as they were packing up to leave, Tessa still looked nervous but was no longer hunched over. She seemed more confident. She and Valentina hugged each other. Will hung back.

"Good job," he told Tessa.

"Do you know when I'll have to testify?" she asked.

"Probably week after next."

"Can I attend the trial on the days I'm not on the stand?"

"No. Before you testify in a criminal trial, you're not allowed to hear what other witnesses say."

Tessa frowned. "I wanted to show up in court every minute I could get off work. I wanted Nick to know I was watching him."

"Not allowed. And you can't read news reports, or watch TV coverage, or talk with other witnesses about the trial. Any of those things could influence your own testimony. You have to stay away. Is that clear?"

"Yes, but I still *want* to be there."

"You can't. Rules are rules."

Tessa looked so determined. Though she was skittish, underneath her fear was strength. Will didn't often get a fighter, and he appreciated that she'd not lost courage and faded away, as Maria had done and Abbey Greenwood almost did. It made him want to win even more.

CHAPTER 46

On Monday afternoon in the courthouse lobby, Will asked Hope, "Ready to go home?"

She wagged her tail with the rapid horizontal sweeps of a housecleaner polishing a tabletop. *Hurrah!*

Sandy handed over her end of the leash for the Hope Transfer. "She's had a rough day with a sad little girl. You need to take her for a major walk before she goes to bed."

"I need a walk as badly as she does. Warfield didn't let up for a second." With jury selection, Will had been looking for younger people, women especially, who believed in the importance of direct verbal consent. But Warfield had wanted older, more conservative men who believed that women consented by "asking for it" with short skirts and tight pants.

"I never had time for lunch. I'm hungry enough to eat shoe leather," Will said.

"Warfield always fights like a rabid tiger," Sandy said.

"Yeah, he loves to win."

"You think Judge Plodsker will help him? Sometimes he goes easy on assault defendants."

"How well I know," Will said. Judge Plodsker had once handed out a sentence that was barely a hand slap to a DV bully Will had worked hard to send up the river. For days, Will had smoldered about it.

"Why do you think Judge Plodsker can be biased like that?" Sandy asked. "You think he beats his wife or something?"

Will shrugged. "Maybe someone he cared about got wrongfully convicted. Who knows?"

People in the assault business were often personally connected to it, trying to even a score or set straight something in their heart. After Maria, Will surely was. Sandy's ex-husband did time for DV that had sent her to a hospital. Valentina was sexually assaulted on a vacation in Mazatlán. Many of Will's staff were wounded healers, trying to help others who suffered as they had.

Hope tugged the leash to hint of going home. The lobby was bustling with people as eager as she was to leave. At the entrance, officers in khaki uniforms stood around, looking weary after a day of searching briefcases and purses.

Will thanked Sandy for the Hope Transfer, and she trotted along beside him to the exit. But outside, rain was pouring, and she stopped abruptly, like a car screeching to a halt. She stiffened and raised her right front paw as if to spare it from touching the wet stone. She blinked against the rain. It pelted her like the fearsome water in Will's shower, and she wanted no part of it. Her body was as rigid as her opinion: *No way am I subjecting myself to this inclement weather! I am* not *a Portuguese Water Dog.*

Distracted by jury selection, Will had forgotten his umbrella, so he hunched down to meet the elements. As rain splattered his face, he urged Hope down the steps. "Come on. We have to stop at the office for a minute, and then we can go home. The car's just a block away."

Not pleased by the prospect of slogging along for an entire block—and her fur getting soaked—Hope gave in, nonetheless. In the crowd, she gingerly accompanied Will down a couple of steps.

Ahead of them, traffic crept along the street, the cars' windshield wipers going full blast. The collective smell of exhausts thickened the air. Will sloshed through puddles and dodged umbrellas to keep from being poked in the eyes. His shoes sodden, water squished between his toes.

"Hey, Armstrong! Wait up." Justin Warfield's deep bass voice fit the kind of man who wrestled alligators.

Already today, Will had heard far too much of that voice, and he didn't relish hearing more, especially in the rain. Irked, he turned around as Warfield hurried down the steps toward him and Hope. Warfield's brown umbrella looked like a buzzard's wing.

He stopped one step higher than Will, an obvious power play so that he could look down on him. Will didn't particularly like raising his head to meet Warfield's eyes, but at least his umbrella partly sheltered Hope.

"Nice dog." Warfield stooped down and thumped his fingertips on Hope's head.

Will supposed the gesture was meant to be a pat, but it did not contain affection. Clearly, Warfield was not a dog person, and Hope knew it. She eyed him with her most suspicious expression.

"I want to talk with you about the dog," Warfield said.

"The dog's name is Hope. And hurry. She doesn't like getting wet."

Warfield's loud bass laugh came from deep in his chest. "She's a retriever, for God's sake. Don't they like swimming into rivers to fetch dead ducks?"

"Hope is unique."

"She's a wuss."

Knowing she was being discussed in a disparaging way,

Hope flashed Warfield an equally disparaging glance. She pressed back her ears. *Hmmpf.*

"I understand she'll be in the witness box with Tessa Jordan and Abbey Greenwood," Warfield said.

"Yep. I expect you'll make the trial an ordeal for them. She's trained to comfort people when they're stressed."

"How does she know if those women are stressed because I'm asking hard questions or they're lying under oath? She can't tell the difference. Either way, she'd comfort them."

"Comforting is her job," Will said.

"I don't like this deal. Just by being there, she'll sway jurors. One look at that face, and they'll melt," Warfield said. "Every time those women pet her, they'll send an unconscious message to the jury that they're vulnerable and sympathetic. They'll look like they need her because they've been victimized and they're stressed out from telling the truth."

"You don't have to worry," Will said as an impatient driver behind him honked at a cab that cut in front of her.

"What do you mean?" Warfield cocked his head like Hope did when she was trying to understand English.

"When the jury comes in, Hope will be on a down-stay at the women's feet. Judge Plodsker will explain that she's there, but they'll never see her."

"What if her tail hangs out of the witness box? Or she snores? Or she stands up?"

Enjoying the insecurity in Warfield's questions, Will smiled. *Great. Underneath the aggression, he's sweating. Maybe Hope will put him off his stride.* "A tail or snore can't sway anybody. She's trained to stay out of sight. There's no chance she'll reveal herself."

"I'll be watching," Warfield threatened. "She'd be a good excuse for a mistrial."

You jerk. "You can depend on Hope," Will said. "We need to get out of the rain."

As Will walked her, drenched, to the parking lot, he wondered if she ever *would* stand in the witness box. *Surely not.* Still, Warfield had just made a tiny chink in Will's own confidence armor.

Always something to worry about.

At home by seven, Will fed Hope and ate a ham sandwich and some canned bean soup. After he carried his dishes to the kitchen sink, he let Hope out for her evening survey of the field. It had stopped raining. She'd come back muddy, but that was her right as a dog.

From his porch, he saw Tessa refilling her cats' water at the spigot beside the barn. The floodlight glinted on the metal bowl and shone on her hair, which curled in the damp. As she set the bowl on the ground, she turned and looked just beyond the circle of light, then squatted down and held out her hands like she was calling something.

Only then did Will notice a cat, who looked like a small palomino pony, hanging back in the shadows by the woodpile. The cat was Fitzgerald—in the last few months, Will had learned the names of all seven—and Tessa had mentioned that Fitzgerald was the closest to becoming tame. His ears pricked, he crept toward her, but then seemed to think better of it and backed into the shadows again. Tessa called him and patted the grass in front of her. He stepped forward again and crouched down, watching.

Anyone could tell that he wanted to make friends, but he hesitated. The time wasn't right. He didn't quite trust Tessa yet. But she was patient. Anyone could see that, too. She was waiting for Fitzgerald to grow out of his caution and come to her on his own terms.

Tessa kept holding out her hands and murmuring encouragement to him, but he stood his ground. Last week, Will had noticed bits of hamburger at the bottom of the cats' bowls because they'd not been able to finish their dinner. Fitzgerald must realize how fortunate he was.

Will liked Tessa's generosity and her eagerness to nurture the cats. He could tell she was a good person. If they'd met under different circumstances, he'd have asked her out. Now he watched her giving Fitzgerald a pep talk on trust. The love and gentleness she was showing the cat moved Will—but warned him to be careful. Developing feelings for her was not an option.

CHAPTER 47

As Tessa swished a feather duster over her desk in Howard, she realized that her ivy plant's drooping leaves were shouting, *Water me!* Their yellow tinge shamed her for neglect.

"I'm sorry," she whispered to the ivy as she shared her bottled water. With her shirt's cuff, she dabbed at drops that had splashed on the desk. "Today I'm as stressed as you are." The trial had started on this Wednesday morning.

Tessa still wished she could attend, but for the next three days, she couldn't have been there anyway. Last spring, before she'd met Nick Payne, she'd signed up for a Northwest Bookmobile Services Conference in Olympia, starting at two this afternoon. She'd also promised that Howard could be part of a bookmobile exhibit in the conference hall's parking lot. Librarians would visit him for ideas about how bookmobiles could enrich people's lives, and Tessa would explain her programs. She also hoped to sneak away to vendors' exhibits or workshops on such topics as grieving the death of a beloved patron. But she'd have to work to concentrate because her thoughts would be drifting to the courthouse.

For days, Tessa had been gussying up Howard, dusting and cleaning him, washing his windows. She'd arranged a display of large-print books for seniors and struggling young readers. She'd typed up bookmobile drivers' safety tips and stacked them next to Howard's entrance. And to his bulletin board, she'd pinned the covers of story-hour books and photos of children, sitting on each side of his aisle and listening to her read.

Now all she had to do was hurry up and leave. Olympia was calling. As Tessa fired up Howard and rumbled down the highway, she still wanted to turn him around and head to the trial.

The three days in Olympia passed in a blur. Every morning, Tessa got up at five o'clock, fed her cats, and drove half an hour to pick up Howard at the library's main branch. Then she drove him an hour and a half to Olympia, where she stood and answered questions all day. At five o'clock, she drove back, fed the cats, and dragged, exhausted, into her cottage after eight for leftover minestrone. All through each day, she was hungry for trial news.

Emma kept her informed in a vague and general way. Tessa knew, for example, that Will and Justin Warfield had given their opening statements, and Sandy and Mary O'Malley had testified. One of Nick's neighbors had taken the stand and described seeing him on his deck with a woman in clothes that matched what Tessa had been wearing that night.

These generalities were not the same as being at the trial. Tessa felt like she was watching it through an opaque window that allowed her to see only shadowy forms. She couldn't judge for herself what was said, and her negligible understanding frustrated her.

When she got home on Friday night, someone knocked on her door. Through her peephole with a fisheye lens for a wider view, she saw Emma on the porch holding out a pie. "Pecan. You up for a pig-out?"

Tessa opened the door and moved aside so Emma could come in. "I could use some comfort food," Tessa said.

"So could I. I've had a grueling day, compliments of Nick Payne's defense attorney." Emma set her pie on the table, and they began their ritual of cutting pieces and making tea.

Tessa knew that Emma had testified today. As they were sitting down, she asked, "Can you tell me anything that happened?"

"Will Armstrong was even more attractive in court than when we went to his barn. You should see how impressive he is," Emma said.

"I'm not thinking about him." Tessa sounded impatient. "I want to know if everything went all right."

"I'm not sure," Emma said. "I explained talking with you after you came home from Nick's house and then taking you to the police. I definitely pointed out how traumatized you were when I drove you home late that night. I said you were *still* traumatized."

"You think the jury believed you?"

"No idea. Warfield accused me of exaggerating because you're my best friend and I was playing for the jury's sympathy. He asked me, 'Are you always a drama queen?' Can you believe that?"

"Such a hateful man!" Tessa stabbed a bite of pie.

"I had to sit there and take it. He twisted around everything I said to make us look bad."

"That's what he's going to do to me."

"You've got to gear up for it. You have to make up your mind to keep your cool no matter what he says. You can't let him get the best of you."

"I'm afraid he will."

"Not if you tell the truth and stick to your guns."

Tessa realized that she was digging her nails into her palms. She wanted the chance to stand up to Nick and make him pay for what he did, but after her practice session with Will, she'd understood that taking the stand would not be easy. Just how hard it would be was starting to sink in.

CHAPTER 48

"All rise," shouted the strapping bailiff.

Nodding to him and the court reporter, Judge Plodsker lumbered in. He placed his hands on his chair's arms to support his weight as he fitted his plump body into his seat. When he greeted everyone, his pink cheeks made him look overheated. The jury, a collection of ordinary-looking people, appeared fresh and alert after the weekend off.

As Will rose, a few moth wings fluttered in his stomach as they sometimes did on Monday mornings before he'd gotten back into his prosecutor's groove. Standing as tall and strong as an oak tree, he called Dr. Henri Aurand to the witness stand.

Dr. Aurand sported a goatee, and a red silk handkerchief that matched his tie peeped out of his suit's breast pocket. He looked like the sort of man who went around kissing women's hands. Will's initial questions established that he was a professor in the University of Washington's School of Medicine and an expert witness on drugs.

"I'd like to talk with you about zolpidem, Dr. Aurand. As you know, most people recognize it by its brand name, Ambien, so let's just call it that." Will pivoted to the right to check that the jury understood; then he turned back. "Can you tell us how Ambien works?"

Dr. Aurand rested his right hand's knuckles behind his goatee so he looked like *The Thinker.* "Ambien increases the activity of people's gamma-aminobutyric acid, which slows the brain so they can fall asleep. Usually in fifteen to thirty minutes."

"Does Ambien have side effects?"

"Sometimes dizziness or unsteadiness. Headaches, nausea, diarrhea. The most common side effect is memory loss."

Will raised an eyebrow. "Memory loss," he repeated, looking at the jury. "I've read that some people take Ambien and carry out ordinary, everyday tasks, even driving, and they don't remember it. Is that right?"

"Yes. Sometimes the part of the brain responsible for complex thought and decision making remains asleep, even though the person is walking around and seems perfectly functional."

"What about having sex?" Will asked. "Could someone on Ambien have sex while her brain is asleep and then forget it ever happened?"

"Indeed. And the memory loss can be worse if Ambien is mixed with alcohol."

"Is that why it's supposed to be an ideal drug for sexual assault?"

"Yes. The victim often doesn't remember it after being given Ambien. The drug is also easy to get—over ten million prescriptions are written for it every year. And it can leave the body quickly, so it's undetectable. That's an important plus for an assailant."

"Mmhumm." Will acted like he found these facts fascinating. "Tell me, how quickly *does* Ambien leave the body?"

"Often in eight to fourteen hours. Some people excrete it in the morning after's first urine. The drug might still remain in other people for up to forty-eight hours, but after that, it's usually gone."

"So people vary in the time Ambien takes to leave their body?" Will asked.

"Yes."

"Could that variation account for one of this case's alleged victims testing positive for Ambien approximately fourteen hours after her assault, and the other claiming she was drugged but having no trace forty-eight hours later?"

"Yes."

"What would account for Ambien leaving some women's bodies sooner than others?"

"Age. A millennial might metabolize the drug more quickly than a senior citizen. And fluids. If someone drank a lot of water, it would increase urine output and flush Ambien out of the system." Dr. Aurand smoothed his hand over his tie.

"What about food? One alleged victim had eaten nothing for seven hours before she believes she was drugged."

"Food makes a difference. If the woman was metabolizing it at the same time as Ambien, it would stay in her longer. Conversely, if she'd not eaten and was not metabolizing food, the drug would leave her body faster."

"Interesting." Will turned toward the jury again, emphasizing the point. "So let me make sure we understand. When we consider age and water and food intake, we can explain how one alleged victim could have Ambien in her body after fourteen hours, and another could have none after forty-eight. Am I correct?"

"You are." Dr. Aurand leaned forward. "Basically, you must keep in mind two essential facts. First, individuals vary in how they metabolize Ambien. Second, they vary for logical, proven reasons."

"Thank you, Dr. Aurand." *May you have put to rest why Mary O'Malley did not find traces of the Ambien Tessa claims Nick gave her.*

Judge Plodsker nodded at Warfield. "Counsel, your witness."

"Thank you, Your Honor." Warfield charged the witness stand like a center who's snapped the football to his quarterback and is taking on the defensive line. "Mr. Armstrong has been keen to prove why a forensic nurse found no Ambien in one of Mr. Payne's alleged victims forty-eight hours after she'd been supposedly drugged. I have just two questions for you, Dr. Aurand," Warfield said. "If she'd been given another drug to knock her out, could it still have been in her body after that time?"

"Depends on what drug it was. But, yes, some remain longer."

"Could we look at all this in another way—that one of the alleged victims had no Ambien in her body because Mr. Payne *never gave it to her* in the first place?"

"Yes. You can argue either way," Dr. Aurand said.

Several jurors nodded approval. Murmurs rippled through the gallery. Judge Plodsker tapped his gavel lightly on his bench. "No talking allowed. If you persist, you'll be asked to leave the courtroom."

"Thank you, Dr. Aurand." Warfield swaggered to his seat, his chest puffed out after his seemingly effortless defense.

Will thought, *Thank you, Warfield, for being a jerk, as usual.*

CHAPTER 49

On Tuesday morning, Hope was hidden in the witness box, ready for Abbey Greenwood. Will waited at the prosecutor's desk for the day's proceedings to begin. Across the aisle, Nick was straining the seams of his suit's coat as he leaned forward and rested his elbows on the defense's table. He was sitting so still that he could have been forged from steel. His head was bent as if he were reading the tabletop's mahogany grains, like tea leaves, for a prediction of the jury's verdict.

Judge Plodsker arrived, and everybody rose. After a few "good mornings," Will called Abbey to the stand. She walked to it with grace, but she looked shy and tense. She wore a gray herringbone business suit, and her hair was twisted up into a tight knot. As she took her seat, she looked nervously around the courtroom but never at Nick.

"Good morning, Ms. Greenwood." Will smiled, intending to put her at ease.

When she didn't smile back, he assumed she regretted coming forward and agreeing to appear in court. Nearly every assault survivor did.

"I'd like for you to tell us what happened on Saturday night, April seventh of this year. Let's go through it step-by-step, all right?" Will asked.

Abbey nodded. Maybe she thought her voice would shake if she spoke.

"You went to the Nisqually Food and Wine Festival?"

"I attend every year. The woman who usually accompanies me had to go out of town, so I decided to go ahead on my own."

"So what happened next?"

"I went around to booths and tasted wine. I talked with a few people I know from work and some of the vintners I've met before."

"So you felt comfortable there?" Will asked.

"Very."

"Did you meet your alleged assailant there that night?"

At the reference to Nick Payne, Abbey did not give him even a cursory glance. She seemed like she'd go blind if her eyes turned in his direction. "Yes, I met him."

"Is he in the courtroom now?"

"Yes."

"Can you point to him?"

Abbey looked like she'd rather swallow lye. She aimed a pale index finger at Nick, and murmurs arose all over the courtroom.

"Let the record reflect that the witness has identified the defendant, Nick Payne." Will shook his head as if Nick's very existence was a shame. "Tell me, Ms. Greenwood, how did you meet him?"

"I was talking with a vendor, and he came over and took one of the wine samples lined up on the booth. Pretty soon he joined our conversation."

"Did you feel ill at ease or stalked?"

"No. At the festival, it's not unusual to talk with people you don't know. He was well-dressed. He told me he was a professor. We talked about the polarization in U.S. politics, and our views were similar."

"So you had something in common. You felt comfortable with him?"

"Yes."

Will glanced at the jury with a knowing expression, which asked, *Do you see that Nick Payne set her up?* The nods of a few jurors' heads signaled agreement. To Abbey, Will said, "So you liked the defendant. Were you attracted to him?"

She paused, clearly collecting her thoughts about how to answer such an uncomfortable question. "Yes," she said to her lap. "But it wasn't some wild heartthrob attraction. It was a stupid lapse on my part."

"What did he do next?"

"He told me he collected wine, and he had a bottle he wanted me to try, and I said, 'Okay.' The festival has rules against bringing your own wine into the Conference Center, so the bottle was in his car. He asked if I knew anywhere we could go to drink it—he said he lived in Seattle and didn't know places in Nisqually County very well."

"How did you respond?"

"Foolishly, I said we could go to my house."

A wave of whispers traveled through the gallery. It was clear where Abbey's testimony was going. The spectators were probably either worried about her or eager for the lascivious recounting ahead. Will hoped the jury was concerned.

"Ms. Greenwood, did you feel you were what some people might call 'picking up' the defendant?" he asked.

"Absolutely not! I've never picked up a man in my life," Abbey protested. "I was just thinking, you know, he wanted me to try the wine, and we couldn't drink it at the festival—and he seemed nice. So why not go to my house?"

"How did you get there?"

"He walked me to my car in the parking lot and said he'd get his and follow me home. In a few minutes, I heard a tap on a horn behind me. The defendant stuck his hand out the window and waved."

"Did you see what kind of car he was driving?"

"No. He stayed pretty far behind me all the way. It had gotten dark, so all I know is the car looked black or gray or brown."

Will glanced at the jury to check out their absorbed expressions. "What happened next?"

"I parked in my garage, and he parked down the street."

"Did you have any reaction to that?"

"Not at the time, but I understand now that I couldn't identify his car when it was parked there. He hurried into the garage, and we walked through the kitchen door together."

"He had the wine with him?"

"Yes, in a travel wine cooler that could hold two or three bottles—it had zippers and a strap. It was odd for a single bottle, but I didn't think much about it."

"Then what happened?"

"I got two glasses out of my cupboard and went to hang up our jackets while he poured the wine and brought it to the living room. We sat there and talked and looked for the deer and raccoons that come to my yard at night. Everybody loves to watch them."

"Where were you sitting?"

"On my sofa. He was across from me in a club chair."

"Did you have another glass of wine?"

"Yes. He went into the kitchen and refilled our glasses. He kept watching me. At the time, I thought he liked seeing me enjoy his wine, but now I think he was looking for signs his drug was working."

Warfield hefted his body out of his chair and loudly proclaimed, "Objection! Assumes a fact not in evidence."

"Sustained," Judge Plodsker said.

"Ms. Greenwood, did you ever sense that the defendant had put something into the wine?"

"Yes. I know what I feel like when I've been drinking. That night I was stifling yawns, and my eyes closed, and I was gone. That's never happened to me before. I believe something in the wine knocked me out." Abbey hurriedly wiped tears off her cheeks with the back of her hand.

Will did not enjoy making victims relive the worst experience of their lives. He offered Abbey water or a break, but she declined. When she'd composed herself, he asked in a kind voice, "Before you passed out, did you consent to sex with the defendant?"

"No! Never! Absolutely not!"

"Would you tell us when and where you woke up?"

"The next morning. About six. On the sofa."

"Were you dressed?"

"I still had on my socks and shirt, but I was naked from the waist down. I knew immediately that the defendant had raped me." For the first time, Abbey glared at Nick. The jury could not have missed her hate.

"Did the defendant leave anything in your house?"

"Nothing. He even stole my wine glasses! The thief!"

"What did you do next?"

"I called the police. They came with a sexual assault advocate, and we went to the forensic nurse."

After more testimony, Will thanked Abbey for her forthright answers to sensitive questions and acknowledged the courage it had taken her to appear there today. He'd hardly had a chance to breathe before Warfield sprang to his feet.

"Ms. Greenwood," he boomed. "When you brought the defendant home, did you know who he was?"

Abbey's cheeks seemed to grow taut. "Of course, I did."

"What was his name?"

"Nick."

"No last name?"

Abbey visibly drooped. "He must have told me, but I'm not sure."

Warfield's smirk looked sadistic. "Do you often invite men home when you don't know their name? At *night*?"

"I do not," Abbey said. "I admit it was a lapse of judgment on my part."

Warfield turned toward the jurors. They were hanging on his every word. "You have identified the defendant as the man who assaulted you, is that right?"

"Yes."

"You're sure he's your assailant? You have no doubt?"

"I'm sure."

"Tell me, at the festival, were the lights dimmed as they might be in a restaurant?"

Abbey paused as if she were trying to picture it again. "Yes, I think so."

"You said when you brought the defendant to your house, you watched for wildlife. Did you turn on outdoor lights?"

"Yes."

"Did they shine into your living room?"

"A little. Mostly near the plate glass window."

"And where was it in relation to where you and the defendant were sitting?"

"Across the room."

"How many lights did you turn on *in*side the house?"

Abbey seemed to count in her head. "I turned on the kitchen light and a living room lamp. An overhead light was already on in the hall."

"Where was the living room lamp located?"

"Next to the sofa."

"So you didn't turn on a light by the club chair where you said the defendant was sitting?"

"No. It's more fun to watch the animals if the room isn't too bright."

"So how far was the defendant from you when he was sitting in the club chair?"

"Maybe eight feet."

"Could you see his face clearly?"

"Yes."

From his considerable height, Warfield peered down on Abbey. "When you went to the police, were you asked to describe the man who assaulted you in as much detail as you could?"

"Yes."

"You knew your description would help the police catch him, didn't you?"

"Yes."

"So you tried your best to describe what the man looked like?"

"I did."

"Yet all you said was that he was a white male, approximately forty-five, brown hair, about six feet," Warfield said. "Are you aware that your description fits millions of men in the state of Washington?"

Abbey stared at her lap as if she wished she could dive into it and hide. "Yes."

"Speak up, Ms. Greenwood," Warfield demanded.

Abbey glared at him as harshly as she had at Nick. "YES!"

"With such dim light in your living room, are you sure you *saw* the defendant well enough to identify him?"

"I saw him," Abbey spat.

"But you didn't know his name, Ms. Greenwood, and you brought him into a semi-dark house. I don't think you could be sure *who* he was." Warfield turned to the jury and shook his head as if he felt sorry for Abbey, being so pathetic.

You snake! Will slapped the tabletop as he stood. "Objection! Argumentative. Counsel is testifying and badgering the witness."

"Sustained," Judge Plodsker said.

"So tell the jury, how much had you drunk before you brought the defendant home?"

"It's hard to say. At the festival, wine comes in tiny cups."

"What would you estimate your samples added up to?"

"A couple of glasses. Maybe a little more."

"What was their effect on you?"

"I was hardly drunk, but I could tell I'd had a little alcohol."

"So to you, more than two glasses is just 'a little alcohol'?"

Abbey flinched. She surely knew as well as everyone in the courtroom did that Warfield was boxing her in. "I guess not."

"So at home, you had another drink and a refill. That would make a total of four at least," Warfield said. "Could all that wine have blurred your memory of the nameless man you brought home?"

"It wasn't blurred! I identified him in the photo lineup, and I can identify him here today."

Warfield paced back and forth in front of her, leaving her hanging. Finally, he asked, "Ms. Greenwood, would you say you have a drinking problem?"

"I do *not!*"

"Do you take drugs?"

"Prescription drugs, sometimes."

"Do you take Ambien?"

"Never."

"What about illegal drugs? Any history with them?"

"Of course not."

Warfield's sly smile must have maddened Abbey. Will detested watching him go after her. No wonder victims had a difficult time in court.

Adding discomfort, Warfield towered over Abbey and peered down at her as if she were a cockroach. "If you have no history with illegal drugs, can you tell us why on April third of twenty-eleven, you were arrested for heroin possession?"

Abbey looked like she'd like to strangle Warfield. "It was not *my* heroin. My little brother was living with me at the time. I didn't know he was dealing drugs."

"How convenient to blame it on him when he's not here to defend himself." Warfield sounded snide.

Outrageous! The weasel. Will shot to his feet. "Objection, your honor!"

Will had counted on Abbey to be his slam dunk for this case. "Judge Plodsker, we need to send the jury out."

At the end of the day, Will walked Hope outside and met the press, gathered like a flock of vultures on the courthouse steps. In the fewest possible words, he assured them of his confidence that Nick Payne would be going to prison. But that was only bluster. Truth be told, he was not confident of that at all.

Inside his head, a hammer seemed to slam on iron. The ache had come from anger at Warfield, Will supposed, but of course, he could never let the bully—or the press—sniff a trace of it. Abbey had never talked with Will about her drug arrest. Warfield had blindsided him.

After the jury had been removed from the courtroom, Warfield said, innocent as a newborn lamb, "I never intended to ask her about the arrest, Your Honor. I thought she'd be honest about her drug history. I didn't know I'd have to impeach her."

Give me a break. Will that jackass try to sell me the Space Needle next?

Will clenched his fist on Judge Plodsker's bench. "A drug arrest from three-and-a-half years ago doesn't prove or disprove that Nick Payne sexually assaulted Ms. Greenwood. It's irrelevant."

"It casts doubt on her veracity. She lied about her drug history," Warfield countered. "We can't believe the only way she had a drug in her body that night was because Mr. Payne gave it to her."

Will and Warfield argued. Sweat moistened Will's forehead. He couldn't remember another time when he'd been so fed up with a defense attorney.

"All right. All right." His face puffy, Judge Plodsker swatted the air as if to tell them he was tired of the conversation. "I'm ruling the arrest inadmissible, and I will instruct the jury to disregard that line of questioning and Ms. Greenwood's answers."

Thank God.

But the damage had been done. There was no going back and undoing what the jury had heard. With heavy steps, Will led Hope to his Jeep. In comfort mode, she pressed against his leg.

CHAPTER 50

Making her way to the witness stand on Wednesday may have been the hardest thing Tessa ever did—all those eyes on her, ears eager for every sordid word, opinions about her whispered through the gallery. Reporters and jurors were seated there with notepads, ready for intimate details of her life. She may as well have been walking naked with a sign around her neck: *I am scared.*

Outside in the hall, Valentina had reminded her that Nick would be there, but Tessa was not prepared for the unnerving feeling of his eyes on her; his gaze felt like acid burning her skin. Though she did not look at him, their hate for each other chained them together and distracted her. When she tried to swallow, her throat wouldn't work.

But when she stepped into the stand, Hope was lying on the floor in her library-lion position, out of sight of the jury, as required. She was a gift wrapped in cream-colored fur. Tessa eased into the mahogany chair and rested a grateful hand on Hope's soft ear. When she set her chin on Tessa's foot, Hope announced, *I am here. Don't you worry. I care.*

Tessa insisted to herself, *I can do this!* Hope was there, and Tessa was as ready as she'd ever be. She'd dressed in a white blouse, black blazer, and gray tweed slacks—the conservative-librarian look Will had suggested. She'd reminded herself of his advice: *Take your time, and don't show anger.*

"Good morning, Ms. Jordan." Will's smile was surely meant to give her courage.

"Good morning," she said. She cleared her throat—*I can do this.* She locked her eyes on Will as if one errant glance at Nick would prompt a migraine.

"Let's start with questions that will help the jury get to know you," Will began. He asked about her library work and her love for her patrons. His questions, similar to those he'd asked in their practice session, seemed designed to give her confidence. They did, a little.

Next, he led her through her story from meeting Nick online to waking in his bed. If the telling seemed too rough as they worked their way through the chronology, he asked if she wanted a break. But what Tessa wanted was to get off the stand, the sooner the better.

Then, as the jury scribbled notes in their tablets, Will circled back to topics for her to clarify. "When you met Mr. Payne for the first time, what was your impression?" Will looked over at Nick.

Tessa kept her eyes on Will. "He seemed okay. We talked about his run for our town's City Council. He was interesting."

"Were you impressed?"

Tessa hated admitting it. "I suppose so."

"Did you think someone like him could sexually assault anybody?"

"No. That was the last thing that would have occurred to me."

"Mmhmm . . ." Will seemed to absorb that idea. A bald man in the jury looked down at his feet, as if he were thinking about it, too. "I don't mean to embarrass you, Ms. Jordan, but I want to ask you some personal questions. You take whatever time you need to answer, all right?"

Though Tessa had been expecting personal questions, a shiver of apprehension zigzagged through her. She reminded herself, *I can do this.*

"Were you dating anybody before you met the defendant?"

"I'd broken up with my fiancé two years before. After that, I'd gone out with a couple of men, but nothing very serious."

"What about sex? This question isn't meant to make you feel awkward, but how long had it been since you'd had sex?"

"Maybe six, seven months."

"So would it be fair to say that you don't get into bed with just anybody?"

"Definitely fair. I need to know and trust a man before I get involved."

"That makes sense." Will nodded toward the jury. A nervous-looking woman on the front row nodded back. "What about the defendant? When you went to his house, were you hoping to have sex with *him?*"

"No!" Tessa's stomach lurched at the thought. Hope raised her head off Tessa's foot as if to check that she was all right. "I hardly knew him."

"So you'd say you're not the type for one-night stands?"

"I am definitely not the type."

"Mmhmm." Will seemed to let that thought sink in. "Tell me, Ms. Jordan, did you consent to sex with the defendant?"

"No."

"Do you think you might have consented and forgotten it?"

"No. And I could never have consented if I was drugged."

"You're sure you didn't imply that you wanted sex? Or let him know indirectly that you were willing? We need to get absolutely clear on that."

"I'm sure. I didn't intend to have sex with him. I didn't

want to have sex. I didn't consent to it. I'd just gone there for dinner, which we never had."

"All right. You didn't intend, want, or consent to sex with the defendant," Will repeated, partly facing the jury. Though they seemed to listen intently to him, Tessa couldn't tell if they viewed her with sympathy or distrust. "After you went home that morning, what did you do?"

"I slept for a long time. When I woke up, I showered and tried to figure out what had happened. I still wasn't sure till the next day, when I could think straight. It was obvious from my bruises and soreness that the defendant had raped me," Tessa stated through gritted teeth.

"Did you have any contact with him at that time? For example, did he call to make sure you were all right?"

Tessa scoffed. *Are you kidding?* "He called but not till after the police had questioned him."

"What did he say?"

"He said he'd taken photos of me naked in bed. If I didn't withdraw my accusation, he'd post them on the Internet and send them to my boss."

"Did you believe him?"

"Yes. I could tell he was furious, and I was terrified." Though Tessa had avoided looking at Nick, now she glowered at him. He was leaning back in his chair, his eyes on her, his legs manspread under the table as if he ruled the world. His smirk taunted her with arrogance and condescension— and defiance. *He's odious! Reprehensible!* Tessa laced her fingers, squeezed her palms together, willed herself to breathe.

"Was the fear hard to live with?" Will asked gently.

"Yes. Extremely hard. It still is."

Hope looked up at Tessa with eyes that urged, *Don't be afraid. I am here. I want you to be all right.*

After more questions that seemed like they would never end, Will said, "Thank you very much, Ms. Jordan. I know this morning was not easy for you. You've shown admirable courage."

Judge Plodsker covered his mouth with his bear's paw when he yawned. "Okay, your witness, Mr. Warfield."

As Will returned to his table, Warfield rose, a mountain of flesh. He swaggered toward the witness stand. Tessa shrank back, then forced herself to sit forward to meet him. Her pulse raced. A steel band seemed to tighten around her chest.

"Ms. Jordan, since you just mentioned the photos my client supposedly took of you naked in his bed, let's start with that. Are you aware that no pictures were ever found in his house or on his electronics?"

"Yes."

"Are you aware there's no link between his cell and landline numbers and the number of the incoming call you claim threatened you with photos?"

"Yes."

"Was there no link because the defendant never made that call? No photos because there never were any?" Warfield sneered.

Will rose. "Objection. Argumentative and calls for speculation."

"I'll rephrase. Ms. Jordan, are you *sure* the defendant called you? Remember, you've sworn to tell the truth."

Tessa bristled. "He called me."

"Are you aware that lying under oath is perjury?"

"I'm not lying!"

Warfield rolled his eyes toward the ceiling and turned to face the jury as if he wanted her out of his sight. When he turned back, he asked, "Ms. Jordan, Mr. Payne's hands would have been all over your naked skin as he changed your positions for the camera. Did you fantasize about that?"

"No! The thought makes me sick." Remembering that Will had warned her not to argue, Tessa bit her tongue.

"Did it make you feel good to think that an important man like Mr. Payne would *want* nude photos of you?"

"No."

"Did you invent the photos so you could feel that Mr. Payne found you attractive and desired you, Ms. Jordan?"

"I didn't invent them!" *Don't argue.* But what was Tessa supposed to do? She couldn't just sit there and let Warfield steamroll her.

He turned toward the jury again. As if he were tossing a question to Tessa over his shoulder, he asked, "Have you ever been married, Ms. Jordan?"

"No."

"Why is that?"

Tessa hated that question. She'd heard it enough from her mother. "I haven't met the right man."

"You're what? Thirty-*six*?" He spat out her age as if it were something she should be ashamed of; he might as well have called her a spinster. "Weren't you hoping to find a husband when you signed up for Northwest Singles?"

"I was mostly open to finding men to go out with."

"In other words, you were trolling for men? Hunting?"

"Objection. Badgering the witness," Will said.

Judge Plodsker said, "Sustained."

"But you wanted to find attractive, impressive men, didn't you?" Warfield asked.

"I was just seeing how Northwest Singles might turn out."

"Of course. We understand." Warfield's exaggerated agreement let everybody know that he was ridiculing her. For Tessa, it set off a slow burn.

Hope must have felt the anger. She leaned against Tessa's calves and her eyes encouraged Tessa, *I understand. I care.*

"So you met Mr. Payne for a glass of wine, and you found him—what did you just tell the prosecutor—*interesting?* You agreed that you were impressed," Warfield said. "What was appealing about him?"

"He seemed nice."

"'Nice' is a lukewarm adjective, Ms. Jordan. Weren't you thrilled that an important man who was about to be elected to the San Julian City Council paid attention to you, a librarian?" Warfield said "librarian" as if Tessa were a mouse, brushing her whiskers against the baseboards of life.

"I was pleased to have met him," she said.

"When he invited you to his house the following week, were you"—Warfield cleared his throat—"*pleased* about that, too?"

"I wanted to get to know him better."

"Did you feel you'd accomplished that goal when you woke the next morning in Mr. Payne's bed?"

"That was *not* my goal! I didn't *want* to be in bed with him!" Tessa said too loudly. Immediately, she was sorry to have lost control. Warfield was playing with her, tormenting her, turning her words around, so she now believed the legal process was inherently ruthless. Too upset even for Hope's presence to calm her, she stiffened and wrapped an arm protectively around her waist.

"What did you say to Mr. Payne when you woke up beside him?"

"I can't remember. I just hurried into the bathroom and got dressed. I wanted to leave."

"Did Mr. Payne try to stop you from leaving?"

"No."

"Did that hurt your feelings?"

"No."

"Did you think he didn't care that you left?"

"Objection!" Will said. "Speculation. She can't have known what was in his mind."

"Sustained," Judge Plodsker said.

"Let me rephrase," Warfield said. "Ms. Jordan, did you worry that Mr. Payne had not enjoyed his night with you? Maybe the sex hadn't been all that great?"

You evil man! "I didn't know if he'd enjoyed it. I was drugged."

"Were you angry that Mr. Payne didn't want you to linger in his bed for more sex?"

"No."

"Did you leave his house to take care of your wounded feelings?"

"They weren't wounded. I just wanted to go."

Warfield paced toward the jury, turned around, paced back. "Ms. Jordan, let's return to your breakup with your ex-boyfriend a couple of years earlier. Who ended the relationship? You or him?"

"We both did. We agreed to split."

"Why?"

"We'd grown apart."

Warfield's raised eyebrow seemed to imply her reason was lame. "Which one of you wanted out of the engagement most?"

It's history. What difference does it make? "I guess he did," Tessa admitted.

"Were you hurt about that? Did you feel rejected?"

"No . . . well, yes. Maybe a little at the time."

Warfield looked like he was trying to suppress a smile. "Ms. Jordan, when some women get dumped by a fiancé, they seek revenge. Some women hang onto the rejection, nurse the grudge, and later overreact if they feel *any* man wrongs them. You think that describes you?"

"No!" Tessa fumed. *How dare you even suggest that?*

"Did the defendant's indifference to you that morning feel like another rejection?"

"No."

"Did you decide to get back at him?"

"I never thought about getting back at anybody. It was the last thing on my mind!"

"But you went to the police and claimed that Mr. Payne had drugged and raped you. That sounds to me like vengeance."

Will jumped to his feet. "Objection! Badgering."

"Sustained. What's your question, Warfield?" Judge Plodsker asked.

"Why did you go to the police, Ms. Jordan?"

"To report what the defendant had done."

"To report and make trouble for him? To ruin his chances to win the City Council election?"

"No!"

"How long did you wait before you went to the police with your *accusations*?"

"Two days."

Warfield's snort made clear that, to him, two days was like two years. "Why so *long*?"

"I wasn't sure what had happened. I needed time to get it clear in my mind."

"Some people might think you were figuring out how to pay him back for hurting you. Isn't it easier to play the victim than to be rejected?"

Tessa's hackles rose at the question. She knew how an animal felt, cornered by hateful boys who were poking it with sticks. Warfield had torn apart the mettle she relied upon to get her through hard times. She pressed her lips together to keep from lashing out at him, and petted Hope's head with urgent sweeps of her hand. "Look, I was just trying to remember what had happened."

"Yeah, sure."

"Yeah, SURE! No matter what I say, you try to make me

look bad!" Tessa shouted in fury. Trying to regain her composure, she squeezed her hands into fists. She was enraged at Warfield and mad at herself for letting him bait her into exactly what Will had warned her against. Now the jury would have no doubt: She was a nasty, angry woman. Desperate, she rubbed Hope's shoulder as intensely as someone rubs two sticks to get a spark.

The ends of Warfield's fat lips quivered slightly and turned up into a leer. In his eyes was glee.

Nick's eyes glittered with cold-blooded pleasure. They told Tessa, *You piece of trash. We've put you in your place.*

Will's eyes were despondent. Tessa felt guilty, sorry, dismayed. What if she'd lost the trial for him? Never mind that she'd been reinjured in the name of justice or that her modesty and honor had been trampled on. Today had been a judicial form of Sherman's March to the Sea, and she was Georgia, razed to the ground.

"That'll be all, Ms. Jordan," Warfield said.

CHAPTER 51

After a fifteen-minute recess, Judge Plodsker reconvened the court. All there would be time for this afternoon was Warfield's first witness. Will wanted to get this difficult day behind him so he could go home and lick his wounds. Maybe he'd have a couple of beers, try to get over the deplorable fact that Warfield had tanned his legal hide. Abbey Greenwood hadn't been the game changer he'd expected, and Tessa hadn't helped. In other words, as his boss, Bret Bailey, had threatened, from now on, Will would be prosecuting traffic violators.

Warfield stood at the defense table and buttoned his suit's coat as men do to look proper, a sharp contrast to his underhanded moves. He called Abbey Greenwood's ex-boyfriend, Martin Slipman, to the witness stand. Will could not see how an attractive woman like her had gotten together with a man who slouched to the front of the room, bent forward like a Neanderthal, a forest of chest hair growing from his open collar.

"Mr. Slipman, did you and Ms. Greenwood live together?" Warfield asked.

"Yes."

"When was that?"

When Slipman rubbed his chin, gazed at the ceiling, and mulled over the dates, his shaggy eyebrows may have partly blocked his view. "I'd say from about two thousand eight to two thousand ten."

"So about two years," Warfield said. "In that time, did you get to know Ms. Greenwood well?"

"Very well. We worked at the same place, so we were together almost every day, morning to night. Not that it was all that great."

A couple of titters traveled from the gallery to the witness stand. Warfield scowled.

"I'm not interested in exploring your relationship, Mr. Slipman," he said. "I want to know how aware you were of Ms. Greenwood's habits. For instance, can you tell us, did she sleep soundly?"

"No. She had real bad insomnia. I'd get up at three a.m. to go to the bathroom, and I'd find her reading in the living room because she couldn't sleep."

"So insomnia was a big problem for her?"

"Yes, and sometimes it made her grouchy as hell."

"Did she take medication for it?"

"Yes."

"Can you tell us what kind?"

"Ambien."

From the gallery floated murmurs and the surprised catching of breaths.

"How do you know the exact medication?" Warfield asked.

"We shared the same medicine cabinet. I saw the Ambien every time I got out my toothbrush."

"Yesterday I asked Ms. Greenwood if she ever took Ambien, and she said, 'Never.' Would that be true?"

"No. She *did* take it," Slipman insisted. "On plenty of

nights I saw her open the plastic container, shake an Ambien onto her palm, and swallow the pill."

"Thank you," Warfield said.

"Redirect, Mr. Armstrong?" Judge Plodsker pointed vaguely in Will's direction.

As he walked to the witness stand, Will thought, *You slime*. Normally, Abbey's prior use of Ambien would not have been considered relevant, but when she'd claimed she'd never taken it, Warfield had filed a motion to allow Slipman to testify. She'd opened a can of worms, and now Will had to get the worms back in and close it again. And Warfield was sitting there, smug, sure he had the trial sewn up.

"Mr. Slipman, you just testified that you and Ms. Greenwood lived together until two thousand ten. So you broke up about four years ago?"

"Yes. I don't know the exact date, but four years sounds about right. I still see her at work."

"In the last four years, has she ever mentioned taking Ambien?"

"No."

"So you have no knowledge that she continued using it after you quit living together?"

"Correct."

"You have no knowledge that she uses it now?"

"Correct."

"So if she told us yesterday that she never takes Ambien, could she have meant that she never takes it *now*?"

"It's possible, but she still has a major sleeping problem. Sometimes when she drags into the office, I can tell she hasn't slept more than a few hours."

"But you can't say whether she does or doesn't take Ambien now?"

"Correct."

"Thank you, Mr. Slipman."

"Mr. Warfield, do you have any questions for recross?" Judge Plodsker asked.

"No."

Grateful for this day to end, Will walked back to the prosecutor's table. He didn't see Tessa in the gallery—she must have hurried out to escape the pressure—but he did notice a woman in the back row. She was dressed in an unremarkable black down coat, and a black muffler hung from her neck. He was struck by her face, white as a cotton ball against the black. An eraser might have come down from the sky and rubbed away her skin's flesh tones.

She looks like how I feel, Will thought, as he wearily packed up his notes to leave.

CHAPTER 52

Tessa did not stay at the trial to see Warfield's first witness. She'd had enough of courtrooms for a lifetime. And why observe more when Warfield had won a resounding victory over her? And when the trial seemed like a wreck in the making? And when, once again, behind her anger had been helplessness and fear?

Will had watched her leave the witness stand, and the enigmatic expression on his face had also disconcerted her. At first, she'd thought he must be feeling disappointment, maybe even resentment. Hard as it was, she could live with those—and she might have earned them. But after a couple of hours' reflection, she felt certain that his look had been about neither of those things. It had been about pity, and that she could not bear. Being felt sorry for, especially by him, was a terrible thing to add to her guilt and shame.

But what could she do about it? What could she do about *anything*?

Too mentally jumbled to answer those questions, Tessa changed out of the clothes she'd worn to court and walked outside to clear her head. She went to her kale patch, which was just below her kitchen window and illuminated by her porch light.

The plants were scraggly and as beaten down by winter storms as Tessa felt by Warfield. But the plants had valiantly kept trying to grow and produce at this time of year. The kitties loved kale. Tessa would cut it fine and steam it with tuna for their supper. It helped her to focus on them instead of on her pain.

From each plant, Tessa snipped off only a leaf or two, taking care that enough remained for the kale not to feel abused. Her plants were her friends. She always talked with them, though tonight she was too shaken for a lengthy conversation. She told them only, "I've just had the second most terrible experience of my life."

Tessa believed that on a primitive level, they picked up her energy, which tonight radiated from her in tortured waves. And who knew? They might even feel some sort of empathy. She placed their leaves in her wicker basket and thanked the plants for their generosity.

When it started to rain, she hurried inside, wishing her survivors' group were meeting tonight or Emma would drop in with another pie.

CHAPTER 53

When Will walked out of the courtroom, he took the back stairs to the lobby so he wouldn't have to talk with anyone but Valentina, who'd be waiting to hand over Hope. He did not want to meet Warfield on this sorry afternoon, not after the man had found legal loopholes to spring Abbey's drug arrest and prior Ambien use on Will. Warfield was so confident about winning this case that he'd chosen not to risk Nick testifying. And Will had no rabbits to pull out of his hat. *Win some, lose some*, Will thought, but he had wanted not to lose in this trial. Exhausted, he felt like he'd placed last in a decathlon that afternoon.

In the lobby, Will found Valentina standing near the entrance, scrolling through her cell phone messages. She looked chipper, but Hope, standing by her feet, was slumping, and her ears were pressed back. Her tail hung down without a wag left in it. Tessa's emotions on the witness stand had worn her out.

Valentina looked up from her phone and smiled. "Your girl's had a hard day." She handed Will her end of Hope's leash.

"I'll play fetch with her in my living room." Hope's slobbery tennis ball was right up there with the yellow duck for cajoling her out of stress.

"Warfield's a bastard," Valentina said.

"No argument there."

"As soon as he was through with Tessa, she left here about to cry."

The news grieved Will. "I was worried about that."

"You nailed Warfield's last witness, though."

"It's kind of you to say, but I just introduced a reason for doubt. Jurors can choose which interpretation they want."

"You never know how things will shake out, Will. Don't lose hope."

"Yeah," Will said, glum as the rain that had been falling all day. The rain had stopped, but the autumn sky was bleak, and tires hissed on the asphalt. In the damp, the rays from the headlights of passing cars looked fuzzy.

Hope lifted her front right paw out of a dreaded puddle. When Will pulled up his trench coat's collar and led her across the wet street, she did not look pleased. Standing under a so-dium lamp just ahead of them was the same woman in black he'd noticed in the gallery. Her breath fogged in the cold as she dabbed a tissue at tears on her cheeks.

Hope clearly recognized the sign of need. Though damp and tired, she tugged on her leash and proclaimed to Will, *That woman needs help. I have to comfort her!*

Though trained not to pull, Hope tugged Will toward the woman. Mystified by Hope's urgency, he let himself be led. When she leaned against the woman's knees, she bent down and petted her. Tears hung on the woman's long, dark lashes.

"Are you all right?" Will asked.

"Oh, you know—or maybe you don't. I'm upset and con-fused."

"I saw a lot of that in court today," Will said, leaving her a chance to explain if she wished.

"I was there. I heard Tessa Jordan's testimony. I'm Eliza-beth Burgess." She fished in her purse, pulled out a business card, and handed it to Will. "My husband and I own the Ferndale Winery."

He glanced at the card. "I know where you are. Just off Madrona Road."

"That's us," she said. "All day, I've been trying to decide what to do."

"About what?"

"About letting you know I've met the defendant. He visited our tasting room several times."

Interesting, but why are you telling me this? "Nick Payne does seem to like wine."

"That's the thing. One afternoon last fall, he hung around when I was closing up. He said he'd brought a bottle of wine he wanted me to try. He was friendly. Charming. I thought, my husband's out of town. I don't have to rush home and make dinner. What the heck?" Elizabeth raked her fingers through her wavy hair. "I never dreamed Nick Payne would rape me."

As she poured out her story, her tissue disintegrated and left sodden white flecks under her eyes. She stuffed it into her coat pocket and pulled another tissue from her purse. Hope nosed Elizabeth's hand to volunteer for more therapeutic pets. *I'm here. I want to support you.* Elizabeth absently stroked Hope's ears.

Will said, "I'm sorry. None of that should have happened to you." Exhaling a heavy breath of disgust, he felt once again like punching Nick Payne senseless.

Elizabeth swallowed like she was trying to hold back more tears. "I've never told a living soul about this. Not my husband, not anybody. I didn't report it to the police."

"It would have helped us. I wish we'd known about you."

"Nobody knows, and it has to stay that way. I've been so ashamed."

"There's nothing to be ashamed about. He's a predator. You didn't do anything wrong," Will said.

"I didn't read the signals. I should never have let myself be alone after hours with him, but he seemed like a perfectly respectable man."

"That's what the other women thought. He had his act down pat, that's for sure."

"My story's just like Tessa's." Elizabeth blew her nose. "I've followed Nick's arrest and trial in the *Review*. Every day, I've thought I should talk with you, but I couldn't make myself do it."

"Everybody says it's hard to come forward."

"I'm *not* coming forward. I'd die before I'd take part in a trial."

Then why are you telling me all this? She'd raised Will's hope for getting Nick convicted after all. She might have been his trump card. But in Will's heart, hope gurgled down a drain as he watched Elizabeth rummage through her purse.

She dropped a thumb drive into his hand.

He folded his fingers around it. "What's on it?"

"Watch."

CHAPTER 54

After Tessa had left her cats' kale and tuna in Will's barn—and thank goodness, he'd not yet gotten home from court—she drove back to her cottage, free to rest at last. She felt like she'd been in combat all day. Body and soul, she ached. She wasn't sure she'd have the strength to go to work in the morning.

She was pondering what to eat for dinner when the phone rang, and once again, the caller ID revealed that Margaret Jordan was trying to reach her. Tessa did not want to answer. She'd not told her mother about the assault; making conversation while tiptoeing around that monumental incident had been a strain. Margaret was not the type in whom a daughter could confide. But all the way across the country, she'd suspected something was amiss, and since May, she'd asked Tessa repeatedly if anything was wrong.

On a day when so much was indeed wrong, Tessa was unsure that she could protect herself from her mother. She stared at the phone, prim in its cradle, yet capable of causing harm. A responsible daughter, however, she owed it to her mother—and to the memory of her father—to be available. Duty won out over hesitation. "Hi, Mother," she said.

"I've been leaving messages, but you haven't gotten back." Margaret sounded grumpy.

"Sorry. I've been super busy. I had to go to a bookmobile conference in Olympia. Too many complicated things going on at once."

A pause. A worrisome sign. Her mother was probably computing "complicated things" and deciding how hard to press to find out what they were.

"Tessa, I don't believe you've been so busy at work. I can tell something's the matter. I've heard it in your voice for a long time."

"Nothing's the matter. I'm fine."

"Have you broken up with somebody?"

"No." *There may never* be *another "somebody."*

"I'm your mother. What's going on? I can tell when you're upset."

Tessa sank into her Bentwood rocker next to the fire in her wood-burning stove. She rested her elbow on the arm to prop herself up and stared at her father's photo on her desk. In the months after his death, she'd hidden him in a drawer because looking at him stirred up too much grief. But in the last few weeks, she'd taken him out again because she badly needed him. Tonight she'd have given anything to talk with *him* instead of her pushy mother.

Margaret kept insisting, "What's wrong? You can tell me. I know something's bothering you."

Tessa felt like a sapling facing down a bulldozer. She was sick of people running over her. Nick. Warfield. Now her own mother. It was all too much. She didn't feel like squelching her pent-up anger anymore.

"Okay, Mother, you want to know what's wrong? I'll tell you. I've been attending the trial of a man accused of sexual assault."

"Why were *you* there, for Pete's sake?"

"Because I'm one of the women he raped."

Tessa heard a gasp. She could picture her mother's face and neck turning red as her blood pressure inevitably rose. Margaret had asked for it. Tessa hadn't wanted to tell her.

Margaret sputtered, "How did you let that happen?"

How could *you, Mother? As if I haven't already blamed myself enough!* Tessa needed an ally, not another defense attorney's attack. "I didn't *let* anything happen. I got drugged on a date. I had no way to fight back."

"Who was the man? Did you know his family?" What family someone came from was paramount in the small town where Margaret lived.

"No, I didn't know them."

"How in heaven's name did you meet an awful person like that?"

"Online."

"Oh, Tessa, no. You mean one of those dating things? We were talking about them at bridge club last week."

"It was a website. Plenty of decent people find perfectly good dates online these days, Mother. I just had bad luck."

"It's worse than bad luck. How could he have drugged you?"

"He put something in my wine."

"Where were you?"

"At his house."

"You didn't have enough sense to stay away from that man's house? You didn't know his family!"

When her mother's inquisition finally wound down, Tessa felt like a rag wrung out and wiped across a filthy floor. She'd never missed her father so much. Grief over his death seemed greater than ever, now that she was so angry at her mother. Louann might say Tessa's anger masked shame; from clear across the country, Margaret Jordan's shaming finger had shrunk Tessa to a moral miniature of herself—a failure, a disgrace.

"You've got to come home for Christmas," Margaret insisted.

No way in hell. "We'll see."

After Tessa hung up, she climbed into bed with her clothes on.

CHAPTER 55

After playing fetch and feeding Hope, Will opened a beer and went to his computer. Usually, Hope padded along behind him and curled up at his feet, but tonight she needed time to unwind. She poked her nose around in her toy basket and found her yellow duck, then disappeared. Later, Will would find her, conked out on his bed in her super-sprawl position, the duck between her front paws.

Will booted up his computer and worked the thumb drive into the USB port. When the drive's icon showed up on his desktop, he clicked and opened the only available file. Elizabeth Burgess and Nick Payne appeared on his screen. *Wow!* Though he wasn't sure exactly what he'd expected, they hadn't been it. He leaned forward for a closer look.

Nick and Elizabeth were sitting on opposite ends of a sleek brown leather sofa, talking, smiling, underscoring bits of their animated conversation with sweeps of their hands through the air. In front of them was a low table, covered with wine magazines. Behind the sofa at the end of the room was a bar with chairs and a counter, at which Elizabeth must have poured tastes of Ferndale wine and collected payments for bottles of it lined up along one wall. Along the other wall were framed poster-sized photos of vineyards with luscious clusters of ripe grapes, about to be plucked from the vines.

So this is Ferndale's tasting room. Will had driven by it countless times but never gone inside. A security camera must be hidden behind one of the dark oak beams, set Tudor style across the white plaster ceiling. Nick hadn't noticed that his every move was being recorded.

He seemed to enjoy Elizabeth. Relaxing against a plum-colored pillow, he took stock of her every move. And she did move. She laughed, clapped her hands together, and bent toward him, a flirtatious distance away. It was not a seduction, but it may have been something Elizabeth would rather her husband not see.

A few minutes later, Nick got up and took the glass from her hand. He walked behind her down the long room to the bar. On it was a carrying case, from which he took two open wine bottles. He poured from each into a different glass and returned Elizabeth's to her. As he took his seat, he brushed his fingertips across her shoulder.

Will felt like a voyeur. They'd done nothing untoward, but he feared what was coming, and he felt squeamish watching. Elizabeth kept sipping, and Nick kept observing. As they continued talking, she yawned, and her eyelids began to sag. When only a swallow was left inside her glass, she put it down and leaned back into the sofa again. She started to speak, then stopped as if words were too hard. She closed her eyes, and Nick sprang to life.

Oh, man. Will hated what was about to happen to Elizabeth. If only he could have warned her.

Nick stood, looked down into Elizabeth's face, seemed to study her for signs of consciousness. He shook her shoulder, perhaps to see if she'd wake. It was as if he'd shaken a rag doll, no bones, her body floppy and relaxed. Smiling, Nick sat next to her and began unbuttoning her blouse . . .

Will heard, "Hey, big brother, I've brought you some en-chiladas! You forget to eat when you have a trial." Maria let herself in the front door.

Nobody had to tell Hope that company had arrived. Will heard her barrel down the stairs. *A visitor! A visitor!* Hope loved guests almost as much as her yellow duck.

Will called out, "Maria, can you wait a minute? I have to finish something."

"No problemo. I'll turn on the oven. Hope and I can have a chat."

Will thought that his sister's arrival might be a good thing. He hadn't relished watching porn all evening, but he did have to know what was on the video before he fought to show it to the jury. He set the video on fast-forward, the quicker to get through what he was sure Nick was going to do.

Even when Nick ripping off Elizabeth's skirt was sped into a blur, Will wanted to shout at him to stop. It appeared that Nick was taking no pleasure in what he was doing. *It's more about dominance than satisfaction.* Maybe in Nick's warped mind, Elizabeth was a substitute for a woman he wanted to punish—perhaps a fiancée who'd broken their engagement and set him on a path of violence, a sexual-assault version of the Golden State Killer.

Will tried to detach himself and take a purely professional stance, but Nick resurrected his anger at the football star who'd assaulted Maria—and it was worse when, at that very moment, she was rummaging around in the kitchen. Will could not mentally disconnect, and his loathing intensified when Nick finally finished, pulled up his pants, and fastened his belt, visibly indifferent to the trauma he'd inflicted.

Without a backward glance, Nick left Elizabeth on her back, deep in a drugged sleep, her skirt askew, her panties on the floor. Her mouth hung open, and her arm flopped off the sofa. He strutted over to the bar like a cock at sunrise and set his wine bottles back into the carrier, along with Ferndale's glasses that he and Elizabeth had just used. If she woke and went to the police, he would rely on his sure-fire MO and claim that their encounter, if it could be called that, was consensual. He walked out the door.

"You snake," Will muttered. "By God, we're going to get you."

"I can't wait all night. You done?" Maria asked as she came into Will's study with Hope trailing behind her.

Unclenching his teeth, Will shut down his computer and rose from his chair.

"What's the matter?" Maria asked.

"A video. It's connected to my trial. It was disgusting."

"Why?"

How much should he tell her? It could dredge up her worst memory, but Will needed to explain. "I just watched a sexual assault. At least, I had the video on fast forward. I got through it quickly."

Maria's face looked like she'd just bitten into a lemon. "I've been reading about Nick Payne's trial. You think he's guilty?"

"No question about it. And now I've got him in a video assaulting another woman the jury hasn't heard of yet. I hope to God the judge will rule it admissible."

"I hope so, too, for the sake of the victims."

"I'm counting on your sisterly discretion. Don't talk about it with anyone."

"You know I won't," Maria said. "Let's go get you an enchilada." She led Will back to the kitchen, where she'd set a single place.

"You're not having any?" He pulled out his chair.

"I already ate." Hope's nostrils quivered at the delicious smells emanating from the pan Maria took from the oven.

"You know, I'm proud of you going after those despicable men."

"Somebody has to do it."

"It takes a lot of determination." Maria set the pan on the tiled kitchen counter and took a spatula from the drawer. She held it in the air for a moment before speaking quietly. "I wish I'd gone to the police and turned in the evil thug who raped me. I should have had the courage to do it."

Will was surprised to hear her say so. She'd been so adamant for so long. "Don't beat yourself up. You did the best you could at the time."

"I should have been stronger." Maria dug the spatula around three enchiladas and set them on one of Will's scruffy-looking thrift-store plates. "It took me a long time to get back my confidence. Four years ago, I did write him a scathing letter."

Another surprise. "You never told me."

"I wanted to send it off and forget it."

"Did you ever hear from him?" Will knew Louann recommended letters—sent or not.

"No. I didn't expect anything. I figured he wouldn't have the decency to apologize." Maria set the plate in front of Will. "Getting a response wasn't the point of writing him, anyway. I just wanted to put my feelings out there. Maybe someday he'll be sorry, but I'm not holding my breath."

"I wish he'd rot in hell."

"I do, too, but anger doesn't help anything. It was hurting me, not him."

Will took a grateful bite. "I hate for you to carry around the trauma." He looked at her and noticed Hope watching them closely.

Maria flicked her wrist as if she were shooing away the whole miserable experience. "I'll never get totally over it, but time and therapy have helped. And trying to make as many happy memories as I can to reduce the power of what happened." Maria brushed crumbs from Will's breakfast toast off the table. "You don't have to worry about me. Actually, I worry about *you*."

"No reason for you to worry about me. And by the way, these enchiladas are great."

"You look a little thin. You probably haven't eaten all week. That's the kind of thing that bothers me." Maria got up and went to the refrigerator, which contained little more than milk for Will's coffee and a couple of white cardboard takeout containers of ancient Chinese food. "Want another beer?"

"Okay."

She got out two and opened them. As she sat back down, she handed one to Will and kept one for herself. "I worry that you're working yourself into an early grave. And you'll land in it without ever having lived a full life. *That* gives me more pain these days than my thoughts about the high school jerk."

"I have a great life," Will protested. Yet as he spoke, doubt cracked his certainty. For years, Maria had been lecturing him about working too hard, but she'd always talked in terms of what it was doing to his health. She'd never tied it to keeping him from a full life.

"There's so much you're missing," she said. "Getting married and starting a family has given me joy I didn't think I could feel after what happened to me. I want you to have joy like that. It's your turn."

"Easier said than done."

"Not necessarily. You just have to be open to it. Joy will come and find you if you let it."

Will thought about that when he finally climbed into bed at midnight, drained from long, hard, demanding days. Alone in the dark, he admitted to himself that there was more to life than his job. No doubt about it—he wished he had that "more."

Hope snored softly next to him, her head on her own pillow. Wondering how a wife would feel about sharing the bed with Hope, he stretched his arm across her and felt the rising and falling of her chest as she breathed.

CHAPTER 56

Tessa slouched in her gallery seat and pulled her crocheted hat down over her brows. To further disguise herself, she wore her reading glasses and a baggy coat over her jeans. She hoped no one would recognize her, the angry woman who'd lost control on the stand last week and handed her assailant a free pass out of jail. Even now, six days later, she burned with humiliation at her lamentable performance. It didn't make her feel better that Warfield had doubtless left plenty of victims like her in his wake.

Hope was napping, her head in Tessa's lap, and to pass the time, Valentina was answering email messages. Though it had been snowing when Tessa arrived, the courtroom was hot and steamy. Spectators were crammed together, every seat in the gallery filled. Tension was palpable.

Tessa had told herself that snorting bison could not drag her back to this place. But early that morning, Valentina had called and painted the last few trial days with a broad brush for her and urged her to come for the verdict, which would be given at eleven. Surprised the jury had reached it after only a day of deliberation, Tessa had concluded that deciding on Nick's innocence must have been a no-brainer for them.

She'd insisted, "I don't want to be there when Nick Payne is acquitted."

"He might not be," Valentina said. "Will mentioned a video he fought like mad to get admitted as evidence. The jury finally saw it. Will thought it could help."

Nothing could help. "Will Abbey Greenwood be there?"

"She's in Denver."

"I'm supposed to go to Downhill, Washington in a little while."

"Couldn't you take off work? It might help you to see this trial to its end," Valentina argued.

"Why go hear bad news?"

"It might not *be* bad."

Tessa had not entirely bought that possibility, but reluctantly, she'd taken a sick-leave day.

Now, as she waited and Valentina typed text messages with her thumbs, Tessa glanced around the courtroom. The judge's bench and jury box were empty. Will was shuffling through papers at the prosecutor's table, and Warfield was thrumming his fat fingers on the defense's table. Nick, his shoulders squared, looked like he might be doodling on a yellow legal pad. Tessa hoped that was a sign of nerves.

For comfort, she petted Hope, who opened an eye and, finding nothing amiss, went back to sleep. A few minutes later, the bailiff entered through a side door and strode into the courtroom. Standing in front of the flags, he boomed, "All rise" in his baritone voice, which woke Hope again. Judge Plodsker trundled to his bench, his robe fluttering around him. Silently, the jury filed in, and the courtroom's tension thickened.

Without looking at Will, Warfield, or Nick, the jurors seemed to have drawn into themselves. Their gaze went to the floor, or to their hands folded on their laps, or to some vague vanishing point in the courtroom's corner. By refusing to meet anybody's eyes, perhaps the jurors wanted to be inscrutable, their faces a tabula rasa on which could be written anything. Tessa searched them for signs of what was about to be revealed, but she saw no hint of it.

"Have you reached a verdict?" Judge Plodsker asked the jury foreman, a tall, angular man with a scarecrow physique.

"We have, Your Honor." He handed a piece of paper, folded into a square, to the matronly clerk, who brought it to Judge Plodsker.

Judge Plodsker opened the verdict, read it, and, like the jury, showed no reaction. The verdict might as well have been the ingredients that nobody reads on a cereal box. He refolded the paper and handed it back to the clerk, who returned it to the foreman. "How do you find the defendant, sir?" Judge Plodsker asked.

Tessa braced herself. *Get it over with.* As Valentina put a reassuring hand on Tessa's arm, she hung onto Hope.

Looking solemn, the foreman took rimless glasses from his jacket's pocket and fitted the temple tips behind his ears. He coughed. *Hack, hack.* He took a handkerchief from his coat pocket and wiped his forehead. Slowly, he unfolded the verdict. The courtroom was so quiet that spectators could hear his paper crinkle.

"On count one of rape in the second degree," he began, "we find the defendant Nicholas Payne . . ." The foreman ran his fingers through his remaining wisp of hair. *Hack, hack.* "We find the defendant Nicholas Payne . . . guilty."

Murmurs flew around the courtroom. People glanced at each other as Tessa's pounding heart skidded to her throat. A jowly man in the seat ahead of her whispered to the woman next to him, "Guilty on both counts? Or just one?" Tessa stopped breathing while she waited for the answer.

Plodsker tapped his gavel on the bench, and the foreman waited for silence. He began again. "On count two of rape in the second degree, we find the defendant Nicholas Payne . . ." The foreman cleared his throat. *Ahem.* "Guilty."

CHAPTER 57

Will may have decided long ago to keep a professional distance from Tessa, but when her yellow VW zoomed down the drive through his field, he had to fight himself from going out and hugging her. Before his eyes in court this afternoon, the guilty verdict had changed her. In tears, she'd fallen into Valentina's arms and buried her face in Hope's neck. When Tessa had waved to him, her smile could have lit up Seattle for a week.

Along with the pleasure of knowing Nick Payne was going to bide his time in a prison cell, Tessa's smile had been Will's biggest reward for the work and worry he'd put into the case. When he'd called Abbey Greenwood and Elizabeth Burgess, they'd been happy about the verdict, but nothing like Tessa. Will hoped it would help her get over the havoc that Nick Payne had wreaked in her life.

Tessa parked and got out of her car with a wicker picnic basket. When she walked into the barn, even her posture had changed. A new confidence seemed to have replaced her beaten-dog bearing. She stood up straighter and pushed back her shoulders. Her movements seemed lighter, freer.

As Will watched from his kitchen window, he longed to talk with her. He called Hope, and they crossed the yard and found her spooning the cats' supper into their tins. The instant the seven ferals saw him, they vanished through the open door—and *poof!* No cats!

"We did it!" Will told Tessa. *Forget hello.*

"I know!" Smiling broadly, she stood up and started toward him like she wanted to hug him, too. But seeming to think better of it, she stopped and preserved their usual distance. "I was afraid my anger ruined everything. I felt awful. I couldn't get myself to apologize to you."

"No need for that. The jury saw you're human—and Warfield's a bully."

That smile again. It's who Tessa must have been before Nick.

She set her plastic container on Will's workbench. The whole barn smelled of fish. "Valentina mentioned a video. What was that about?"

"It was from a security camera. It recorded Nick Payne sexually assaulting another woman."

"There were *three* of us?"

"And probably others we don't know about. He's a serial rapist. The video was the next best thing to a confession."

"Wow." Tessa pulled at the striped muffler hanging around her neck. " 'Thank you' doesn't seem like enough for all you did."

"It's my job." Will did not mention he'd wanted to win partly for her sake. "No big deal."

"It's a huge deal for me."

It was Will's turn to smile. He looked around for Hope—who, he only now noticed, had gone off with the cats. Clearly, he'd gotten carried away by joy about the verdict. He didn't want to eat alone on such a happy night. "All I've got in the house are a couple of moldy enchiladas," he said. "I was about to go for a pizza. Want to come along and celebrate Nick Payne behind bars?"

The question seemed to flip a switch inside Tessa. Her

smile lost its curve, and in her forehead, anxious furrows re-appeared. The sudden shift startled Will. She could turn on a dime. He regretted asking her to go for the damned pizza—maybe it had been a momentary lapse of judgment—but he was too far in it now to back out. He folded his arms across his chest and fumbled to recover.

"Look. Don't take my invitation the wrong way. I'm not, um, coming onto you. I'm talking a spontaneous pizza, not a date. Just a quick dinner between two acquaintances." He'd almost said "friends," but that may have spooked her, too.

The dime turned again. Tessa's face softened. "Pizza sounds good."

Let's hope we get through it without me accidentally terrorizing you. "Okay. Let's go."

Say Cheese was located in a small white row house, built in 1902, according to a framed sign beside the door. Like Will's farmhouse, this one seemed to slump on its foundation, as if weary after all those years. Except for two women rapt in conversation, the place was empty on the weeknight. As Will led Tessa through the main dining area, the floorboards creaked under their footsteps.

He walked to a small square table, covered with a red-and-white checked cloth, in a corner toward the back. "This okay?"

"Fine." Tessa pulled out her own chair, as if to remind him that this was *not* a date.

Will took the seat across the table instead of next to her, to remind her that he didn't consider it a date, either. He handed her a menu and opened his own. She chose a small Big Cheesy with mozzarella, provolone, and Parmesan, and he settled on a medium Pizza My Heart, heavy on sausage, pepperoni, and mushrooms.

The waiter, whose apron looked like he'd been at war

with an army of tomatoes, took their pizza order, then asked, "Beer? House wine? Soft drink?"

Will asked Tessa, "Wine? The merlot is fairly decent here."

Her flinch reminded him that Nick had served red wine. Anguish appeared in the outside corners of her eyes. Will backtracked. "How about a beer or coke? Or we could have some chardonnay."

"Chardonnay," she agreed.

Will looked up at the waiter. "A carafe of that."

After a final flourish of the pencil on his small white pad, the waiter disappeared into the kitchen.

"Sorry I suggested merlot. I wasn't thinking," Will said.

Tessa looked down at the tabletop. "Red wine is what Louann calls a trigger. Some little thing can distress me, even if I don't mean for it to."

"It'll take time," Will said. "Eventually, you won't be mired in all that's happened."

Tessa's eyebrows moved toward each other in a frown. "I'm not *mired*! You make it sound like I'm wallowing in my misfortune. It's not like that. I'm trying with everything I've got to move on."

Will raised his palm toward her, a gesture implying peace. "Poor word choice. I understand. Really."

"You can't understand what it's like to be raped. You don't know how hard it is for a woman to—"

The waiter interrupted by setting the table and pouring the wine. Will felt like the celebratory evening he'd intended was slipping through his fingers and falling into his lap. When the waiter walked away, Will couldn't decide if he should change the subject or pick up where they'd left off.

Finally, he said, "I admit I don't know how hard it is for you because I'm not a woman who's been through it. What I do know is that it's hard on a man who cares about her."

"What do you mean?"

"A high school punk sexually assaulted my sister, Maria."
Will took a swallow of wine. "I wanted to kill that kid. Liter-
ally. If murder were legal, I'd have done it in a heartbeat. But
I couldn't. The best I could do was try to comfort her."

Will stopped and searched Tessa's face for signs of her reaction. Perhaps he'd been too honest. Maybe she didn't want
to hear about another woman's rape when she was trying to
recover from her own. "I hope I haven't distressed you."

"No. No . . . I've never thought about assault from a man's
point of view—a sympathetic man's."

"If a man loves a woman who's gone through what you
have, he's . . . perturbed at the very least, I promise you. I still
get upset thinking about it."

"Has Maria recovered?"

"Yes, as much as any woman can, but it took her a few
years to work through the trauma. She's married and has two
kids now. She'll never forget what happened, and it probably
changed her forever in some ways. But she's learned to work
around it. She's made a good life for herself."

"I can't imagine doing that."

"Didn't Hemingway say you get strong in the broken
places?" Will asked.

"Yes, but it seems impossible right now."

Tessa looked vulnerable again. Will wanted to reach over
and cover her folded hands with his and reassure her. But he
was afraid he might frighten her another time. "I know I can't
speak for you, but I'm sure you'll find peace someday."

"I hope."

The waiter arrived bearing two pizzas parallel to his
shoulders, like shot puts he was about to rest against his neck
and hurl. He set them between Will and Tessa. "You want
Parmesan? Hot pepper flakes?"

Will looked at Tessa to see if she was interested. She shook
her head. Will said, "Thanks. Just the pizzas are fine."

Unburdened from them, the waiter said, "Buon appetito,"
and passed through the swinging door back into the kitchen.
With cheese stringing from the slices Will and Tessa pulled
from their respective pies, they started to eat. Tessa was re-
fined about it, cutting bite-sized pieces with her knife and
fork and dabbing grease off her fingertips onto her napkin.
Will dug in with gusto like Hope attacked a Puppuccino.
Holding his slice in one hand, he chomped lusty mouthfuls
and washed them down with eager gulps of wine.

"We should have had a toast to celebrate the verdict." After he wiped his mouth and raised his glass, she lifted hers to
his and clinked. "Here's to Nick Payne in the pen," he said.

"I like the sound of that!"

Tessa's eyes shone. She was beaming as if someone had
flipped a switch inside her again. Will thought how pretty she
looked when she was happy. Still, it was a challenge always to
be careful. He felt like he was walking a razor's edge.

He cleared his throat, knowing he was about to risk upset-
ting Tessa again. "Now that we have a guilty verdict, Judge
Plodsker needs to decide Nick's punishment," Will began.
"In a week or two, there'll be a sentencing hearing. It would
help if you wrote a letter for it."

"What would I say?"

"You could address it to Nick and tell him what you've
been through. You know, the physical and emotional hardship, your feelings about what he did," Will said. "Do you
think you could do that? It doesn't have to be long or complicated. It could be just a page."

"I tried to write him a while back, but I couldn't get the
words out."

"Could you try again? Nick would read it and maybe admit to himself what a sicko he is. Judge Plodsker would see
the price you've paid. Your letter would also counter the ones
Warfield might get from Nick's friends about his 'sterling

character.' You could help persuade Judge Plodsker to throw the book at him."

Tessa said nothing. She stared at her pizza, the cheese cooling into a solid layer. *Did I upset her again?*

"You don't have to write the letter, but it would help." *Come on, Tessa. Say you will.*

CHAPTER 58

Home from her evening with Will, Tessa booted up her computer to write the letter he requested. At first, she wasn't sure she was brave enough to stand up to Nick—not with Warfield behind him—but she resolved that, no matter the stress, she would tell him how she felt.

Her memory of Nick's reaction to the verdict would stay with her forever. Even his back to her showed his devastation. At *guilty*, he flinched like he'd been shot. Then he froze like a block of ice and one tap on his shoulder would splinter him into a thousand shards. He bowed his head and covered his face with his hands. Warfield had not been able to save him. At last, he would get what he deserved.

Now, instead of being Nick's victim, Tessa would claim her hard-won role as victor. She would write her letter and count on Judge Plodsker to do the rest. The key for her was setting the right tone—being measured and assertive without whining, blasting him, or rambling on. She would be brief, to the point. She would keep her cool better than she had in court.

With a solemn formality, she raised her hands to the keyboard and began.

To Nick Payne:

Now that you've been found guilty, you may pity yourself and believe the verdict was unfair. After all, in your warped mind you probably think that all you did was have sex with me—a minor matter. Who cares about consent? Why all the fuss?

But let me tell you, the fuss is because what you did completely upset my life. It wasn't just that hideous night, which will revolt me forever. It was also what came afterwards—the hours of explaining what had happened, the invasive forensic exam, my long fight for justice, and a second assault at the hands of Mr. Warfield in the ordeal of your trial.

Mr. Warfield tried to make me out as a liar, a desperate spinster, a slut. He suggested that I falsely reported your crime to retaliate for your supposed rejection of me. In front of a crowd, he made me relive the most shattering and humiliating experience of my life while you sat there, smirking, showing not a sliver of remorse, and feigning innocence.

But I now know that you carefully planned assaulting me, and I walked into your ambush. You manipulated me into trusting you, the biggest mistake of my life. You drugged me so I was defenseless, and you raped me— and after I went to the police, you tried to bully me into retracting my accusation. Yet I was determined to get you. It was my duty to myself and to other women you might assault. I refused to let you intimidate me or stifle my voice.

For all you did, you should go to prison, sit in your cell for years, and reflect on your sadistic and criminal behavior. I hope you think about how much you've lost, and you remember your fall from grace, and you come to understand that you deserve it. Maybe you will also suffer some of the pain you have caused others, including me.

Because of you, I will never be free of my terrible
memories or my injuries from your assault. You may think
they were only to my body, but they were also to my mind
and spirit. You wounded my confidence, dignity, and self-
worth. You made me lose my sense of safety and my trust in
life. You cost me months of time and energy and countless
nights of sleep.

But I will not allow you to cost me my future or define
who I am. I will not let you destroy me, and I will not
waste my life hating you because you are not worth the
effort. Still, while you sit wasting your life in prison, I will
take comfort in knowing that I helped put you there. And
I intend to heal and move on. My greatest wish is that you
will get what you deserve: to be locked behind bars for many,
many years.

When Tessa printed her letter, she was sweating from the
emotions that writing Nick had stirred in her. In order to put
down her thoughts calmly, she'd kept her fury in check. De-
spite the verdict and insights from her survivors' group, anger
could still leap out and overwhelm her sometimes—and it
probably always would.

Still, the thought of Nick serving time soothed Tessa. It
was a perfect antidote to rage. She wondered just how many
years Nick would be sentenced to prison. Of course, she expected it to be a very long time, but exactly *how* long?

To find out, she Googled "sentence for rape in Washington State." She clicked on a government website and read
definitions for legal degrees of rape. First-degree required
the assailant to have used a weapon, kidnapped the victim,
or caused serious injury. In second-degree, which had been
Nick's charge, the victim had to be rendered physically helpless or mentally incapacitated—just as she had been with his
Ambien.

Farther down on the website was a sentencing grid, which suggested a complicated range of possibilities for a single second-degree rape. They hinged on the offender's score on such things as prior convictions and length of time between crimes. The higher his score, the longer his sentence.

As far as Tessa could figure, the average for a second-degree rape ranged from seven years and six months to twenty years and five months, give or take a little time. If she doubled those estimates for Nick's two counts, he could be in prison for fifteen to almost forty-one years!

For Tessa, fifteen would not be enough. Nick's actions should earn him a high offender's score, and fairness to her and Abbey also required Judge Plodsker to give him a longer sentence. Though Tessa usually wished the best for people, she wanted Nick to be eighty by the time he was released from prison, and that would mean forty years of nasty food, no wine, a mere one hour out of his cell each afternoon. Perhaps turnabout would be fair play, and inmates would sexually assault *him*.

Justice at last! The prospect cheered her.

CHAPTER 59

A pine with silver balls and tinsel hanging from its branches in the lobby had suggested that Christmas was coming, but the holidays were the last thing on Tessa's mind. Since she'd written her letter to Nick, thoughts of his sentence had hounded her. Now that she, Valentina, and Hope were sitting in the gallery to hear Judge Plodsker pronounce his sentence, she was obsessing.

"Want a mint?" Valentina whispered.

"Thanks." Tessa popped it into her mouth. The mint was something sweet to counter her burning stomach. Hope's soft ears and most loving I-am-here expression were not enough to displace the strain of suspense.

Perhaps Abbey Greenwood had been wise to stay home, but nothing could have stopped Tessa from attending today. Every gallery seat was taken, and people were standing outside in the hall. Will, turned slightly in his chair toward Nick and Warfield, draped his arm over the prosecutor's table so his hand dangled from the edge.

Judge Plodsker peered down at Nick over his half-glasses. "Before you receive your sentence, Mr. Payne, do you have anything to say?"

When Nick stood to speak, even from behind him, Tessa

was shocked at his appearance. He must not have eaten since the guilty verdict. He seemed to have shrunk; his rumpled suit's coat bagged on him. He hunched his shoulders forward as if to protect his heart.

He glanced at an index card from his coat pocket, then looked up at Judge Plodsker. "Your Honor, I'd like to apologize. I didn't consider the impact of my actions, and I made poor choices, which I regret. I wish I could live this year over again without hurting anyone. I'm sorry for any pain I caused the victims and their families."

You don't seem very sorry, you jerk, and you wouldn't regret your choices if you hadn't been caught. Tessa ran cold fingers through Hope's fur.

"I believe my attorney has informed you that I acknowledge having a sex addiction," Nick continued. "To help me overcome it, I've attended an evening program this last month. I will never hurt anyone again. You have my word."

Your word is worth nothing. And, by the way, a sex addiction is a sorry excuse for your crimes. Nick's feigned remorse had the resonance of tin. With disgust, Tessa watched him take his seat again.

"Thank you, Mr. Payne," Judge Plodsker said. "We appreciate your apology. It's important."

The judge sipped water from a glass. Addressing the courtroom assembly, he said, "I've reviewed all the sentencing memoranda, including letters condemning and supporting the defendant. One victim wrote to Mr. Payne—and I'll read—'Your assault was not just on my body. It was on my confidence, my self-worth, my dignity, my sense of safety, my hope.' Another victim pointed out, 'I never expect to recover. The trauma runs too deep to heal.'"

Judge Plodsker aimed his gaze at Nick and raised his index finger. "Those are compelling words, sir. It's clear to me that you caused grave physical and emotional injury and long-lasting pain."

Tessa scoffed when Nick hung his head and Warfield set his hand on Nick's shoulder as if to comfort him. *The hypocrites!*

Judge Plodsker continued, "There clearly is another side to you, however, Mr. Payne. I note that in the past, you had a respectable academic career, and you served your college and community well. You also had an unblemished record and no history of misconduct or convictions for previous crimes. I believe that your proactive measures for rehabilitation are sincere."

Tessa whispered to Valentina, "Judge Plodsker can't really believe that!" Valentina shrugged like she didn't know.

Judge Plodsker took off his glasses. "These mitigating factors lead me to hope that in prison, you will respond well to counseling and the prescribed treatment for sex offenders, and once released, your risk of re-offending could be less. However, because of your crimes' seriousness, I will require you upon release to register as a sex offender."

Valentina whispered, "The sex offender thing is *great!* It'll ruin his life."

Everyone else in the gallery was whispering, too. Looking impatient at the disruption, Judge Plodsker slammed his gavel on the bench. "Quiet. Order in the court!"

When silence resumed, Judge Plodsker stared down at Nick again. "Mr. Payne, correcting your attitude is only part of what's needed in your case. You must also make restitution to the women you've harmed, and that requires punishment in the form of a prison sentence. I've weighed your mitigating factors when determining the length of time you should serve.

"On count one for second-degree sexual assault, I sentence you to seventy-eight months in prison. On count two for second-degree sexual assault, I sentence you to seventy-eight months in prison."

Tessa's mouth dropped open. Remembering her calculations, she knew the sentences added up to less than fifteen years.

Judge Plodsker continued, "These sentences will run concurrently."

That can't be! A total *of seventy-eight months?*

Judge Plodsker told Nick, "I wish you luck and productive years of reflection and rehabilitation." He tapped his gavel on the bench. "This court is adjourned."

As excited conversations started up around her, Tessa yanked a pen and pad out of her purse and quickly figured that Nick would serve only six years and six months. Stunned, she told Valentina, "That's just three years and three months *each* for Abbey Greenwood and me."

"It's the shortest possible sentence," Valentina said.

"It's wrong!"

Tessa watched a sheriff's deputy pull Nick to his feet, handcuff him, and start toward the exit. When Nick turned back to say one last thing to Warfield, Tessa got a glimpse of his face. It was the cold gray of a winter sky. Deep creases marked his cheeks. His eyes showed a wolf's fear when a trap's steel teeth have bitten through its paw; like the wolf, Nick knew he couldn't free himself.

That should have given Tessa satisfaction, but she was too shocked to feel anything. THE LAW HATES WRONG, in the plaster above the courthouse entrance, flashed through her mind. It was a lie. The law didn't hate the wrong done to her at all.

CHAPTER 60

On the courthouse steps, Will grinned over a forest of micro-phones at cameras and reporters. He never expected so many to turn out today. From Seattle and all over the county, they testified to just how much interest Nick Payne's sentence had attracted. It felt so good to stand here and claim success.

Just before Will had taken his place at the microphones, he'd seen Warfield grousing about the verdict to the news crews. That had felt good, too.

"Today is a great day. There's much to celebrate," Will told the crowd. "Nick Payne has received a just sentence, and his two sexual assault victims will now see him locked up in prison for years. Achieving that victory has been hard, but we've prevailed because the women were brave enough to come forward and confront Mr. Payne in court. They give hope to other assault victims that justice is possible. A crimi-nal is getting his due."

"Will Warfield appeal?" asked a reporter in a black trench coat.

"It would be wasted effort. Warfield knows it's a lost cause. The evidence we brought forth proves Mr. Payne is a rapist—and even Warfield couldn't get him out of it!"

As Will fielded a few more questions, Tessa crossed his

mind. Surely, she'd be pleased with Nick's sentence, he thought. But after the press cleared out and he saw her coming down the courthouse steps, he knew something was wrong. Tessa's eyes met his, and she paused as if she were trying to decide if she should hurry away in the opposite direction. But then she must have chosen to continue toward him.

Valentina, who was with her, let Hope loose, and she bounded down the steps to Will. Careful to keep her wet paws off his trench coat, he stooped down and petted her as she whimpered with joy at their reunion.

"Congratulations, Will!" Valentina said as they caught up. "Great job!"

"That's good to hear," Will said with a smile of triumph. "Nick Payne will cool his heels behind bars for a while."

"Not for long enough," Tessa said, flat as plywood.

So that was the problem. She didn't waste any time letting him know. Little did she understand that he could not dictate Nick's sentence. Or that getting him convicted at all had taken hard work—and luck.

"Judge Plodsker explained why he chose the length of time he did," Valentina reminded Tessa.

Tessa's huff dismissed Judge Plodsker's mitigating factors. "Nick wasn't remorseful. His sex-addiction program was a ploy for a shorter sentence. His 'unblemished record' is just because nobody accused him of rape till now."

"I'm grateful we got Nick at all," Valentina said.

Tessa's sigh was loud enough to be heard over passing cars. "How long will he actually serve?"

"It depends on how well he behaves," Will said.

"What if he's a model prisoner?"

"He could get a year off for good behavior and more than that if he cooperates in the sex offender program. They might let him finish his sentence in a halfway house—that could give him another year."

Before Will's eyes, Tessa's face flushed from her neck to her forehead. She sputtered, "So that could be two and a half years off his six and a half?"

"Maybe." *No use tiptoeing around the eggshells of facts.*

"I can't believe it. It's not fair!"

Will had heard her say "it's not fair" so many times that it was getting annoying. He was sorry she was disillusioned, but he'd done the best he could. The least she could do was appreciate his effort.

"Nick will have to register as a sex offender, Tessa. That's huge. He'll never teach again. People will look at him like he's a pervert," Valentina said.

"That's fine, but he should also have the maximum prison time. I saw online that two counts could get him up to forty years."

"Is *that* what you expected?" Will asked, incredulous.

"It's what he deserves."

"Maybe, but it's pie in the sky," Will said.

Tessa gasped. Hope stepped in and fixed her with adoring eyes.

"I know this is hard, but the sentence isn't up to you, Tessa," Valentina soothed.

But Tessa didn't seem up for soothing, not even from Valentina and Hope.

"Look," Will said, exasperated. "In Washington, for every criminal conviction, there are sentencing guidelines. Maybe Judge Plodsker chose the shortest time, and he decided on concurrent sentences. But what Nick got is legal and way better than nothing. We got justice. That was the goal, not to put Nick behind bars for life."

Tessa screwed up her face in indignation. "You're talking just like a lawyer."

"I *am* a lawyer!" Will said. "And I did all I could for this trial."

"Well, it wasn't enough," Tessa snapped. She stormed toward the parking lot.

Will watched her go. As Valentina followed, Hope turned her face up toward him and let her opinion of his exchange with Tessa be known. Hope did not like conflict because it stressed her, and sometimes she was unsure whom to comfort. But today, Hope, who usually kept her judgments to herself, bristled her eyebrows in disapproval.

As Will walked Hope toward his Jeep, parked on the street two blocks away, he also disapproved. Tessa was ungrateful! She had no idea how much he'd put into sending Nick Payne to prison. But then Will reminded himself that he got Nick's guilty verdict for the good of Nisqually County and Washington State, not Tessa Jordan. He was glad the trial was over, and he wouldn't have to deal with her anymore.

But then there were those cats in his barn. Of all the stupid things! He was going to tell her to find them a permanent home. It was time for an eviction. He wanted Tessa Jordan gone.

CHAPTER 61

Hope was an exceptionally forgiving dog. She could no more hold her grudge against Tessa than she could sprout wings and fly. When Tessa walked into the survivors' group meeting on the night after Nick was sentenced, Hope picked up her distress from across the room and hurried over, swishing her tail and exuding goodwill. She seemed eager to smooth Tessa's ruffled feathers.

And they were, indeed, ruffled. All the women must have seen it. A drizzle had flattened Tessa's hair, her mascara had smeared, and she had the start of a raccoon's mask beneath her eyes. The last to arrive, she sagged into her chair. "Defeat" and "disappointment" were written in her forehead's horizontal lines.

"What? They let Nick Payne go free?" LaKeisha asked her.

"No, but his sentence was ridiculous. With good behavior, he could be out of prison in four years. That's nothing! They'll probably feed him caviar and invite dancing girls to visit him."

Louann passed Tessa the evening's brownies. "Here. This'll help."

Tessa took one, bit into it, and passed the plate on to Carmen.

"At least your assailant's going to prison," Sam said. "You're the only one of us who can say that."

Though Sam had spoken gently, her simple fact chastised Tessa, and she added guilt to her list of the day's emotions. With her thumbnail, she dented her Styrofoam cup of tea. It was like Valentina had said. Nick's punishment wasn't up to her.

"I'm sorry for complaining. I know I'm fortunate Nick Payne got any sentence at all. It's just that I was shocked. I expected it to be much longer."

"We all wish it had been longer for you, Tessa, but perfect is the enemy of good. Any sentence for that pervert is positive," Sam said.

"You can't control the length of time any more than you can control whether he gets around to feeling remorse," Gail said.

"I guess you're right," Tessa conceded, though she could still feel tightness in her chest and knew it would probably be there for a while. "At least he's going to have to register as a sex offender."

LaKeisha, in a Parks and Rec Department sweatshirt from her new job, whooped. "Hallelujah, girl! You're going to be a drag on that man's ass!"

Gleeful chortles from all the women. The brownies made another round.

Being a drag on Nick's ass was cheering. "It helps me so much to talk with all of you," Tessa said.

"I can't talk with anybody *except* our group," Carmen said. "When I bring up anything about the rape, my friends look at me like I'm a prostitute. Or they judge me. They act like I asked to be assaulted by jogging alone. And then my family! You'd think they'd be supportive, but one word about anything, and they get upset."

"Does that make you feel lonely, Carmen?" Louann asked.

"It does."

"Are any of the rest of you not getting support from people you expect it from?" Louann asked.

When everybody nodded, Sam said, "I guess that's unanimous." Tonight, she was still working on her afghan.

"A few weeks ago, my own *mother* blamed me for Nick's assault. I'll never get over it. As if I hadn't blamed myself enough!" Tessa said.

"That must be very painful for you," Louann said.

"Like I've been stabbed in the heart," Tessa admitted.

"These betrayals are tough. They're why assault survivors sometimes cut themselves off from relatives and friends," Louann said. "You're not sure whom to trust with your story. And when you make yourself vulnerable and do talk about it, people don't always know how to handle it."

"Total bummer," LaKeisha said.

"Yeah, but we've got our group," Sam said.

"Groups like ours are pretty new. Imagine what it was like for survivors decades ago," Louann said. "After an assault in those days, a woman didn't get support like this, and everything was hush-hush. The few people who knew about it viewed her as an outcast and thought her life was over. They didn't even name a sexual assault for what it was. They just said, 'He took advantage of her.'"

"That's so wrong," Sam said.

"Agreed," Louann said. "I don't usually talk about my own experiences in here because this is your time, but maybe you'd be interested in a dinner I had with two of my closest friends a few months ago." She reached for a brownie. "We're all in our fifties. We've known each other for years and told each other everything. But that night, we got to talking about sexual assault. And you know what?"

A chorus of *whats?* from around the table. All ears were cocked.

"One of my friends admitted she'd been raped in college. The other said she'd gotten into her car one night and a man jumped up from the backseat and put a knife to her throat—she managed to wriggle out of his grasp and run. And, P.S., a few years before our dinner, her daughter had been drugged and raped. I told my friends that I'd been groped and attacked a number of times, but by the grace of God, I always managed to escape."

"You'd never talked about that with each other *before*?" Sam looked amazed.

"Never. It shocks and saddens me now. We missed years of supporting each other," Louann said. "I've told you about that dinner, so you can see how women had little choice but to suffer alone in silence. There certainly were no survivors' groups. No carefully trained forensic nurses or police interviewers. No assault advocates. Women were intimidated. Even fewer came forward than they do today."

"That must have been awful," LaKeisha said. "As hard as everything has been for me, it would be so much worse without this support."

Louann nodded. "Change may be coming at glacial speed, but at least now there's some progress."

For one of the first times ever, everybody got quiet. You could hear Carmen chewing her brownie, Hope softly snoring, Sam's knitting needles clicking. Tessa was feeling grateful for the group—and sorry about all the untold stories of women who'd never been able to talk about what an assailant had done. It occurred to her that her mother belonged to the hush-hush generation that viewed rape victims as pariahs. That didn't excuse her reaction to Nick's assault, but it did explain her attitude.

Finally, Gail cleared her throat and said, "Louann, you mentioned that women used to be intimidated. I've decided that a lot of us still are."

"Want to share your thoughts about that, Gail?" Louann asked.

"Yes. But first I have to tell everybody something."

"We're listening," LaKeisha said.

"I've never mentioned this before, but I'm a nun. I was afraid if I told you, you might feel like you had to be extra virtuous around me. But now I hope you know I'm an ordinary person."

"We know," Tessa reassured her with a smile.

Gail pushed a stray lock of hair off her forehead. "Okay. Yesterday at mass, we had a Bible reading from St. Luke. An evil spirit crippled some poor woman so she hobbled around, bent over—for eighteen miserable years. One day, Jesus saw her, laid his hands on her, and said, 'Woman, you are set free from your infirmity.'

"He didn't physically *help* her up. He just pointed out to her that she could walk tall if she wanted to. For standing up straight to mean anything to her, she had to do it on her own. So all by herself, for the first time in those terrible years, she stood up proud—no more hunching, bending, shuffling of feet, looking at the ground. I like to think she never stooped down again."

"I don't see how that applies to us," LaKeisha said.

"Or what it has to do with intimidation," Carmen said.

"I got to thinking about myself," Gail said. "An evil man assaulted me and made me stoop. Not literally, but psychologically. Because of him, I've been emotionally hobbling around, feeling ashamed and bad about myself. I think we're all the same. See the connection?"

"Yeah," LaKeisha said with a nod. "I agree. I'm stooped."

"When we're stooped down, we're intimidated and humiliated and devalued. We have a poor self-image, low self-esteem. Maybe that's what our rapists wanted—to put us in our place and take away our power," Gail said.

"We can't let them do that!" Sam said.

"You're right," Louann said. "So how can all of you fight against being stooped?"

"By standing up for ourselves. Believing in our value." *If only I'd done that with my mother*, Tessa thought.

"By speaking truth. Being honest about what we think and feel," Carmen said.

"Carmen, what about standing straight when your friends act like you're a prostitute or imply you were 'asking for it' by jogging alone?" Louann asked.

"I can do like you said about anger a few weeks ago. State my grievance and tell my friends how they can set things right."

"Perfect. You want to practice? What could you say to them now?" Louann asked.

Carmen exhaled a long, slow breath. "Well . . . I confided in a friend I've known since elementary school. She blurted out, 'Don't you know better than to jog alone early like that?' Like I was some kind of moron. Like I had no right to use the street except between noon and five, and I'd gotten what I deserved."

"The jerk," Sam muttered.

"I should have told her—sorry, Louann, I just said 'should'—I *wish* I'd told her, 'I feel like you're judging me, and it hurts my feelings. I want you to be more sensitive and treat me with respect.'" Carmen looked at Louann. "Does that sound right?"

"Does it to you?" Louann passed the spirit-lifting brownies around one more time.

"Yes." Carmen smiled. "I get it now."

Tessa thought that she was getting it, too. From now on, when she walked into a room, she would *not* allow herself to want to hide. She would tell herself that she was allowed to take up space like everybody else. She would walk tall and proud, and she would remember that her life was so much more than a sexual assault.

And why *shouldn't* she do these things? She'd lived through a horrible ordeal, but with the help of the group, she'd survived! And now that she'd thought about it, she was stronger than she'd ever been. Though she'd never be the same person she once was, she may be better. Even if she still had miles of healing to go, she knew she would walk them, and she'd be all right.

CHAPTER 62

Later that night, Tessa tossed under the covers, trying to get comfortable. Her thoughts bounced from Nick's first hours in prison, to Will's lawyer-speak this afternoon, to the survivors' group tonight. When she pondered all she'd learned in meetings, she remembered something Gail had said months ago: "You have to handle your pain, or it will handle you. You have to be in charge."

Tessa stared at the ceiling and considered that idea. The more she thought about it, the firmer became her conviction that she hadn't handled her pain well at all. She'd masked it with anger. Instead of being pain's master, she'd been its slave. *It* had been in charge.

Tessa flipped over her pillow and told herself that she had to stand up straight in order to deal with pain. She had to be strong. She pulled her covers up to her chin and imagined her pain as an injured mythical beast with antlers, webbed feet, black-and-orange scales, and a haunch branded with two teardrops inside a heart. The pain was licking its wounds at the bottom of her bed.

Tessa tried to shoo the pain away, but it bared its teeth and snapped at her. She waved her hands to frighten it, but it growled. Under the covers, she kicked to send it to the floor, but it raised a webbed foot to kick her back and hissed.

The thought occurred to Tessa that fighting the pain into submission would never work because it would fight back to defend itself, and she would be caught forever in a battle that made no sense. She had to make friends with her pain and accept it.

So Tessa welcomed the pain into her heart. Together in the dark, she and the pain worked out a truce. Starting now, the pain would go off on its own some of the time; of course, it would also return, perhaps with less and less force as years went by, but she would never be rid of it forever. To expect that outcome would be more pie in the sky, and she'd had enough of that for today.

Tessa closed her eyes. She imagined the beast nodding, climbing down from her bed, and settling for a spot in the corner, giving Tessa room to stretch her legs. It was a start. Maybe she was ready for a new life.

CHAPTER 63

On a chilly afternoon, Tessa was putting up a new display of books across from a scrawny Christmas tree, squashed between her desk and Howard's starboard side. For decorations, she and Emma had strung popcorn and cranberries because ornaments would not survive Howard's thundering along the highway. The tree filled the air with a fresh cedar smell and boosted everybody's Christmas spirits. On Tessa's desk were jars of jam, plates of cookies, and loaves of cranberry and persimmon bread, left by her people.

Perhaps the book display clashed in tone with her tree and gifts, but it was timely, too. Across the top of one of Howard's shelves, she'd taped letters spelling out *Once Upon a Crime*. She'd cut "once upon a" from black construction paper and "crime" from red foil so it looked like dripping blood. Lined up face-out on the shelf were detective and true-crime novels that patrons always requested to take on holidays.

When Howard's door opened, a cold, damp whoosh of air gusted in, along with Mona Upton, who had defended Nick last summer when she'd checked out *To Kill a Mockingbird* for her daughter. At that time, she'd been wearing tennis togs, but today, her pants and parka suggested that she might be headed for a ski slope. She shook rain off her closed umbrella and stomped her hiking boots on Howard's welcome mat.

"I need some light Christmas reading. For once we're getting out of here to escape the holiday frenzy," she said.

"Where will you go?"

"We've rented a condo at Whistler. We'll have a whole week to play in the snow and sit by a fire."

"That sounds like heaven," Tessa said, but then she thought that Emma's annual Christmas potluck for waifs and strays was as much fun as a ski trip. "What light reading were you thinking of?"

"Romance! Escape!"

Tessa steered Mona down Howard's aisle to the fiction shelves and handed her books by Danielle Steel and Nicholas Sparks.

Mona studied the covers and asked, "Do you have any bodice rippers?"

Tessa squirmed, and her discomfort grew when Mona pulled one out of her animal-print tote bag.

"My neighbor loaned me this for the trip." Mona showed Tessa the cover, on which was a bad boy, who looked like a young Sean Penn, panting on the neck of a white-robed maiden. As he ravished her, she swooned in his arms, clearly in no condition to consent.

"Bodice rippers have sexual assault as a plot device." Tessa made herself sound casual, as if she were speaking of the raindrops pinging on Howard's roof.

"Yikes. I hadn't thought of that. Let's forget bodice rippers. These two books will be fine." As Mona followed Tessa back to her desk to check them out, she dropped the bad boy back into her tote bag, thankfully out of sight, and asked, "Have you read about that awful Nick Payne?"

The question didn't surprise Tessa—she was ready for it.

After the recent trial publicity, he'd come up in conversations. In the small towns she visited, her patrons were used to the *Nisqually Crier's* police logs, which listed traffic accidents, DUIs, or calls to rescue frightened cats in trees. A prominent person going to prison for violent and salacious crimes had shocked her people, and many had wanted to talk about it.

"Yes, I read about Nick Payne," Tessa said impassively as she scanned the barcode on Mona's books.

"Who would have thought someone like him would assault anybody? You don't know who you can trust in this world anymore."

"Yes," Tessa agreed. Outwardly, she showed no feelings, but inwardly she rejoiced that Mona Upton, who'd once maligned the unidentified woman claiming rape, had seen Nick Payne for what he was. Though Tessa had been feeling less shame about the assault, she did not feel like revealing it to Mona or any of her people. For now, she would talk about Nick Payne only with her survivors' group. She would protect herself.

Tessa handed the two romances to Mona. "Here you go."

"I'm glad they put Nick Payne in prison! At least they got him off the street," she said.

"A lot of women tell me that," Tessa responded, an octopus unashamed to hide behind her ink.

"I wonder when he'll get out."

"Who knows?"

As Mona was leaving, Tessa called after her, "Merry Christmas!"

CHAPTER 64

In downtown San Julian, Christmas floated through the crisp, cold air. Will smelled it in the swags of evergreen festooning the shops' paned windows, and he heard it in the happy shrieks of children in a cart, drawn down Rainier Avenue by veterinarian Dr. Vargas's chestnut horse. Outside Mel's Market, a shivering Rotarian in a Santa suit rang a bell beside a brass pot, into which passersby could toss donations for needy families' Christmas dinners.

Will threw in a five-dollar bill. Always a last-minute shopper, he'd just ordered whale-watching tickets online for Maria and her family, and he'd bought catchers' mitts and baseballs at Totally Toys for gifts his nephews could unwrap. Now all he had to do was buy Hope's favorite gourmet biscuits for her Christmas dessert, and wine for tomorrow's family dinner. He'd pick up two pecan pies and a little something for himself at the Sweet Time Bakery before it closed at six—and he'd be done. *Relief!*

Mel's was full of harried shoppers, zooming down the aisles and searching for last-minute dinner items. Will made his way to the pet department, then to the wine department, which was as packed with people as the rest of the store. A frazzled woman in a hairnet and white apron was setting out sample cheddar cubes for a crowd hovering like birds of prey over her demo table.

Though Will needed to hurry and get the pies, he was hungry, so he waited his turn for a sample. He'd take a couple—the woman didn't look like she'd slap his hand. As he jostled his way through the crowd, he glanced around at the wine, and his gaze landed on Tessa, studying the chardonnays displayed in shelves along one wall.

Of all the departments where he might find her, wine was the last he'd have expected, but probably she'd steeled herself to come here and, like him, was shopping for tomorrow. She picked up one bottle, then another, and studied the labels. If she were anything like Maria, she'd buy the bottle with the prettiest one, and that would be that.

Will was still a bit bruised by Tessa's lack of appreciation for his efforts, but now he felt almost protective toward her, alone in the crowd. Most of the people surrounding her had never lived through anything so damaging as sexual assault. Thanks to Nick Payne, Tessa would be forever different from them. As Will knew from Maria, Tessa would live with the emotional injury for the rest of her life.

That injury didn't mean he had to be overly friendly to her, however. Will intended to tell her to take her cats and go. But he had no time right now to get into it, and after all, it was Christmas Eve. It wasn't in Will to be mean. He could not be Scrooge.

After he ate three cubes of cheese—and the sample lady didn't slap his hand—Tessa was still there. He had no choice but to pass her in order to pick out his own wine. Not one to slink by unnoticed, he decided to walk up, say a quick hello, and move on.

"Excuse me, Tessa," he said, ready to pass her in the narrow aisle.

She looked up, and her eyes brightened. She was standing so close to him that he could smell her soap, which was as fresh and clean as a florist shop. "Sorry." She turned sideways toward the shelf to allow him plenty of room to go by.

"Merry Christmas," he said.

"Same to you."

He'd feel awkward if that was all they said to each other after they'd shared the pizza and an evening together. "What are you doing tomorrow?" he asked.

"The usual. Dinner with Emma and some of our friends." Tessa fidgeted with the fringe on her paisley scarf.

Am I standing too close and making her nervous? To keep from threatening her, Will took a couple of steps down the aisle.

"What about you?" she asked, as if she were calling him back.

"Dinner. My sister and her family and my crazy Uncle George. He's been married five times. We're waiting to see if he brings a date."

Will was drawn to Tessa's smile. But then, in two minutes, she might fly off the handle.

"Do you think your uncle *will* bring a date?" she asked.

"No idea. Often when he tells a story about his past, he can't remember the name of his wife at the time."

"That's funny." Tessa smiled again. "Will you bring Hope?"

"She's part of the family. She belongs around the table with the rest of us."

Now Tessa looked sad. Will figured he must have done something wrong again. "I've . . . um . . . got to get wine for tomorrow. Good to see you, Tessa." Will sounded stiffer than he intended.

"Good to see you, too."

As Will made his way to the red wine, he could have sworn that her soap's smell followed him. Too bad that things had worked out the way they had. Her mood may shift in a blink, but still, he'd like to have known her.

CHAPTER 65

Tessa was scrambling eggs for her kitties' Christmas breakfast when the phone rang. She had no time to talk with anyone. Tuna Yummies for her cats' dessert were in the oven, and she had to bake an apple crisp for Emma's potluck at noon.

That has to be my mother. The prospect made Tessa weary. She'd considered phoning her mother this morning to wish her a happy Christmas, but so far had not gathered the strength. Tessa turned off the fire under the cats' eggs, wiped her hands on her apron, and picked up the phone.

"Merry Christmas, Tessa."

The tone of those three words told Tessa that her mother resented her not spending the holidays in Maine. "Hi, Mother. Merry Christmas back."

"I'm at your Aunt Rose's. We're roasting a turkey. All *her* kids will be here in a little while."

But I won't. "That sounds like fun. Tell everybody hello," Tessa said, avoiding the purple, bearded elephant hanging from the phone line.

Margaret took umbrage at avoiding. "It's embarrassing that you're not home for Christmas. My friends think we don't get along."

"Um . . ." What could she say? They hadn't been getting

along since Tessa had told Margaret about Nick. She could not forget her mother's heartless lack of support. It still upset her.

Margaret asked, "Any plans for today?"

"A potluck at a friend's."

"Will any nice men be there?"

Tessa should have expected the question—a leopard couldn't change its spots. But her mother's insensitivity knocked the breath out of her. She closed her eyes and told herself, *Forgive! Let it go!* But then she thought that she could not let the comment pass. She had to stand tall, be proud, no stooping. As Louann had suggested, Tessa had to state her grievance and speak the truth.

"Mother, are you asking if men I might date will be there today?"

"Well . . ." She coughed. "Yes, I suppose I am. For your own good, I always wish you'd find someone and settle down."

"*I* always wish you'd remember that I was raped. I wish you'd keep in mind what I've been through. I want you to stop hounding me about men."

"I—I'm not *hounding* you!" Margaret stammered. "I never hound anyone."

"Sorry if that offends you, but it feels like hounding to me." Tessa's pulse throbbed at her temples. "I know you want me to get married, but after all that's happened, I'm not sure I ever will. And if I do, it will be in my own time. I'd like for you to stop bringing it up."

Silence. Now that the purple, bearded elephant had been addressed, icicles hung from the phone line instead. Still, as Tessa had taken up for herself, she'd felt her power return, and now she also felt clean inside, as if she'd swept and mopped and dusted her heart. With the dirt and cobwebs gone, she could see Margaret less as a threat and more as a sad, lonely woman who had old-fashioned ideas about victims of assault. But that was Margaret's problem, not Tessa's. For once, she didn't feel that she had to compromise herself in order to appease her mother.

"I'm sorry," Margaret said.

Cactus needles seemed to prickle from her expression of regret, but they couldn't hurt Tessa anymore. She said, "Apology accepted."

After today's overdue shift in the relationship, she added, "No promises, but I might come for a visit at Easter. I'll have to see how things go."

As she hung up, she thought, *Thank you, Louann! Thank you, my survivors' group!*

Chapter 66

Hardly anyone would be in the office during Christmas week, but Will had work to catch up on after all the holiday distractions. At least he could go in today wearing jeans. He put on his down jacket, went to the door, and called Hope, who'd been out wandering her field. Today she would not have to wear her vest.

She ran to him from the barn, then ran partway back. She stopped and turned to look at him. When he called her, she moved closer to the barn and looked back at him another time. Her face was intent about something. *Odd.* She seemed to ask him to follow her. He felt like he was in an episode of *Lassie.*

Will zipped up his jacket and struck out across the grass. Inside the barn, he understood what she wanted him to see. One of Tessa's cats—he thought it was the one she called Fitzgerald—fled through an open window, but not in time for Will to miss that his face was bloody and something terrible was wrong with his leg.

Oh, man. What am I supposed to do?

Will had not seen Tessa since Christmas Eve, and he had no idea when she'd be coming here next or if the cat would appear when she came. It would be wrong not to let her know that the cat was hurt. She needed to get over here and trap him and take him to the vet.

Will sighed, went back into his house, and called her.

When Will got home late that afternoon, he saw that Tessa had set a trap in the barn. *Good.* He hoped Fitzgerald would cooperate. As Will was making pasta for his dinner, he heard Tessa drive up and park. A few minutes later, she knocked on his door. Wondering what she wanted, he turned off the fire under his boiling pasta water and answered.

"Thank you for calling me this morning. It was really nice of you." Tessa's eyes were scrunched down at the edges so she looked grateful and sincere.

"I was glad to help," Will said. "Have you caught Fitzgerald?"

"Not yet. I just found Bronte in the trap. I let her loose and reset it. Maybe Fitzgerald will come back tonight."

"Let's hope," Will said.

Tessa looked like she was about to say something else but thought better of it. "I'll let you know."

"Good luck with your cat."

The next morning, Will was about to leave for the office when Hope whined and ran back and forth to the barn to get him to follow again. He should have known.

In the trap, Fitzgerald was hissing like a cussing stevedore, $%#@*^! When Hope sniffed the metal bars that incarcerated him, he slashed his paw through the air, clearly intending to claw her nose. *I'm going to kill you,* he snarled as loud and clear as an ambulance siren.

Where is Tessa? This cat is not *my responsibility.* Still, he couldn't leave the cat in such a sorry state. Fitzgerald was suffering. Tessa needed to get over here and take care of him.

Will whipped out his cell. He was tired of being taken

advantage of! "Tessa, your cat's here in the trap. His face looks like hamburger. You need to get him to the vet."

"I can't leave now. I've got half a dozen toddlers and their mothers here for story hour." Tessa's voice was full of stress. "I'll have to call my boss. I'm over an hour away. Maybe I can get there by two."

How did I ever get myself into this situation? "We can't leave this cat here for hours." *Did I say "we"? It's SHE! She can't leave the cat. The cat is hers, not ours.*

"I'll get there as fast as I can. I promise," Tessa said.

She sounded well-meaning, but Will doubted that she'd make it by two. He was a decent human being, and he'd loved animals since childhood. He couldn't leave an injured cat in misery. As Hope stood guard, he put the trap in the back of his Jeep.

After a harrowing drive, punctuated with Fitzgerald's furious hisses and snarls—and Hope's worried whimpers—Will arrived at Dr. Vargas's veterinary clinic. He handed over the cat to a receptionist in a scrub suit with animals printed on the fabric.

"This cat belongs to Tessa Jordan," Will said. Only then did he realize that he hadn't told her that he'd bring her cat here.

CHAPTER 67

When someone knocked on his door on a Saturday night, Will thought Maria must be stopping by unannounced. He set his biography of Clarence Darrow on the table beside his faded wingback reading chair and went to the entry. Hope had beaten him there. She was prancing in a circle, shaking her yellow duck senseless with excitement at a visitor. Her shining eyes shouted, *Company! A friend! Whoopeee!*

Will flipped on the front porch light. As he opened the door, it squawked on its hinges, and the winter damp hit his face. Tessa was standing there in a red knitted hat, navy pea coat, and jeans. Her breath was fogging in the cold. She held a wicker basket out to him.

"Here." Its contents were covered with a red-and-white checked cloth. "I baked you some oatmeal bread. To thank you for taking care of Fitzgerald."

She looked earnest. And grateful. That was not what Will would have expected from her. But then, he reminded himself, she was grateful that he'd taken Fitzgerald to the vet, not that he'd gotten Nick Payne put away. "Thanks, but you didn't need to bake me bread."

"I wanted to."

"I couldn't leave your cat to suffer."

"I'm thankful you didn't," she said. "And you were kind to call me from Dr. Vargas's office and let me know where Fitzgerald was."

Would the real Tessa Jordan please stand up? One day she was mad at him, and the next she was bringing him what seemed like a peace offering, at least as far as her cat was concerned. He looked at the basket in his hand. No matter what had prompted her to bake for him, it was a nice gesture. The warm loaf's aroma made him want to run for his bread knife and jam.

As Hope dropped her yellow duck at his feet and sniffed the wicker, Will asked, "Is Fitzgerald okay?"

"He will be. I just went to visit him. Dr. Vargas said he was in a fight. He's got three stitches on his head and a splint on his leg."

"The poor cat," Will said.

"It broke my heart to see him. He was too doped up to hiss like he usually does if I get too close. He even let me pet him," Tessa said.

"How are you going to trap him again and take off the splint?"

"He has to stay at the clinic till he heals. He won't be coming back here for a while."

"Coming back" reminded Will that he'd intended to evict the cats. If he did, Fitzgerald wouldn't have a colony left here to rejoin, and Will would lose contact with Tessa. Once again, he didn't feel like telling her to find the cats another home. What was it about her that made him so easily let go of resentment? He was as unpredictable as she was—aggrieved one minute and drawn to her the next.

"Um . . . do you want to come in? I've got strawberry jam we could eat with the bread. I could make some coffee," Will said.

The goodwill that had lit up Tessa's face darkened to caution. "I don't drink coffee."

"Okay, tea. My sister must have left a few bags around here somewhere."

At least Tessa hasn't run off.

"I'm not sure . . ."

Will knew what her hesitation was about. "We can sit out here on the steps. You can hold your car keys in your hand. I won't be offended if you suddenly bolt to get away from me." He smiled his confident courtroom smile.

"You don't have to make fun of me," Tessa said.

"I'm not. How about the tea?"

"Okay, but let's sit in the barn with the cats."

He handed her back the basket. "I'll meet you there in a minute. Sugar or cream?"

"A teaspoon of sugar."

"Coming right up."

In the barn, Will set two steaming mugs of tea on his workbench, followed by a jar of strawberry jam from one of his fleece coat's pockets and a pile of napkins, a spoon, and a small serrated knife from the other. "If you want more sugar, I can go back and get it."

"I'm sure what you put in my tea will be fine."

A trusting statement. At least she's not scared I'll drug her tea and assault her. He set two wooden apple crates facing each other in front of the bench. "Have a seat."

Hope was checking around Will's boxes, tools, and field mower for her cat friends, though all of them had fled outside. They may have warmed up to Hope and almost learned to trust Tessa, but clearly, in their opinion, Will was to be avoided. With no one to play with, Hope stationed herself next to the apple crates—as close as she could get to the bread. Her steady stare at it told anyone who cared to notice that she would enjoy a bite.

At the workbench, Tessa set the loaf on her checked cloth and sliced two pieces. She handed one on a napkin to Will and kept one for herself.

"This smells so good when it's still warm," Will said.

"Oatmeal bread is one of my favorites."

"My favorite is any bread. And pies, cakes, and cookies. It takes all my discipline not to stop at the Sweet Time Bakery every time I go downtown," Will said.

"I bake bread and some kind of sweet every weekend."

You do? "Do you make jam, too?"

"In the summer." Tessa dolloped some on her bread. "Mostly from blackberries I pick around the island."

"Hope picks blackberries with her teeth. By August, there's not a berry left on the thickets near my fence."

Knowing she was being talked about, Hope glanced at Will and crumpled her brows. Her eyes went back to the bread. Just as she'd told him that he should come to the barn and help Fitzgerald, her relentless stare now urged, *You must give me bread! I want. I want.*

"Shouldn't we let Hope have a small piece?" Tessa asked.

"One bite, and we're doomed. She'll never give up." Will smeared jam on his own slice.

"I'll sneak her a bite as I leave."

"Don't rush off," Will said.

When Tessa got quiet, he wondered if his simple statement had been too friendly, and he'd scared her again. He let the silence sit there between them because he wasn't sure how to fill it. Was the only safe topic the weather? He and Tessa chewed their bread.

"Will . . ."

It did not escape him that this was the first time Tessa had addressed him by name.

"I need to say something," she said.

"Fire away." Will braced himself for more complaints about Nick Payne's sentence. It would be a shame to spoil tonight with talk of him.

"I need to apologize."

"For what?"

"For being snippy outside of court the week before last. I've had time to think about Nick's sentence, and you were right. Four years—or however long he ends up in prison—is enough. His conviction will follow him all his life, like registering as a sex offender." Tessa picked a bread crumb off her knee. "My survivors' group convinced me that I should be thankful Nick's going to prison at all. And I *am* thankful. I want you to know I appreciate what you did. A whole lot."

Amazing. The very words Will had wanted to hear, straight from her mouth. "Trust me, I didn't want Nick to get away with what he did to you." Will swallowed some tea. "Sexual assault is so hard to prove. Judge Plodsker has a reputation for going easy on assailants, but he couldn't ignore the video. It was a godsend. Luck like that doesn't come along very often."

"So you accept my apology?"

If she were anyone but Tessa, he'd hug her or squeeze her hand to reassure her with touch and not just words that he forgave her. But he held back. "Of course, I accept your apology. And don't worry. I'm tough. I've gotten lots worse on my job than a little snippiness." Will handed her his napkin. "And I'd like more of your fantastic bread."

Tessa smiled as she handed him another piece. Hope watched it as Will spread more jam with the back of the spoon.

"It's great to see you smiling. When I first met you, you looked like you'd never smile again," he said.

"I've learned a lot from my survivors' group."

"Like what?"

"Resilience. Dealing with anger. Standing up for myself," Tessa said. "I love those women. And Hope. She came every time and encouraged us. She showed us how to get through emotional storms."

"And how do you do that?"

"By being like her. Quiet. Brave. Patient. I wait for the bad feelings to pass. I realized if I get distressed and Hope isn't there, I can calm myself by acting like her," Tessa said. "She taught us about hope, too. I'm starting to trust that somehow, in its own good time, life works out."

Tessa leaned forward, put her arm around Hope, and stroked her biscuit-beige ears. As Will watched, Tessa kissed Hope's forehead and left a faint lipstick heart.

"Sorry. I didn't mean to leave lipstick on her," Tessa said.

Though lipstick prints on Hope had always perturbed Will because he had to clean them off, he said, "It's an occupational hazard. No problem." And he meant it. He ate the last of his bread and stuffed his napkin into his fleece coat's pocket. "Tessa?" he asked. "You said you'd learned to trust that life could work out. Do you think yours has?"

Her brows lowered as she seemed to ponder how to answer. "I guess it's worked out—as much as it can for now. I've still got a long way to go about Nick, but I've already come pretty far, and I'm starting to have faith I'll find peace someday, like you once told me." Tessa folded her napkin in half, then half again, and again like she was trying to make it disappear.

She looked up at Will. "We're being too serious. How about your Christmas? Was it fun?"

"It always is."

"Did your Uncle George bring a date?"

Will chuckled. "He did. Lola. When she went into the kitchen, he told me that she was 'the one.' That'll make his sixth 'the one.'"

Tessa laughed out loud, a first since Will had met her. *Wow.*

"I'm surprised he can keep all his wives straight," she said.

"Sometimes he doesn't. Uncle George gives new meaning to 'serial monogamy.' We'll probably have another family wedding soon."

"Maybe he'll elope."

"Don't count on it. We'll see what the new year brings."

"Speaking of which, Happy Almost New Year." Tessa held out her teacup for a toast.

Will tapped his cup against hers. "To new beginnings." He took his last remaining slug of tea. He wanted to say something, but he was afraid she'd run. Then the guiding angel who resides in everyone plinked on her harp and urged, *Go ahead! Do it! Sometimes you risk more by* not *risking than by going ahead and taking a chance.*

Holding his empty cup in both hands, Will asked Tessa, "Can we be friends?"

EPILOGUE

July 4, 2019

Tessa and Will may have enjoyed the Grand Old Fourth of July celebration every year, but Hope was downright passionate about it. It started early in the morning with the San Julian Rotary Club's pancake breakfast, where under crepe paper–covered tables, she foraged for crumbs. Next, at the Stars and Strikes Old Geezers' Baseball Game, everybody ate—and dropped—kernels of kettle corn. After that came Say Cheese's pizza-eating contest, and bits of crust littered the grass. From food booths at Waterfront Park's street fair, delicious smells of hamburgers and hot dogs beckoned Hope at lunchtime.

At two o'clock, the Mile-Long Parade, led by grand marshal Clarence Kowalczyk and the San Julian High School Band, started at the library and would travel down Rainier Avenue to the Nisqually Wellness Clinic. Along the route, people were lined up on both sides of the street, but Tessa and Will had arrived early enough for front row seats on the curb. Hope watched the parade in her sphinx position next to her personal people.

After Clarence Kowalczyk and the band came a motorcycle escort and Police Chief Mario Romano and Officer Chelsea Bishop, throwing candy corn in cellophane packets from his black-and-white SUV. Then came the Strawberry Festival Queen, perched on the back of a red Mustang convertible in a satin puff-sleeved dress and rhinestone tiara. Oldsters from the Senior Center waved from their bus windows, the Jumping Rope Club skipped by, the Gear Grinders Club waved from their bicycles, and everybody in town who had a basset hound in the family trundled along with their dogs—in the heat, their tongues hung nearly to the asphalt.

Dr. Andrew Hardesty, DDS, wore a huge white Styrofoam tooth around his chest and waved his cowboy hat at the crowd. A fire truck and ambulance came along, followed by the vans and trucks of San Julian's best-loved businesses: DIY Hardware, where Mr. Allen gave Hope biscuits. The Chat 'n' Chew Cafe, where Tessa and Will went for Saturday breakfasts. The Sweet Time Bakery, where he bought her Valentine fudge. Mel's Market, where they'd run into each other on Christmas Eve, before that important night when she'd brought him oatmeal bread and everything started to change.

After the trucks of Nisqually Moss Removal and You-Shovel-It Gravel and Soil passed by, the parade abruptly stopped. Whatever the next attraction was, it had been delayed somewhere down the block, and everyone was going to have to wait.

Tessa nestled against Will, her favorite place on earth to be—and where she belonged, she'd finally realized last year. "Don't get dehydrated in this heat," he said and handed her the bottled water they'd been sharing. He'd learned they were pregnant soon after their wedding, and since then, he'd been extra vigilant about her health.

Tessa drank some water and re-screwed the cap. As she handed the plastic bottle back to Will, she glanced across the street. Staring at her from under Totally Toys' blue-and-white-striped awning was Nick Payne—a salt-and-pepper-haired, paunchy, older version, but she would know him anywhere.

Startled, she froze like a solitary camper who hears a twig snap in the night outside the tent. Tessa's stomach clamped into a fist. In the hot sun, she felt like sleet was falling on her, its needles prickling her cheeks and freezing her hands.

Both Will and Hope picked up that something was amiss. Hope rested her chin on Tessa's knee as Will turned to her. "What's wrong?"

She cupped her hand around his ear and said, "Don't look, but Nick Payne's across the street."

The sound that came from Will was almost a growl. "I didn't think he'd dare show his face in this town again," Will said. "I'd like to cross the street and club him, Tess, but we should ignore him. Don't let him frighten you."

"I won't," Tessa said—and she wasn't frightened, not anymore. The shift that began for Tessa in her survivors' group years before had found its way across the country and the world in the wake of the #MeToo movement—it was the shift of women standing tall and reclaiming their power. She'd gained strength from the solidarity of women.

Still, thrown back so suddenly to the past, she was shocked. And she was disgusted that Nick had the gall to interfere today in the beautiful life that she and Will had slowly created for themselves in the last three years. Two of them had been as friends while he'd waited patiently for her to heal. Last summer they'd gotten serious.

She looked back across the street at Nick. At first, he tried to stare her down, intimidate her, and get her to look away.

But she refused. And she would not give him the satisfaction of glaring at him because he'd think he could upset her—and she realized now that he no longer could. She noted that his face was puffed and pasty, and she thought that he did not deserve the oxygen he was breathing, but she felt no need to hate or run. With no expression, she stared at him.

I know what you did, and you know what you did. You have to live with yourself, and I doubt you'll ever find peace. I feel sorry for you. You're a sick man.

Tessa sat up straighter, her gaze unmoving. *Men like you can't get away with assaulting women like me so easily anymore. We've learned to speak up and expose you for what you are. We refuse to be docile or passive or silenced.*

Tessa knew there was still a ways to go, even after #MeToo. *But now we've got a reason for hope.*

Nick broke the stare and looked at his feet.

Tessa won.

Oh, it was so good. Delicious, really. She felt as if the evening's fireworks had started early, and showers of congratulatory golden sparks rained down on her and Will. In her mind, a rocket streaked across the sky and exploded in a silver celebration.

Her gaze still locked on Nick, Tessa reached for Will's hand, which felt warm and familiar now that it had touched every inch of her. His hand was like part of her own body. Out of the corner of her eye, she saw him smile.

Hope leaned against Tessa as the parade started up again and the delayed staff of Sun Joy Chinese Restaurant finally ran down the street under a fire-breathing dragon the length of five cars. Momentarily, it blocked Tessa's view of Nick, but once it passed, she looked for him again. He'd melted back into the crowd and was nowhere to be seen.

Will let go of Tessa's hand and put his arm around her shoulder. He drew her closer and whispered, "Well done."

"Thanks," she said, but she hadn't needed Will to tell her because she knew she'd handled Nick just right. Without speaking a word to him, she'd shown her strength. It may have taken her a while to claim, but now no one could take it from her. It would be a hard-won part of her forever.

ACKNOWLEDGMENTS

As usual, many kind people helped me write this book, and for all of them I am supremely grateful. I can't imagine writing anything without turning to others with my questions. Any mistakes I may have made with the answers I got are mine alone.

From a vague idea to the final book, my agent Cullen Stanley, my editor Michaela Hamilton, and my publisher Lynn Cully thoughtfully shepherded me through the publishing process. Along the way, Alexander Kovats, my longtime friend, talked with me about hope, which is fundamental to the story. And Julie Miesionczek, another friend, answered countless questions as I wrote.

Several assistance dog handlers allowed me to get to know their beautiful retrievers while they told me how they worked as teams. The extraordinary bond between these dedicated dogs and women impressed me greatly: Astro and Tambra Donohue, director of Monarch Children's Justice and Advocacy Center in Lacy, Washington. Marshall and Kim Carrol, senior victim advocate at the Thurston County Prosecutor's Office in Olympia, Washington. Harper and Gina Coslet, child interview specialist at Dawson Place in Everett, Washington. Wilson and Sheryl Speight, former outreach coordinator at the Courthouse Dog Foundation in Bellevue, Washington.

The judicial and legal process for perpetrators of sexual assault is complicated, and the Internet could take me only so far. Graciously filling in the gaps were: Retired Judge J. Robin Hunt, the State of Washington Court of Appeals.

Bob Langbehn, deputy prosecuting attorney for Snohomish County, Washington. J. Kirkham Johns, an attorney in Bainbridge Island, Washington. And Peter Wolf, a detective with the New Jersey State Police.

I've been fortunate to count three local police officers as friends, and this story is the second of mine that these generous people have contributed to: Officer Aimee LaClaire in Seattle, and Sargant Trevor Ziemba and former Officer Carla Sias in Bainbridge Island, Washington.

Mo Maurer, executive director of Bainbridge Island's Assistance Dogs Northwest, helped me network with experts and showed me how the dogs are trained to respond to special commands, such as "snuggle" and "kiss." Mo's tireless effort for the dogs and their people is inspirational. I'd never have begun this book without her and our mutual friend Paul Zuckerman, who in the grocery store one afternoon first told me about courthouse dogs.

Last but by no means least, without my husband John I'd never have written a word for this or any other book. For decades, he has encouraged me as I've made my way as a writer. For him, "thank you" hardly begins to express my gratitude.

A REASON FOR HOPE

Kristin von Kreisler

ABOUT THIS GUIDE

The suggested questions are included to enhance your group's reading of Kristin von Kreisler's *A Reason for Hope*.

DISCUSSION QUESTIONS

1. According to the National Sexual Violence Resource Center, in the U.S. nearly one in five women and one in seventy-one men have been the victim of attempted or completed rape in their lifetime. The Rape, Abuse and Incest National Network reports that an American is sexually assaulted every seventy-three seconds. Do these statistics surprise you? Or are they what you would expect? Why do you think that sexual assault is such a problem in the U.S. today?

2. Why do some of the women in *A Reason for Hope* never report that they were sexually assaulted? What other reasons might there be for not going to the police? Was Tessa's choice courageous or foolhardy? What would you have done? Could you sympathize with her delay in reporting the assault?

3. A moral dilemma at the heart of this story is based on the conflict between the assault victim and perpetrator's legal rights. Tessa believes that the laws are unfair to the victim. Do you agree? Should proving consent be so important? How could this conflict of rights be resolved?

4. Some people might say that Tessa was "asking for it" by going to Nick's house when she hardly knew him—at night. How do you feel about that? Could she be blamed in any way for what happened to her?

5. Do you agree or disagree with Tessa that the judicial system is inherently sadistic? Why? In court, does everyone come out worse even if they're on the winning side? Or is justice meted out fairly? Was Nick Payne's sentence fair?

6. How did Tessa grow and change as a result of the assault? Did any good come from it? Or is it going to hurt her for

life? What about the other women in her group? How do you think their futures will be?

7. Louann says that anger often masks deeper emotions that are too frightening to feel. What might be some of those emotions? Why do women have problems expressing anger or letting it fuel constructive action, such as standing up for themselves? Could Tessa have done that in court?

8. How would you define *hope*? How does it play a part in the story? What are some of the reasons the characters might feel it? Do you believe that women can have hope about justice for sexual assaults today?

9. If we assume that we can't escape physical and psychological pain at some time in our lives, do we need to make peace with it? Does fighting it make it harder to bear? Does it help to surrender as Tessa did? Is that possible?

10. Do you think that hardship makes you stronger—and that if you've gained strength from it, nobody can take the strength away? How does this apply to Tessa? Have you ever taken pride in strength you've gained at a cost to yourself?

Kristin von Kreisler will be happy to meet with your reading group via Skype, Zoom, or FaceTime—or in person, if you're in the Seattle area.

Contact her at kristin@kristinvonkreisler.com

Connect with

Visit us online at
KensingtonBooks.com
to read more from your favorite authors, see books
by series, view reading group guides, and more.

for sneak peeks, chances to win books and prize packs,
and to share your thoughts with other readers.

facebook.com/kensingtonpublishing
twitter.com/kensingtonbooks

Tell us what you think!
To share your thoughts, submit a review,
or sign up for our eNewsletters, please visit:
KensingtonBooks.com/TellUs.